"I'll be right there," he called, probably mistaking Marian for someone else so she tried again. He turned slightly, "Did you see a ring lying about anywhere about this room? I looked earlier, but no luck then. I was hoping to be wrong."

"Yes, I have it," she answered as she slipped the ring from her finger.

"Thank you!" he cried, sagging before he spun about to face Marian at last.

His mouth dropped open though when he spotted her standing across the room.

But before he could close it or even speak, light footsteps rushed along the hall toward them.

Marian darted for the closest hiding place, behind a velvet curtain.

NO ORDINARY LADY © 2024 by Heather Boyd
ISBN: 978-1-922733-39–9
Editing by Kelli Collins

HEATHER BOYD

USA TODAY BESTSELLING AUTHOR

No Ordinary Lady

Distinguished Rogues

20

Chapter One

"Turn in here," Daniel Dawkin, Lord Scarsdale, called to his coachman as they reached a familiar crossroads.

"We could still go on," his valet, Sunday Paul, murmured, looking hopefully toward the long, empty road ahead. "There's plenty of daylight left."

"No. We spend the night here," Daniel said firmly.

"But home is only an hour away," Sunday argued.

"Your ma will still be there tomorrow," Daniel promised, patting the fellow's knee. Daniel's valet was more friend than servant, and he was eager to reach home and his doting mother. Sunday was bouncing in his seat with impatience.

Daniel was less eager, although this journey home had been entirely his idea. "Cheer up. It's just one more night."

"You keep saying that every time we stop. Lady Scarsdale will be none too pleased by these delays of yours," Sunday warned.

"Well, my mother wouldn't have known I was even coming home if you hadn't written to warn them to expect us," Daniel shot back. "I told you I'd take care of the matter of informing them."

"By writing the night before we arrive?"

"My mother didn't need weeks to prepare her litany of complaints for my arrival," Daniel replied, his humor for Sunday's grumbles evaporating. "I'm sure she has made an even longer list since I saw her last year in London now."

"It's been five years since you've been home to the estate. Maybe she'll be happy to see you finally return," Sunday suggested with a hopeful expression, because he must know that would be impossible for Daniel's mama.

"Once every other year has been more than enough time to spend in close proximity with my mother," Daniel announced with a nod as the carriage rolled to a stop in a muddy inn yard. "By all reports, the estate has thrived without my personal oversight. Secure lodgings for us."

Daniel glared at Sunday until he exited the carriage and left him to the task of speaking with the innkeeper to secure rooms for the night for himself and his servants. But it was mostly so Daniel wouldn't have to look upon Sunday's disappointed face again.

Daniel had enjoyed his week's long journey homeward. Sunday had not. They had meandered from London into Somerset, visiting any friends within a reasonable distance from the main roadways.

Daniel had a lot of friends and had taken an abundance of enjoyment in their company.

He'd ate well, slept sufficiently, and flirting with as many pretty women as possible. His journey was almost at an end, but he wanted one more night, more or less to himself.

Eventually, he got out of the carriage too and looked about the village of Wraxall. He had never actually stopped here before since it was so close to home, but would make the time to explore now. He doubted he'd ever have leisure to do so again.

The night before he announced to his family that he intended to marry was his last night of complete freedom as a gentleman. After tonight, he would never be unencumbered by a source of guilt again.

He intended to please himself one last time and then he'd buckle under like all his friends had done recently and devote himself to obeying the whims of just one woman. Marriage was the only reason he'd come home and there was no time for doubts any longer.

Yet they persisted.

He grimaced and then shook his head. Tomorrow he'd arrive home, hopefully at peace with his decision by then, and perhaps mother would actually smile at him for once when he told her his news.

But he wouldn't hold his breath for that outcome. Mama had not smiled at him since his father had gotten sick and died. From then on, it had been one frown after another and constant disagreements about the careless way he lived his life. It was the main reason he avoided her and the estate. He'd done nothing there that made her happy since he'd inherited the title.

"The accommodation at the inn is not what you're accustomed to," Sunday announced when he returned, his expression and manner still sour.

"That actually is the point of staying at unknown inns," he replied. "It'll be adequate for one night and perhaps even memorable."

"I highly doubt that," Sunday grumbled. "There is only one small room available for the night. I'll have to sleep in the carriage with the grooms."

"Those are well-sprung seats in there. A place to rest our heads is all any of us need," he assured his valet. "We'll stay one night and then, refreshed, we'll finish the journey together tomorrow."

Sunday's eyes narrowed on him. "Do you promise? No more detours? No more distractions? No more pretty women in your bed that you simply cannot part with after just one night?"

Daniel laughed at the picture he painted. He knew Daniel's nature very well. "I promise."

Yet Sunday turned back to the inn with a muttered curse about foolishness and wasting time.

It was Daniel's time. Precious and not to be squandered by rushing anywhere. Shabby surroundings or not, he intended to enjoy his stay.

He smiled to himself as he removed his hat to enter the low-beamed establishment. But promptly smacked his head on the next beam, anyway. He let out a soft curse, shrank down a little more, and rubbed his poor head.

"Got to keep an eye on things in this place," the balding innkeeper warned, rushing forward to welcome him. "Welcome, my lord. What can I get for you?"

"A pair of tankards to begin with," he murmured, looking around the dim room. It seemed a cramped sort of place and hardly anyone obviously important or wealthy appeared to be present. That suited him just fine.

Daniel had no wish to meet anyone he knew too well from the area. He was here to have fun, not mind his manners and worry what gossip might spring from his stay and find its way back to Mother. There would be time enough for having his ears blistered for tardiness later.

Once Mother had exhausted herself of her complaints, Daniel would make haste to call upon his nearest widowed neighbor, and the man's unmarried daughter, Amy. He would be the best version of himself from then on.

But not tonight.

He took a seat at a table by the small, dirty front window that looked out over the stable yard. He sat facing the room, a habit he'd picked up in London when drinking alone in low places, and hoped for some excitement to liven up the place.

Wraxall did seem rather ordinary on the surface but, in his experience, first impressions were often wholly inaccurate. He was constantly surprised by how flawed his own judgement could be about places, and especially people.

Men routinely lied, and betrayed even their best friends for money or to gain power over others. Women were not immune either. They always wanted to have what other man could give them. His own poor judgement where women were concerned seemed to be something he could never save himself from, either. He lived in hope of love, but Daniel had never had much luck with women so far.

His brief affairs of the heart had only ever led to disappointment for him. He'd made friends of many women, but nothing deeper seemed possible in London. Which was why he was going home at last.

Daniel was resigned to make a proper match with a woman who would meet his basic needs and please his mother. He would set aside his preference for more exciting women for the sake of immediate peace in his family.

That meant he would finally settle down and lead a dull and unexciting life, the same his own father had lived when he'd married Mama.

The prospect of such a fate almost had him turning tail for London again.

Yet, he could not shirk his duty forever. A marriage must be made soon, and an heir produced in short order after that to ensure the succession.

He was getting closer and closer in age to what his own father had been when Daniel was born. Father had only lasted ten years more, and he barely recalled his face now.

Daniel was the last direct male descendant of his line, and he had a family of women to worry about, too. He could not have his estate and title revert to the crown or have some far-distant unknown relation come forward to inherit it all after he was gone. Mother would never forgive him if that came to pass.

He took a long swallow of his ale when it arrived and pondered where his valet had taken himself off to. Probably sulking up in the rented chamber because he couldn't kiss his mama good night tonight. Daniel exhaled and shook his head. He had never done that. Hugged or kissed his mother good night. At least, not that he could ever remember. A head nod was their habit.

All the love and comfort Daniel had ever known had come from his Granny Nolan, a feisty old wench who seemed to embarrass her daughter with every breath and recounted her past deed with such glee. Granny had come to live with them when Papa had died and never left, or left for long. She had visited her old friends in Portishead a few times over the years—but not lately.

He had missed Granny a great deal. He was looking forward to seeing her and hearing her wild tales once more.

A figure ran past his window, catching Daniel's attention. When two more followed, running too, he grinned. *Finally.* Something exciting must be going on.

He rose and put his face closer to the dirty windowpane.

There seemed to be some sort of commotion taking place just out of sight.

A cheer rang out, reaching even the occupants inside the inn, who were on their feet and headed for the door the next moment. Daniel hurried to follow, his curiosity piqued, and eager for any event to enliven his stay.

A wall of people blocked his view of the ruckus in the narrow alleyway beside the inn. But over the din of noise, he heard a woman shouting in outrage. His smiled slipped. The sound of distress drew him farther into the melee.

The woman was incensed about something serious.

Daniel attempted to push his way to the front, not an easy feat since everyone wanted a closer look at what was going on, too.

"You can't do this!"

"Oh, yes, I can," a man answered. "Come along, gentlemen, don't be shy. Who here needs a woman? She's strong, healthy and has all her own teeth. How much will you offer for her?"

There was a profound silence after that, and then the lady blistered the air with a round of remarkable set downs. Her inventiveness impressed the hell out of Daniel. Not even the worst of his friends could match this woman for creativity. *He* certainly couldn't.

He ended up at the front of the crowd and got a better look at the woman.

What surprised him was that she was young—couldn't have been much more than two and twenty years of age—and despite the raggedy dress she wore, Daniel thought her rather handsome. He'd always favored blondes.

But her scowl could crack the earth and her tongue lashed fire over the man holding her by one arm. Their eyes met, and Daniel's breath caught. He licked his lips, and the woman's gaze dipped to his mouth. Attraction sizzled in the air between them, and he took another step forward, intending to rescue her or claim her perhaps.

But the old man must have sensed his intent and wrenched her back against him first, and the moment passed as her gaze left him. Clearly, she wasn't happy with being sold off to the highest bidder like some prized mare at Tattersall's, and Daniel couldn't blame her.

Women were not property to be sold off to the highest bidder, unless they would be married into a good family as part of the process. That seemed hardly likely given this crowd.

Daniel folded his arms over his chest and scowled at the man holding her captive. It was none of his business, but he felt compelled to say something about the matter and put a stop to this ridiculous wife auction. "Have you not the stamina to mount her anymore, sir?"

The crowd laughed at his ribald taunt.

The man turned to face him, and Daniel was taken by surprise by his trodden-down bearing. He was old, his hair peppered with gray, and there were deep lines etched on his face. He seemed weary down to the bone.

The old man looked him up and down and nodded. "I'm dying," he said simply, voice no longer as strong as it had been when he'd addressed the crowd. "I want her to have a good life after I'm gone. Are you married, sir?"

"No," he blurted. *Well, not yet.* But he'd already decided about that. Amy Wilson would be his bride in a few short weeks. Eighteen years of age, bright minded, and a favorite of his mother's, Amy would make a perfectly decent countess. She was already accomplished in household management. Her temperament, though, was sedate, utterly unexcitable, which made her perfect for the role of a country wife.

He glanced at the woman standing between him and the old man. She was more to his taste than Amy, but he couldn't have her.

He was always drawn to outspoken women. The way she

clung to the older man made him a little envious. She seemed to adore the old fellow now, despite his attempt to sell her off just a moment ago.

He gestured to her. "I think she'd rather stay with you until the end."

"Finally, a sensible man speaks," the young woman exclaimed, throwing her hands up in the air. Her manner turned tender toward the old fellow. "I'll be all right," she promised him, softening her tone a lot as she leaned into him. "I need little, and I want to spend our last days together."

"You need a home for after I'm gone, pet," he said, cupping the young woman's cheek. "And a man to protect you from the harm walking the world. I would rest easy in my grave knowing you were taken care of."

"Yeah, but who is going to take care of her poor next husband when she loses her temper again," someone asked from the crowd.

Everyone laughed, and the crowd began to disperse. Clearly, there would be no takers in this village for such a woman.

Daniel remained behind a moment longer, touched by their situation. He couldn't help the woman find a replacement husband, but he could set the old man's mind at ease about their present circumstances. He slipped his fingers into his waistcoat pocket and withdrew some coins. "Here. Take this."

The gold sovereigns were the most he had on him. A fortune to someone of their inferior status, more than likely. More than enough to ensure the comfort of this old man in his dying days, see him buried, and perhaps still leave enough for his widow to live on after he was gone.

"We don't need his money," the woman said, bristling with indignation for Daniel's offer of charity.

But the older man took the coins and tucked them into his waistcoat. "Thank you, sir. Bless you. You've a good heart. A true saint."

"Hardly," he muttered under his breath. "Good day to you."

"Yes, good day," the old man said with a slight smile.

The woman hooked her arm through the old man's. "Let's get you home."

Daniel nodded to himself as he turned away, knowing he'd taken care of someone less fortunate than himself and feeling good about it for a few steps. He was glad he had stopped here today.

But then a small body crashed into him, nearly knocking him over. "Here now."

A boy of maybe eight years struggled to separate from him. Eventually, he pushed against Daniel's chest and then sprinted off through the village.

Daniel frowned at the fellow's haste and then scowled. The least he could have done was apologize.

Daniel straightened his coat as he headed back to the inn, but the feeling of satisfaction faded with every step he took closer to home. Was it his impending marriage that had robbed him of greater satisfaction in a good deed done today, or the discovery of Sunday's anxious face waiting for him on the front step of the inn?

Sunday scowled darkly. "I thought you'd left me here!"

"I would never do that," Daniel promised, laughing at poor Sunday, and pushing his doubts aside yet again. He was doing the right thing, going home to marry, but Sunday was a worrier down to his toes, which made him a perfect valet for a somewhat careless man. "Where did you go? I thought you'd join me in the tavern for an ale."

Sunday's expression turned even more disapproving. "I've had a word with the cook and have arranged for your dinner to be served in your chambers tonight. There's no private dining room. It's only mutton stew, probably bereft of mutton, by the way. You would eat better if only we went home tonight."

"It's good enough for one night," he decided. "Sunday, you've become truly persnickety in your old age."

Sunday was only three and twenty. A few years younger than Daniel, but much more conservative in his opinions and expectations for service. He'd entered Daniel's employ at the tender age of twelve, as a temporary valet, and had never left the position. Over the years of living in London, though, Sunday had gained an appreciation for the finer things in life and always expected Daniel to want the same.

But unlike Sunday, Daniel had had his old granny in his ear, pleading with him to never let his title or wealth go to his head. Granny said if he was too proper, too concerned with his own consequence, he'd miss out on all the fun. So that had compelled Daniel to seek adventure anywhere and everywhere. Gaming hell, brothel, or high society ball.

Daniel had had a surfeit of fun over the years following Granny's advice, much to his mother's chagrin. That was why he was finally ready to settle down. He couldn't think of anything more that was left to experience in the world. Marriage would be his last grand adventure, he supposed. Whether it was fun or not was up to him and his future wife to come to terms with.

He reentered the tavern and sat down at the table by the window, noticing the tankards he'd not finished before were empty. Someone had relieved him of his ale in his absence from the tavern. It was his own damn fault for leaving it behind, of course. But he still threw a scowl at the few occupants in the room now before he ordered another pair of tankards from the innkeeper.

He pulled the tankards close when they arrived. He would not be distracted from them again.

After all, it was to be his last night of total freedom before becoming engaged, and he intended to finish his bachelorhood on his own terms.

He glanced around the room at the other occupants once more and sighed at the obvious lack of potential entertainment and female companionship. There was not even a handsome servant woman who might smile his way tonight or flirt with him.

Daniel slouched in his chair, sipping his ale, but his mind turned to the past and all the women he'd known. He was not sorry to have left them behind, really. He regretted mostly that he'd not found the one woman he might turn heaven and earth over for. Some said love was worth any sacrifice. Daniel would have to wait to find out if that was true or not.

Perhaps he would fall in love with his future wife when he saw her again. It had been a long time since he'd seen Amy, and she was only now old enough to make a marriage.

He finished his ale in solitude and then looked around to see Sunday had returned. "Your dinner is ready."

"Good." Daniel stood and trudged upstairs alone, Sunday disappearing to the stables where he'd spend the night in Daniel's comfortable carriage, probably grumbling or dreaming of being home again in his own feather bed.

He let himself inside his chamber and looked around. A

bed, chair and table, and a fire. Almost everything a bachelor could need. A woman in that bed would have completed the picture.

But there would not be one last wild night of abandon here.

He went directly to the small, battered table by the window and sat himself down with a heavy sigh. He found the promised mutton stew and a hard bread roll beside it. He wasn't as fussy as Sunday and knew it would be enough, but he had to admit that his last meal and night as a bachelor was turning out to be a severe disappointment.

Chapter Two

"DID WE GET EVERYTHING?" Marian asked as she joined the others after taking the long way to their camp so she couldn't be followed. She glanced at the table and grinned. "Pocket watch, pearl-handled knife, and the rest of the coin he carried," she noted with approval, dropping onto a log beside her uncle. But the second gold sovereign the fellow had given them was suspicious by its absence. But Marian knew better than to question her uncle about that. Uncle always put a bit aside for a rainy day.

"Yes, well done, everyone," Uncle Crossman murmured as he pulled it all toward himself and began a careful inspection of each item. He tucked some away in his pockets, others were left out, but as he lifted the gold sovereign, his frown grew. "Was this really all he carried?"

Marian looked around at the youngest member of their troupe, Billy, who nodded vigorously. He was young but already well skilled at picking pockets without detection.

Marian liked young Billy, but she also worried about him. He didn't speak, and no amount of prompting could make him utter a single sound. But he was small and nimble and carried out orders without complaint, so Uncle used him as often as needed.

Uncle and Tommy, a strapping young man in their wandering troupe, planned to take the rich man's carriage on the road tomorrow. Today, they'd tested how deep their target's pockets might be with that little farce between her and Uncle outside the Wraxall Inn.

They were all certain he had more to steal, but the last time they'd met someone like him on the road, it had been an ugly business. Blood was shed, and that wasn't usual for their troupe and something Marian would like to avoid happening ever again.

When she'd seen her chance to perhaps avoid unpleasantness tomorrow, she'd signaled to Billy to crash into the young man. Billy had emptied his pockets with no trouble or hesitation, and it proved he wasn't as well off as they'd all imagined. He certainly didn't act like any of the wealthy toffs she'd ever met on the road.

"I would have thought with the way his valet carried on about the shabby state of the inn that his master would have carried more upon him." Uncle pursed his lips and glanced over at Billy. "Are you sure this is all of it, boy?"

Billy nodded vigorously and inched toward Marian, so she spoke for him. "He never felt a thing."

Beatrice chortled. "Maybe he enjoyed having a strange little boy hold on to him for so long. Maybe Billy should run back and try again."

Billy leaned harder into her side, and Marian put her arm about him. Beatrice could be cruel toward Billy and often said horrible things that often frightened him. Marian scowled at Beatrice. "Leave him be. He did well today."

"Yes, well done, Billy," Uncle Crossman said, smiling fondly at the boy.

Marian ruffled his hair and grinned. She knew so little about Billy's past, but he'd clearly suffered mistreatment at the hands of others before they'd found him. He was afraid of most men, especially men as large as Tommy, yet he'd trusted Uncle Crossman and her from the moment they'd met.

Uncle tossed a few small value coins at each of them, their share of the profit, that they all hastily tucked away in various hidden pockets.

It was a disappointing take for everyone else, but Marian was satisfied with her day. She might just have saved a handsome gentleman from unnecessary harm at their hands tomorrow.

Uncle preferred their targets to be wealthy and foolish, men who drank heavily and noticed little that happened around them until it was far too late. He might be satisfied with only having that secret second gold sovereign in his pocket.

Tommy's eyes fell on her and narrowed with barely concealed irritation. Marian smiled back, but privately worried about his intentions now. Of late, Tommy had been advocating for a more direct approach to filling their pockets. They could get by picking pockets and begging for charity, but he always wanted more. Marian had sensed his interest in the traveling carriage as soon as it had rolled through the last town and knew it would end badly for someone. She'd heard all the arguments for and against taking the carriage by force when and if it left Wraxall tomorrow.

It would go badly for the grooms on the carriage particularly and for the gentleman inside, too. And of course, there would be consequences for her family if they were caught robbing it.

Tommy seemed to think he was invincible and could take anything that caught his fancy these days. Beatrice encouraged him to believe that, too.

She cast a careful glance over at Beatrice, hiding how

she felt about the woman. Everything had changed when Beatrice Woods had joined their little group six months ago. In the beginning, it had been a comfort to have another woman always around. Someone to talk to and knowledgeable of a woman's lot in life. But that was only in the beginning weeks. Once Beatrice had secured her place in their troupe, she'd shown her true colors, disagreeing with Marian at every turn, flirting with Crossman, and because he hadn't discouraged her attentions, she'd started throwing around her opinions more freely.

Lately, though, it seemed to Marian that Beatrice and Tommy had formed a secret alliance. They'd started whispering together when Uncle Crossman was not around and more than a few times had slipped away together at night, though both pretended otherwise the next day. Perhaps it was love, or just a convenient rutting. Either way, Marian had a bad feeling about them growing closer.

"The way one of the servants carried on, his master is rich. I expect he's jewels hidden somewhere," Beatrice said suddenly, narrowing her eyes on Billy.

Marian checked Billy's reaction to her words and shook her head. "He carried none on him, Beatrice, or Billy would have shared that, of course. Perhaps any jewels remained in his carriage."

"No," Tommy answered curtly. "I searched for hidden compartments when the men went in to dinner."

"He must not have had any then," she said, pulling a face. "I'm sorry, Uncle, I know you hoped for more profit than this."

They had been watching fine carriages pass along this road for months, in the high hope that this time, they could retire on their haul. Rich gentlemen hardly ever stopped at this particular village.

"It is, as ever, a gamble," Uncle mused. "Time to go back to what we do best, I think. We've traveled as far west as I care for already. Time to head home."

Uncle's home. A place Marian hadn't seen in so many months, but that wasn't where she'd originally come from. Portishead was where her poor parents were buried and where she'd been when her uncle had come to mourn his beloved brother, though he bore a different surname.

She was lucky to have had someone to take her in as an orphan, family, but Uncle had never stayed in one place or town for long.

Tommy glanced sideways at Uncle, and his jaw set before he stalked away. After a moment, Beatrice set aside her mending and headed in the opposite direction to Tommy.

Marian wasn't fooled, and looked toward her uncle to see if he was at all suspicious. He was too occupied with his pilfered wares to seem to notice.

He glanced in her direction. "You did good today," he said. "No sense taking putting us all at risk for so little gain."

"I doubt we'd catch him unawares a second time," she warned.

"There's more than one way to skin a cat," Uncle said cryptically, smiling as he polished the pocket watch with his handkerchief. "This will fetch a pretty penny. More for your dowry," he promised, but that was only said in jest.

Marian had little of her own or ever expected to have, and nothing of any real value she couldn't live without, either. She liked to always keep her belongs to a minimum and at the ready because she never knew when she'd have to make a quick escape.

She dug into the food sack. "Billy, this is for you," she said, offering him a hunk of bread and then some cheese. He was a growing boy, but he never asked to be fed. Someone had to take care of him, and it had fallen to her to do it.

She noticed her hands were dirty and wrinkled her nose at the state of her gown. She snatched up her satchel. "I need a moment alone to wash and change. I'll go downstream," she murmured, and uncle nodded absently. But Billy hurried to hand over her cloak. She thanked him as he passed it to her, and she walked off alone into the woods.

They traveled as a family, old father and his four motherless children, passing through town after town with none the wiser that they were robbing them as soon as they met.

At the moment, their carriage carried a fortune in stolen goods in hidden compartments under the floorboards and seats. They'd sell their wares later to an acquaintance who knew better than to ask where they came from.

Marian hurried down to the stream, ducked under the low-hanging branch of a large tree to change into traveling clothes and wash. Once dressed again, she settled herself down on a rock to indulge in the peace of her surroundings.

It was rare she was ever entirely alone lately, but she enjoyed these small moments of peace on the road and by herself. At such times, she pondered what her life might have been like if her parents hadn't died so young and orphaned her. Would she be married and living in a fine house somewhere with a half-dozen children underfoot?

It was a secret longing that could never come true. No man would knowingly marry a thief and Marian wouldn't lie about her past just to have a ring on her finger. She had no good reason to change her ways at this point, did she?

She pushed aside any lingering regrets with the toss of her head and thought of the handsome gentleman she'd met today. He'd been too easy to fool. Clearly, he was prosperous and quite kind to strangers in need. But the way he had looked at her first, though, suggested he might be a bit of a rake when it came to women.

Marian approved of that.

She was not overly concerned about the low morals of gentlemen, or even women. In fact, she was always surprised by decency. In her book, as long as a man was kind to his servants, didn't beat his lovers or wife and children, he could do as he pleased everywhere else.

Yet they said most rakes ended up married. Reformed. Marian shuddered. Imagined there might be a man who looked at her, knew her past as a thief, and thought, "I'll make an honest woman of her."

Marian couldn't help but laugh and then immediately pictured the handsome man she'd met today on his knees. Begging for her hand in marriage. Such folly.

But he was a man who might have had a chance to lure her away from the scandalous life she led. There was something in his eyes and his smile that suggested he'd be fun to play with.

Marian let out a soft sigh, and closed her eyes, taking the sounds of the woods into her soul and picturing the fellow's handsome face poised above her. His lips parted right before he kissed her witless. He'd probably be a good lover for someone worthy of the honor.

"We waited too long to strike yet again," Tommy complained suddenly. "He can't even see it."

Marian's eyes flew open, but there was no Tommy

standing in front of her. She turned but stayed hidden, curious to know who he was talking to.

"But you can," Beatrice crooned. "How much longer will you put up with this? Can't you see she's taking over, and the old man is letting her? We decided to take the carriage tomorrow morning, and she thinks a few worthless trinkets today are something to crow about. When that fellow discovers he's had his pockets picked, he'll be on his guard tomorrow and we won't get the rest."

"He'll alert the authorities." Tommy growled darkly. "I should have wrung her neck there and then!"

Marian made herself as small as she could, keeping quiet as she listened to Tommy and Beatrice complain about her actions, her commitment to protecting their lives apparently worthless to them. She was only doing what uncle had taught her to do. Rob the rich, and pass along the wealth to him and make sure they never get caught.

Tommy, Beatrice, and even Billy had been taught the same thing, and each did it in their own way.

"The girl served her purpose, but she's become too soft for this game," Beatrice told him. "It's the boy."

"Never you mind the boy. We need him," Tommy argued. "But not her. Not anymore. One of these days, her loud protests will be remembered and draw too much attention to us."

Marian gaped. She had been with Crossman longer than Tommy. Why, if not for her *soft heart*, Tommy would still be begging on a street corner.

"Crossman won't leave her behind without a good reason," Beatrice warned. "She's his family, and he's sentimental about her."

"She's no more related to him than I am, and I can

guarantee he leaves her behind now," Tommy promised ominously. "Crossman's gotten his money's worth from the chit, but he can't abide disloyalty."

"She seems loyal to me," Beatrice murmured. "What makes you think otherwise?"

"She can't abide disloyalty either," Tommy said, and then he chuckled. "Crossman only took Marian in lieu of a payment when her pa died. He told me he tried to sell Marian off to the highest bidder once, but the child somehow escaped and returned to him, never realizing Crossman was behind it. Since then, he's made a fortune selling her in every village. But he can't do that forever. Soon he'll have to put her to work in other ways and miss high and mighty won't like that one bit. Crossman's first loyalty is always to the money, and if he thinks she betrayed him today, he'll never trust her again. And if she somehow learns the whole truth, she'll be gone by nightfall."

There was a long pause. "What are you going to do?"

"It's done. I've made sure he'll see his pet is a liability he can no longer afford to keep. When we get back to the village, ask to borrow her cloak and make a show of checking her pockets in front of Crossman."

Marian remained still, confused, and outraged by what she'd heard. She'd always been utterly loyal to Uncle Crossman and everyone in their troupe. She had never kept a single thing that her uncle hadn't given her first. She'd held nothing back.

But now Tommy claimed Uncle Crossman wasn't actually her uncle, and he was working on some scheme to set Crossman against her. He'd obviously planted something in her cloak to prove it.

Marian glanced at her cloak, lying just out of reach. She

couldn't move to check and pressed her fingers over her lips to hold in a growl of frustration. Crossman had been like a father to her all these years. She'd thought he had protected her from men like the stranger who had tried to take her away from him when she was a little girl.

But was it all a lie?

Her whole life. Gone in the blink of an eye. How could she not have suspected she was being used? She would never have trusted Crossman if she'd understood.

But she'd been so young, though, when she'd been orphaned and grateful that Crossman had taken her in and put food in her empty belly. But he'd never once said they were not related when she'd called him uncle.

Her eyes stung with tears as she recalled all those moments of affection between them, a twisted lie that made her feel soiled. The pinched cheek, the fond pats on the head when she offered him what she'd taken from strangers.

Marian shrank from those memories as they took on new and horrible meaning. Crossman *had* treated her like a pet. Like property.

"She knows too much for him to simply let her go," Beatrice warned. "We can't risk her running to the authorities and telling tales about us, either."

"No, we can't," Tommy agreed. "If she gives us any trouble, I'll deal with her in my own way. Where is she, anyway?"

"Back with Crossman and the boy, no doubt. She's always cozying up to the old man and spoiling the boy. Whispering to turn them against you," Beatrice suggested, feeding Tommy's insecurities with lies about her loyalties.

If Tommy believed Beatrice, and it seemed that he must, Marian was doomed.

"What are you going to do about tomorrow?"

"Nothing has changed," Tommy promised, and Marian shivered in fear. "I want to wipe that smug smile off that fellow's face."

"We could always take a peek through the room while he sleeps tonight," Beatrice suggested in a wheedling tone. "If he wakes, you could question him thoroughly and we wouldn't have to tell the others about what we might find there."

Marian pulled a face. They would tie him up or threaten him with harm unless he confessed the location of everything of value.

"No. It's too risky. Someone might see us there. You'd go back to camp alone before he comes and finds us together," Tommy said suddenly.

"I wouldn't want that," Beatrice crooned, "I'll dream you are in my bed tonight."

"You'd better," Tommy growled, and then she heard the unmistakable sound of the pair kissing.

Marian pulled a face, trying not to hear Beatrice's theatrical and probably fake moans of pleasure at being kissed on the other side of the tree.

After an excruciatingly long kiss, the pair walked away separately, but a chill was racing through Marian's whole body at the dreadful discussion she'd overheard.

They wanted to get rid of her by any means. They would get rid of her and tonight.

She scrambled for her cloak and searched the pockets, even the secret ones she'd sewn herself.

Marian had almost given up the search when she touched something cold, she did not recognize. Puzzled, she withdrew her hand…and found a pretty lady's ring she did not recognize.

Dull yellow gold band, and a single opal stone.

A pretty bauble meant for a lady.

She cursed under her breath. Billy must have found it in the handsome man's pockets, and Tommy had told him to give it to her and let no one else see it first.

He would never normally have kept such a treasure. He would have given it directly to Crossman, as he had all other things.

She clearly remembered Billy touching her cloak, handing it to her just before she'd left their camp to change. Only Billy could have hidden it in her cloak without her suspecting him.

And Tommy had put him up to it. Threatened him with who knows what to betray her trust.

Marian cursed under her breath. If Crossman found her with this ring, even if she'd not known about it, it would not go well for her. Not well at all. And Billy could never reveal the truth of where it came from either, since he never spoke.

It would be her word against the irrefutable proof of riches in her possession.

She really was doomed.

She couldn't trust anyone anymore. Not Tommy, Beatrice, Billy and not even Crossman.

Until now, she'd thought herself safe, protected, but there might be nothing to stop Tommy from getting rid of her once they convinced Crossman she had stolen from him.

But what was she to do about it?

She could hardly run to Crossman at camp, beg him to believe her and, in the next breath, accuse Tommy and Beatrice of trying to take over, which surely must be his plan. It certainly was Beatrice's.

Marian's instinct for survival had always been strong, and

she checked all the secret pockets she's stitched into her gown for reassurance that she had everything she cared about. Money. She'd always kept a bit of coin on her. Not so much that she jangled, but enough to pay for her next few meals. What she had was more than enough for a carriage ride out of Wraxall, but probably not enough for a room at an inn, too.

But she was a survivor and unconcerned with the strict morals proper ladies lived by. There were plenty of places to find shelter.

Marian hid her old clothing under a pile of fallen leaves and donned her dark cloak over the better-quality gown she was currently wearing.

She had to move quickly, and alone. Keep far away from familiar territory where she might cross the troupe's path again.

She felt a momentary pang for leaving Billy behind because she didn't believe he'd wanted to betray her trust. Tommy could be very persuasive when he wanted to be. The lad would have been given no choice but to obey.

He'd do well enough without her. Tommy said he needed him, and Crossman would ensure he was fed and earned his keep.

As much as she wanted to, Marian did not dare go back to ask Billy about the matter. She either had to bury the ring here and now or run with it.

Marian slipped the ring onto her finger, discovering it was a perfect fit for her hand as she admired it for a moment.

But the pretty bauble was not meant for a thief to keep, and she knew she must take it back. Crossman would never have let her keep it. He would sell it for the money the first chance he got.

Marian would return it to the gentleman at the inn somehow. Had he intended to give the ring to his lover? He would surely want it back. Marian might even be rewarded. Money or a fast carriage away from here would do.

Marian glanced over her shoulder, realizing she was wasting precious time debating. She couldn't remain in the woods to let Tommy or Beatrice find her, given their intentions.

Marian crept out from her hiding place and then hiked up her skirts to keep them clean as she followed the river bed deeper into the woods. Once she judged she'd traveled far enough, she changed direction to head directly toward the inn. The stream meandered around the village and close to the inn.

It would be the perfect hiding place for her tonight. It was the last place they would expect her to go.

Crossman, Tommy and Beatrice, and Billy would spend tonight thinking Marian was lost somewhere in the woods, and never imagine she'd run away from them until it was too late to catch her.

Chapter Three

DANIEL WAS DROWSING by the fire when the door creaked open. "I'm done," he called. "You can take the tray away."

"I'm not here for your tray," a woman said behind him. "May I come in?"

Daniel swiveled in his chair, gaping as he saw the young woman from the inn yard standing in his doorway. The firebrand in his chamber, but she was alone. Her hair was half falling down and in need of a good tidying, and it appeared she had been crying. He burst to his feet. "What has happened?"

"Nothing that I could have anticipated. I had to see you," she said, slipping inside and shutting the door behind her.

"I don't understand," he said, moving toward her, drawn by the tremble in her voice. "Is he dead already?"

"No. At least I don't think so. I have left him. You were so kind to me earlier, and I thought," she said, lowering her chin and watching him from under her lashes, "that you might be again."

"To you or your husband," he said, drawing closer to her. "Where is he, by the way?"

"He's not my husband," she blurted.

Daniel blinked several times. "B-but I thought, given his talk of your future, that he was…"

"He deceived you. Deliberately," she admitted. "He does that."

Daniel frowned. "Why?"

The woman wet her lips. "So he can decide if he can empty your pockets later," she admitted.

Daniel blinked again. Had he been duped into sympathizing with their situation and giving over his money for no good reason? "And I suppose the man was probably not dying, either?" He cursed when she nodded. "So, what are you doing here now? Looking for more charity from me?"

"I've nowhere else to go." She lifted her face, and he saw her cheeks were streaked with tears. "They will kill me for coming to you tonight," she whispered.

He frowned at her. "Why? Because you are talking to a stranger?"

She rushed toward him, pressing her hands against his chest. "I came to warn you. Tomorrow, on the road, make sure your men ride fully armed."

Daniel rocked back from her in shock. "Are you saying they're highwaymen, too?"

"Not exactly, but people like us are anywhere there are riches to take," she warned.

"And you work for them," he asked, knowing the damning answer already. She was a thief, too, and that explained where his pocket watch and knife had gone. He glanced around somewhat nervously. He was alone with a woman professing to be aligned with thieves and possibly cutthroats. He crossed to the door and made sure it was locked tight against further intruders. His men were too far away, but he could defend himself from one small woman easily. "How many are there?"

"We were five, before I left."

Daniel turned back to the woman and leaned against the timber frame before thinking better of it. He'd rather not feel a knife stab him through a crack in the wood. He shifted toward his luggage, where he had a pistol and shot tucked between his waistcoats, trying to hide his nervousness.

"I've thought the leader of our group was family to me for as long as I've known him," she said. "But I've just learned he may not be any relation at all. I'm sorry. I know you can hardly care about my problems, but I don't want to see you hurt. Tomorrow, you must be on your guard as soon as you step out that door."

"I will be. Thanks to you."

She moved a few steps toward the door, her hand lifting for the latch. "Goodbye and good luck to you, sir. Lock this behind me."

Daniel cursed under his breath. "Stop. Where are you going?"

"I don't know, but it has to be somewhere they can't find me. It can hardly matter to you as long as I'm gone away, I suppose. You will never see me again."

Daniel crossed the room and put his hand on the door to hold it shut. "There is more I need to know about your friends. Their skill with weapons. The arms they carry."

She looked up at him and that feeling that stuck him in the inn yard returned. She blinked and glanced down. "An old man past his prime, a man nearer your age, a woman close to mine, and a young boy. The boy is no one to fear."

"He is if he's the one who crashed into me today," Daniel grumbled, and then patted all his pockets, only to be reminded that they were empty. "He took my favorite pocket watch."

"He was only doing what he was told. What I told him to do, and I'm sorry about that, too. Take care tomorrow, sir," she whispered, attempting to open the door and leave. "I would not like you to be hurt."

He kept his weight against the door, refusing to let her pass and trying to catch her eye again. "Does that happen often around you? People getting hurt."

"No, it has not been common. Tommy, the young man in the troupe, is growing impatient with taking orders and his small gains. I think he means to take over soon, whether Crossman likes it or not."

"Crossman?"

"The man I called Uncle," she said with a defiant lift of her chin. "Barricade this door behind me when I'm gone."

"Surely they wouldn't be so brazen as to mount an assault on me here, of all places," he said, half worried that they might.

"I did," she answered, and then smiled quickly. "But not for the same reason as the others might. You should never leave a door unlocked, even if you are wide awake. Let me pass, sir."

"No. Tell me where you are going first."

"I need to find somewhere dry to hide for the night until a carriage comes."

"Which you'll pay for with ill-gotten gains, I assume?"

She nodded.

Daniel ought to let her leave now, but he clearly heard the patter of rain against his window. Daniel finally caught her eye. "So, you really have left them?"

She gulped. "Yes, with all I own upon me and a little money for a carriage ride tomorrow. I'll be running for my life for a long time and with no one to call friend."

He considered her words, likely an exaggeration to garner sympathy and her prospects for a better life elsewhere. A woman traveling alone, leaving the company of thieves and murderers in the hope of a better, safer place to call home, would be grateful for any assistance. He wished her well with her ambition, but feared it was a fairy tale with no happy ending in sight.

She did not seem the type he should trust...but he wanted to help this woman and believe she meant him no further harm. She might have just saved his life tomorrow, and he could repay her in full by offering her shelter for the night. "You seemed fond of the old man," he asked, seeking clarification before he committed himself.

"That was before I learned he actually did sell me once as a child," she said, lifting her chin. But her lips trembled. "Like a fool, I escaped to return to him without knowing he was the reason I was taken."

Daniel reeled back in shock at hearing what had been done to her as a child, but then his eyes narrowed. "He was selling you again today?"

"That was different. It was staged, and we all knew it. A game we play on rich and unsuspecting travelers. I knew what was going to happen today, but the first time, when I was a child, I did not. He made a profit by handing me to a complete stranger," she growled, voice rising. "And I ran back to him for protection thinking him my family. I feel so stupid."

It could all be a lie, but he would bet his life that her anger was entirely real. And he was troubled by what her uncle might do for trying to warn him about tomorrow's ambush when he caught up to her again. She was only a little thing. Barely as high as his shoulder.

A sob escaped her, and she stamped her foot, looking up

and around and anywhere but at him as she wiped at her eyes angrily.

Daniel reached for her—his heart beating faster and faster as he gently cupped her face in one hand. The woman kept her gaze lowered as tears continued to seep from her eyes, but then she leaned into his touch a little harder.

Poor creature. Forced to consort with thieves and scoundrels all her life. Lied to for years. He didn't know what more he could do to help her, but he could be here for her tonight, at least.

Daniel risked attempting to embrace the woman as the instinct to shield her from further harm filled him. "You did the right thing, coming to warn me."

"I hope so," she whispered. "And I hope they never find either one of us. You must believe they won't hesitate to hurt you if you were to get in their way. Leave at dawn. Don't stop for anything or anyone on the road."

"As long as you promise to do the same," he said. "You must be careful tomorrow, too."

She looked up at him, her eyes glassy bright. "Can I come with you in your carriage? Will you help me get away from this place?"

He winced and shook his head. "I am actually on my way home for an important wedding. My family…"

"Oh," she breathed and looked away. "I understand. It would be a scandal, a strange woman like me traveling in your carriage alone."

"You'll be safer on the mail coach," he promised her. "After all, your friends want to take my carriage on the road. Their attention will be on me and not on you going the other way. You'll slip away unnoticed."

"You could be right," she said, and she pulled out of his

arms. "I had better go then. Find somewhere to wait for the coach tomorrow."

"No, you will stay the night with me," he urged, ignoring the guilt that he would leave her behind to an uncertain fate in the morning when he didn't have to. "You'll be safe for the night here, and dry too."

"There's nowhere truly safe, but I would like to stay the night with you," she murmured. "You are so kind. Kinder than anyone I've ever met before."

"That's what he said, too," he noted dryly. "Your uncle."

"That's why he picked you," she answered. "He thinks the kindest, most generous men are always the most easily swayed." The woman turned away from him and moved to the fire, holding her hands out to the flames. "You should be more careful around strangers."

"So should you." He followed her a few steps. "Are you not worried about your reputation by being alone with me?"

She chuckled softly. "I'm not afraid of you. You're a true gentleman toward a woman in peril."

He was flattered by the remark and also annoyed by her faith in him. Most women labeled him a scoundrel from the moment they met. "How can you be so sure I'm a gentleman?"

"Any other man would have assumed I was here to share their bed by now," she suggested. "You haven't said anything yet."

"True."

But now she mentioned it, he couldn't think of any better way to spend a rainy night than together. She wasn't married, after all, and neither was he yet. But her life was in danger, and so was his, it seemed.

And he wasn't free to do more than offer her haven for

one night and he must send her away in the morning with perhaps more of his money in her pocket…hopefully towards a safe and happy life somewhere else.

"The bed is yours if you want it," he offered, moving away from her. "I'll sleep in a chair tonight."

Daniel fetched a spare blanket from his trunk for himself and carried it to the only comfortable chair in the room as she removed her cloak and revealed a remarkably pretty gown beneath. She had a curvaceous figure. A body made for lovemaking, too.

He stopped himself before his imagination could run away with itself. It would be an uncomfortable night in more ways than one, but he'd be a gentleman for her sake. "What's your name?"

"Marian," she said. "And you are?"

"Danny," he answered, omitting mention of his first and last name and especially his title, which would declare him a well-to-do local landowner.

Daniel sat himself down, regretting how his last night as a bachelor would hold no further pleasures besides kindness. He would be on his best behavior tonight and prove himself to be a man of moral character. Just as she assumed. "Well, Marian. Consider yourself at home for the night."

"Thank you." Marian went to the table and promptly finished his meal. As Sunday had predicted earlier, it was barely adequate, and Daniel had found he'd not had enough of an appetite to finish it all.

After Marian had wiped the plate clean with a scrap of hard bread, she stood and headed for the washbasin.

She poured water in the basin, splashed some on her face and scrubbed her hands clean with his sandalwood soap. As she patted her skin dry, she threw a cheeky smile in his direction, and then let her hair down.

Daniel sat up a little straighter, utterly affected by that smile, and spellbound as she combed through her hair with his ivory comb. Her hair was long and blonde, tumbling almost to her waist.

He made a fist, fighting the longing to find out if it was as soft as it looked. Dear God! He'd been without a woman for only a few days, but it felt like an eternity somehow as he watched Marian prepare to sleep in the bed that should have been his, too. He supposed it was a commonplace event, but he'd never done this before—watch a woman prepare for bed with no expectation that he could join her in his immediate future.

She went to the bed and drew back the snowy white sheets Sunday had made his bed with, and tested the bounce of the mattress—all the while watching him from afar with a knowing smile. "It's a nice big bed, sir."

He gulped. "It is."

"Seems a shame that only one of us will enjoy it and alone." Then she returned to him and held out one hand. "I want you to share the bed with me."

He remained seated. "Why?"

"Does there have to be a reason?"

He stood slowly, his breath catching. Anticipation and confusion coursed through him. He ought not to go to bed with Marian, given her warning and her profession. He ought to keep his eyes on her the whole night. A thief did not make a comfortable bed partner—not that he'd ever had one before.

"I don't think it's a good idea for either of us to get more deeply involved."

"I'm not asking you to marry me in the morning," she said, grinning widely. "Just hold me until I fall asleep and if anything else were to happen between us, I want that, too. My entire life has been turned upside down in the last few hours, and I desperately need a distraction. I don't have anyone but you to talk to, and I'm feeling very much alone in the world. Tell me everything will be better in the morning," she said. "Even if it's not true."

"I can do that for you," he decided, as he lifted one hand that trembled to her hair and tucked the strands behind her ear. "Everything will turn out for the best because tomorrow, you and I will go our separate ways and Crossman will never find you again."

"Thank you, Danny," she said as she immediately threw herself into his arms and squeezed him tight.

Daniel held her close, and as his hands skimmed quite naturally down the curve of her back, Marian laughed wickedly. She drew back a little, eyes locking on his. "I was right about you, after all. Not entirely a proper gentleman, after all."

"Old habits," he said in apology as he raised both hands into the air, away from temptation. "It won't happen again."

"I'm not at all offended. I'm flattered," she promised as her own hands slid over his chest and down to stop at his waistcoat pocket, then toy with a button.

Her actions made him suck in his stomach and let out a slow breath as he fought not to become aroused. It was a struggle, and he captured her wandering fingers and kissed them. "Don't taunt me."

"I'm not. You smell nice and you're lovely," she whispered, pressing her face hard against his chest. "I'd forgotten."

"Forgotten?"

"I don't let men get close to me like this very often," she admitted, wriggling against him maddeningly and sighing again. "It's nice to feel completely understood. To want someone even when you know you can't keep them."

"Yes," he agreed, and her hand resumed its wandering over his stomach again. His, however, fell away from her back as his stomach pitted. That was the worst feeling in the world, and it was a shock to discover someone else had been similarly disappointed in love. He drew back.

She looked up at him quickly. Silence stretched as they stared at each other. They clearly wanted each other tonight, but there was nothing to keep them together. They were strangers with nothing in common.

Oddly, Daniel felt the wrongness of that.

Marian licked her lips. "What's wrong?"

"Nothing," he promised with a forced laugh.

This time, he didn't stop her hands when she drew closer. They explored each other. But it was torture and pleasure all rolled into one, thinking that tomorrow he'd never see her again. Marian was exactly the sort of woman that had always appealed to him. Sexually bold, expecting nothing in return.

Before he knew it, he had Marian bent over his arm and she was lifting her lips toward his.

They kissed, and it was glorious. Deep, long, drugging kisses that made his heart race and his body long for a bed beneath them. Marian wrapped herself around him, pressing her hips against his hardness and wriggling with impatience.

When he felt his shirt being pulled at, he almost helped undress himself. But he knew why he should not do that tonight. Marian was not part of his future. She'd come to him because she had nowhere else to go.

"I'm sorry. I can't," he whispered, full of regret for what he was denying himself—one last perfect pleasure before he did his duty.

He smoothed her pale hair back from her face, and then drew back from her body, breathing hard. He could have had one last fling without regret. But there could be consequences for Marian later, and she was fleeing from her former friends, too.

Marian did not attempt to change his mind and dropped her eyes to the floor.

"Where will you go tomorrow?" he whispered, reaching for her face, and lifting her gaze to his again.

"I don't know. Where are *you* going?"

"Home. It's not far," he answered evasively. His lust was under control again, but his heart was full of regret over this woman and all the help he could not offer her. She looked worried. He smiled to lend her some bravado. "I want to tell you something. If it wasn't for my existing plans, I would take you away and we could have had a great deal of fun together."

"I would have liked that," she whispered. She came close again, pressing against his chest as she looked up at him with a shy smile. "What sort of place is home? Since I only have this night to learn everything there is to know about you, tell me about where you grew up."

Daniel considered the wisdom of that, but then scooped her up in his arms and carried the woman to his bed. If he was talking about home, he was sure to never become too excited.

As they lay there together, fully clothed and shod too, he told her about the estate he'd not visited in years.

He described the grounds, the house, and the district. By

the time he told her about his mother and granny awaiting his arrival, Marian was snoring softly.

But he told her about his family anyway, about his father dying so young and his nagging worry that he might not live to see his own son or daughter fully grown, too.

That bothered him late at night, and he drew Marian closer as the candles spluttered and died, throwing them into an intimacy he'd not counted on experiencing with anyone but his future wife.

Holding Marian while he talked worked as he hoped, though. He had not become too excited by sharing his bed with the woman in his arms. But with Marian it was comfortable, being with her, being honest about his fears, so he kept talking long into the night.

Chapter Four

"You're back at last, my dear boy," the housekeeper exclaimed, hugging her only son in the middle of the stable yard, uncaring if anyone saw her display of affection or laughed at them.

The entire estate was aware of Mrs. Paul's excessive fondness for her only son, but if they ever told her about the dangers expected on the last leg of their journey home, she might never release the poor man.

Marian's fears had been for naught in the end, but that might have been because he'd roused his men before dawn. With his men fully armed, and openly brandishing their weapons, they'd concluded their journey without incident.

He hoped Marian's journey turned out to be much the same. He'd left her asleep at the inn, but with enough coin piled by the bed to take her far, far away from any pursuit. He would never know what became of her fate, and that had left him anxious all day long.

Daniel watched mother and son together now with detached amusement and perhaps a little envy, too. They were extremely close. Sunday had written to his mama once a week from London, relating his adventures, and received the same sort of news from the countryside in return.

Mrs. Paul held her son's face between her hands. "You've grown, my boy, and you badly need a shave."

Sunday beamed, loving the parental attention and the

scold most likely, too. "I will shave as soon as I can. His lordship was in such a hurry to reach home that we rode out too early to have time for that."

"It's pleasing to hear you rushed, although I expected you weeks ago," Mrs. Paul said, wiping at her cheeks as she glanced over at Daniel, finally remembering he was still standing nearby. "It's good to have you back home where you belong, too, my lord. If you'll forgive me, you could do with a shave, too, my lord."

Daniel rubbed his jaw and smiled indulgently at the rebuke, and the tears that inevitably followed, as she hugged her son again. The housekeeper wept every time he'd taken her boy away and also cried upon his return on every single occasion so far. Daniel had become used to her emotional outbursts over the years and the occasional scold, too. He remembered well the time her boy fell afoul of the local bully, and they both came home with blackened eyes and other bruises. Mrs. Paul had whipped into a fury and given the boy's parents a piece of her mind. He was a little wistful that he'd never received the same support from his own mama when *he'd* been bullied.

But they'd be home for a good long while, now that he was getting married, and the housekeeper's tears would finally be at an end.

"I'll be off now," Daniel murmured. "You have the rest of the day off, Sunday."

"I'd best unpack for you first," he protested. "And shave you."

"No, don't bother. I'm happy to live out of the trunks for one more night. Be with your mama. She's far from done fussing over you, by the look of it."

"Thank you, my lord," Sunday said, hugging his mama. "I admit I have missed her, too."

"I know you have," Daniel said, giving the pair a wave and sauntering off toward the manor house by himself.

Hammersley Lodge was a tall, neat, four-story country manor house set in a large, formal garden. The lawn was always neatly clipped, and the garden bed filled with blooms cultivated first in the hothouses. There was never a wild unkept bloom or bush to be found anywhere next to the manor. His chambers looked over the drive and clipped lawns on the left side, with an unobstructed view of fields where cows grazed their heads off. His mother and granny occupied the right side, overlooking the kitchen gardens and orchard where most of the servants spent their long days.

It was not a place to relax and laugh, though, or be careless where Daniel left his possessions. Everything had its proper place here and served a purpose, even him now.

Daniel stepped toward the open terrace door into the drawing room to find his mother standing in the doorway, waiting for him already. She must have seen the carriage turn into the stable yard instead of stopping before the manor house, as it ought to have done.

Mother was unhappy.

Daniel could see it in the way she met his gaze as she stood on the threshold of the manor house, blocking his way inside. Although used to such a frosty reception after a period of absence, whether he arrived at the front door or the rear, he fought not to be disappointed that anything more affectionate to celebrate his return had been denied him.

Mother had been a distant figure in his life and was a slave to propriety, too. She was all frost and bristles, night and day. As unlike the housekeeper as it was possible to get.

The way she looked at him now suggested she was disappointed in him and his tardy arrival. Sunday should have let their return be a surprise—as he'd intended all along.

Daniel smiled at her, refusing to be intimidated or apologize. As a young boy, he'd cowered and stammered out endless apologies, clinging to Granny's skirts for protection. Granny had always approved of every wild thing he'd ever done. Mother never forgave her for that.

And somehow, she always knew he'd been up to mischief while they'd been apart. She couldn't know yet about the wild party he'd attended just after leaving London or the woman he'd just left in the last village, either. Yet somehow, Mama would find out and then she'd probably act as if he'd committed great misdeeds. She was utterly terrified of scandal and Daniel refused to be ashamed of his past actions, so they would forever be at odds.

Yet it was the future that mattered now, not the past. He was going to set the ground rules for how their relationship would go from now on. "Good day, Mother."

"Scarsdale," she said. It pained him that she would never call him by anything other than his title. But upon Father's death, she'd grown even more remote when addressing him. "You're looking well, my lord."

"As are you, Mother," he murmured, refusing to continue the use of speaking to each other with only their titles, but he held his place on the threshold until invited inside.

"Please, come in," she said finally. Formally. It had gotten worse when he'd inherited, and he doubted she'd ever change now. But he intended to. The last time they'd spent together in the London town house had been awkward and fraught with constant disagreement between them. He'd gone out often rather than bringing any of his friends home to visit.

He'd been relieved when she'd packed her trunks and gone back to the countryside at the end of that last season, claiming it was a pointless waste of her time being there if he wasn't serious about finding a bride among the debutants fresh on the market.

He hadn't followed her to Lancashire, of course. He'd enjoyed having the town house all to himself for a change. But after a while, loneliness had set in, and he'd spent more time out than in.

When the one woman he'd truly admired, Aurora Hillcrest, had seemed set to choose another man over him, he'd known deep down he wouldn't find what he longed for in London.

Daniel took his first steps into his mother's drawing room. Technically, it was his drawing room, but the first and only time he'd ever dared mention that fact, Mother had pierced him with a look of such coldness, he never wanted to live through it again.

"I'd be pleased to," he answered, striding in, then sitting down in a visitor's chair opposite her. He leaned back as comfortably as he could manage in the ill-padded seat and too-short chair.

Mother took her customary place by the fire, ignoring his discomfort as she always did. "I trust your journey was uneventful."

"Yes," he replied as he retrieved a pillow from the settee to stuff behind his back, causing Mother's expression to flicker with disapproval. The visitor's chair was an object of torture, designed to keep guests alert and their stay in this room as brief as possible.

Mama didn't really care to hear the details of his journey home, and he wasn't about to enlighten her about the dangers he feared he'd encounter. So, he made no further comment on the subject and talked about the weather instead for a time. "I gather the estate continues on in pleasant harmony."

He knew the answer to the question already. Sunday's mother was a great correspondent, telling him things through her son that mother would never dare put into words. There'd been difficulties between Mama and Granny nearly every single week of late. Their squabbling was common but not so frequent as it had been reported about lately.

Her lips pursed momentarily. "Yes, of course. I know my duty. I notified the household staff of your impending arrival weeks ago, and I'm sure your chambers have been aired sufficiently by now for your immediate occupation."

Daniel ignored the subtle dig about his being late and looked around the drawing room. Nothing ever changed here. Not in all the years since Father had passed away.

But there was one notable absence he cared very much about. "Where's Granny?"

"Mrs. Nolan will be along shortly, I'm sure," Mother said with a slight sniff of annoyance at his question.

"Good." Daniel had been hoping to see his granny standing out on the lawn. His grandmother had boundless energy and a rather lax view of proper decorum. Something Mother heartily and frequently mentioned her disapproval of out loud.

He heard an odd sound, an odd creak and groan, and turned slightly to look where it came from.

After a moment or two, Granny burst through the doorway, pushing a young woman seated in the ancient rolling invalid chair rather haphazardly. He'd last seen that chair in the attics and, before that, his father had used it.

He burst to his feet, even as Mother clucked her tongue. "Really, Mrs. Nolan. This is beyond the pale. Young lady, have you no backbone? I told you what must be done with her."

"I'm sorry, my lady. She refused to use it unless I took a turn in the chair, too. She claimed the rolling motion made her sick and vowed to prove it to me today," the young woman murmured, leaping out of the chair with a fiery blush coloring her cheeks. She glanced over at Daniel and blanched. "Forgive me. I didn't know you had company, my lady," she said, dipping him a curtsy.

"Who's this?" Daniel asked as he winked at the young woman when she finally lifted her gaze to him again.

"A nursemaid for Mrs. Nolan," Mother informed him crisply. "Lord Scarsdale, this is Miss Christine Willis, the maid I promoted to tend my mother as her companion."

Daniel excused the unnecessary maid for his grandmother as he moved to approach the older woman. He bent down to hug his tiny granny and then dropped a loud smacking kiss on her upturned cheek as he whispered, "We'll find her a better position later. Darling, how are you?"

"All the better for seeing you, my dear boy," she said, raising a hand to his face and touching his stubbled cheek softly. "You look like you need a drink, Danny."

He didn't but nodded. "I'll fetch us one," he promised, heading for the sideboard.

Mother disapproved of drinking before luncheon, but Granny imbibed freely any time of the day or night. Daniel could hardly keep up with her but usually kept a glass in hand to keep her company and dilute the impact of Mother's scowls.

He was sorry mother and daughter did not get along

better, if they ever had. "Mother, would you care for a glass of something, too?"

"Of course not."

He shrugged. When he turned around, Mother was sitting stiffly and glaring at him, with Granny sitting beside her, smiling.

He passed Granny her drink and sat back down, dangling his glass from his fingers. "Is there anything that requires my immediate attention now that I'm home?"

"I would have said so immediately if there was," Mother quipped.

"The door to my chambers is sticking," Granny murmured, casting mother a searching look. "I should hate to be locked in by mistake again."

"I would not like that to happen, either," he promised, wondering what had been going on to make Granny believe she'd been deliberately locked in her room. "I'll have the carpenter look this very afternoon."

"Such a good boy," Granny murmured approvingly, and he smiled, glad to be of service to someone. It wasn't often that he was given anything to do around here.

"Now, what brings you home?" Granny asked because Mother had fallen silent and watchful.

"I missed you," he said honestly, and encompassed his mother in his glance, too, though he wasn't sure she would believe him. They may not see eye to eye on much these days, but Mother had given birth to him and deserved his respect. He just never managed to show it in a way Mama ever seemed to approve of.

As a boy, a simple gesture of affection, placing wildflowers in her bedchamber, had earned him a severe reprimand for sneaking out of the house and making a mess of petals that the servants had to clean up later. Impulsiveness never seemed to win Mother over as a boy, so he'd stopped making much of an effort to surprise her.

"Well, I am glad to hear it, but I'm more interested in what sent you running from London so early in the season," Granny asked. "It must have been serious to bring you back to this dull place."

"Marriage," he confessed.

"Yes, I'd heard your friends had made several scandalous matches," Mother murmured in a disapproving tone. "I'm glad to know you've ended your association with them."

"My good friends all made matches for the right reasons in recent seasons. They fell in love, Mother," he corrected. "Something I'm sure no one in this family will do again."

Mother frowned at him then, but it was Granny who spoke up. "There's still time, Danny, my boy," she promised. "You'll find someone to steal your heart soon."

He smiled at her optimism, but shook his head. "I doubt that. I've looked around long enough, and it's time to be sensible about certain things. If I cannot have love, then I'll settle for the next best thing."

Mother sucked in a sharp breath.

Granny frowned now. "Daniel, say nothing rash that you'll only regret later."

"It's not rash at all, but it is time to make an acceptable match," he murmured, agitated that his bachelor days had now finally and officially ended.

In London, it had been easier to reconcile his decision to settle down and have a child of his own. Now that he was at home in the countryside, admitting it to those who thought they knew him best, doubts assailed him. He yearned for the excitement of London again, where he could put off his fate a little longer.

But that wild, carefree life was over. He didn't want to live alone anymore. His friends were married and soon to have their own children to inherit their titles. They were far too busy to come out and play with him anymore.

That was what he had to do. He would not be like his father and become an old man, too old to play, when his child arrived in his nursery. It was a miracle the late lord Scarsdale had lived to see Daniel reach even his tenth birthday, he'd been so sick.

And when Papa had passed, everything had changed for the worst. The laughter he'd assumed would always be his had vanished, only returning when Granny landed on their doorstep less than a year later with all her worldly possessions and never left.

But Mama had never laughed with him.

Daniel slipped a finger inside his waistcoat pocket…but did not encounter the object he sought for comfort. He absently checked his other pockets and then frowned as he realized he'd misplaced the promise ring he intended to give his future bride again.

Puzzled by the absence of the family heirloom, he glanced around, assuming he'd dropped it somewhere near his chair by accident. But it wasn't anywhere he could see. He'd surely still had it yesterday when he'd arrived at the inn.

His stomach pitted.

But that was before he met Marian and been run into by the small boy. Both thieves.

When he'd left money beside the bed for Marian's journey, he couldn't recall the ring being in his possession— though it was possible the ring might have been dropped there. Falling to the floor or the bed, which meant Marian could have found the ring!

Daniel groaned under his breath, realizing he might never see the ring and her again. Marian would surely take something so valuable away with her. She was headed in the opposite direction and at this hour she must be miles and miles away from him now.

Marian was the only one who'd gotten close enough to touch him, other than that rude boy and Sunday. And she'd made it clear that she had been mixed up with shady characters all her life.

And she'd begged for his embrace and cried on his shoulder about her fears for the future, and like a fool, he'd not seen a reason to deny her. But had it all been for the purpose of robbing him, pretending she needed his protection when it might have been *him* who'd needed it all along?

Had she feigned sleep and spent the night in his bed waiting for the chance to search him and his trunks? And he'd given her that opportunity, dropping off to sleep without realizing it.

He cursed under his breath again. To think, he'd actually considered remaining at the inn just to protect her or see her safely underway!

He burst to his feet, angry at himself and her.

He needed that ring back. He'd always pictured his wife wearing it.

He'd have to go after the ring, and Marian, too. When he found her again, he wouldn't be listening to any more of her sob stories about hardship and some made-up danger.

But before he left, he would check everywhere he'd been

since leaving the inn just to be sure, and then hurry after her if he did not find it tucked among his belongings.

He headed for the door. There was always a chance he'd merely dropped it in the carriage and not noticed.

"Danny, come back here and talk to us about this," Granny called. "There's no rush, surely, to make a foolish match. You're still young."

"I'm nearly thirty," he growled, turning back to his family at the doorway to the terrace. "Should I wait until sixty like Father did and die before the boy is ten, too?"

"No, of course you should not wait that long," Mother said firmly. "You need an heir."

"Look, I think I left something important in the carriage. I'll be right back, I promise."

"Danny," Granny called. "Daniel!"

But he strode away without offering further explanation and headed directly for the carriage. The men hadn't put it away yet, but snapped to attention as soon as he appeared.

"I lost a ring," he told them. "Small, opals, for a lady's finger. Did any of you see one inside the carriage somewhere?"

"No, my lord," the coachman promised, following him to the carriage door. "But then we never looked for one, either."

Daniel darted inside and searched the conveyance from top to bottom.

The ring wasn't there, and he groaned. Marian had taken it, or the thief she'd consorted with earlier in the day had done so. Either way, one thing was obvious—he'd be leaving the estate today to go fetch it back.

His shortest ever visit yet. Mother would not be pleased about that.

He turned back to the manor and stalked into the drawing room in a terrible mood.

Granny's eyes met his and widened. "I take it you didn't find what you've lost?"

"No. And I'm afraid I must be on my way again. Excuse me."

"No! You cannot leave the estate now," Mama cried. "You only just arrived."

"I've no choice, I'm afraid."

"But what about the marriage? You can't just walk away without telling us more about that," Granny cried out, halting him in his tracks.

"That discussion will have to wait upon my return," he warned.

He never expected Granny to approve of his decision to tie the knot. And Mama had been harping on the subject in her own way for years now. Sly remarks when anyone she favored became unavailable were the usual with her.

They would each have a great deal to say, later and in private, he assumed. Granny had always talked of him making a love match, but it was too late for that. He was impatient and could not wait forever for love to land in his lap. Mutual respect would have to do.

"You cannot leave," Mother ordered, as if he was still a boy who must obey.

"I am."

"We are expecting our nearest neighbors to join us for the afternoon and dinner," she warned. "It will be rude if they see you running away again before you even speak to them."

Daniel gulped. Their nearest neighbor was Amy and her father, Mr. Wilson.

It seems fate was going to deliver his future bride to him

earlier than he'd ever hoped for. And Mother was right, he couldn't possibly leave before he spoke to them. He put his finger in his pocket, hoping the ring would magically reappear so his proposal could occur as smoothly as he'd originally intended.

But it was not to be—the ring, or any proposal without it, either. He would have to slip away at first light tomorrow for his pursuit of his pretty little criminal and hope he would not be too late to catch up with her, and her so-called friends.

Chapter Five

Gravel crunched under Marian's weary feet as she cautiously approached an impressive manor house just as the sun was setting. Glad to finally have arrived at her destination, she stopped a moment to consider what might happen next if it was the right place.

She wanted to be certain that her handsome gentleman friend had arrived home safe and sound, for if he had, he was surely safe from further harm, with so many servants likely to be employed about the estate.

But to find out, she'd have to knock on the carved-oak front door first.

She winced as it occurred to her that he could be quite angry by now. Marian could have easily returned his ring last night to his waistcoat pocket, and not been caught. But had been perplexed to find it on her finger when she'd first woken in his abandoned bed that morning.

She could not keep the ring. It was too valuable for her to sell without guilt, and much too pretty to just let anyone else have it. So, there had been only one thing to do—return the ring and hope he accepted her story of finding it lying forgotten in his room at the inn. The alternative was admitting she had stolen it from him in her sleep—which she could hardly believe herself.

Marian studied the splendid manor house with its golden-yellow stone and many sunlit windows and felt a pang of unease grow inside her. When she'd started out, it had seemed so simple. From his speech and manners, she'd not imagined the young man had come from real wealth like this. But this was a rich man's home, and rich men became suspicious and angry when their possessions were misplaced.

But if he was distrustful of her, at least returning the ring might appease him. She'd come this far, and she was no shrinking violet. She would return the ring to him, or perhaps leave it with a trusted servant if he wouldn't grant her an audience. And then she'd head back to the road, find somewhere to rest for the night before she continued on her way tomorrow somehow.

The money Danny had left her beside the bed would still take her far away from here, and anywhere Uncle Crossman might search for her.

Crossman and the rest would not look for her here. He avoided wealthy landowners' properties like this and favored large market towns where no one knew them. It was easier to get lost in the crowds, he'd said. But he knew she knew that. And he had already said he would head in the opposite direction of this estate, as well, which might have made it the perfect hiding place if circumstances were different.

It was getting late, the sunlight was fading, so she rapped on the front door with the knocker and stood back with a smile plastered on her face. No one came immediately, and she wiggled the ring between her fingers while she waited impatiently. She was unusually nervous about seeing Danny again, and especially here. He hadn't said goodbye at the inn, and had left the door unlocked. Marian hadn't particular cared for that. The man had no sense of the danger she was in. The sooner she gave the ring back, and went on her way, the better.

No one came to answer her second knock, and then she heard laugher. Women twittering nearby. Marian looked from side to side.

All the windows had been sunlit when she'd first walked up to the front door, but now a single window was aglow with light from within.

Curious about the occupants of that room, Marian moved toward the light.

The first thing she saw was a man standing with his back to the door. By his height, build and the color of his wavy hair, it might be her handsome gentleman from the inn, but he was not alone.

Opposite him, with the most fatuous smile on her face, was a beautiful blonde woman, staring up at him. Beyond her, an older pair of ladies, and then what seemed to be an old servant, hovering behind them, holding a silver tray.

She heard Danny's laugh. His voice and let out a sigh of relief. She'd found him.

Marian shrank back a little from the window though as they continued to talk amongst themselves. Although she listened hard, no one mentioned a wedding about to take place or revealed that one already had.

But Danny sounded happy to be home as he laughed again and teased the oldest lady, revealing the great fondness he'd told Marian of last night when he'd spoken of his granny. But to the other regal older woman, he said not a word in jest. That must be his disapproving mother he's spoken of with such sadness in his voice.

Another male voice suddenly joined in the quartet and that moved Marian back from the window a bit farther still for a while. When she dared take another peek, she noticed several other dignified people standing about in the chamber. All of them were focused on Danny's splendid figure, too.

He appeared to be holding court, and Marian sighed at how refined they all seemed. From the cut of their clothes, the riches adorning each woman, it was clear they were all very wealthy. How nice it must be to have acquaintances like that. Refined men and women. No danger, no hardship, no fear of betrayal.

For all her life, Marian had had little to do with women her own age or of higher status. When Beatrice had joined their group, she'd thought they'd become friends and allies for a while, but she soon discovered they were nothing like each other.

With the life she led, it wasn't wise to trust anyone with the details of her situation, and she'd been proven right repeatedly.

She turned her attention back to the older pair of women as she settled to her knees by the glass and confirmed a similarity in their features to Danny's. The grandmother was more expressive, smiled and laughed more often than her daughter beside her.

She turned her attention back to the younger woman in the room. She was truly beautiful in her gown of pure white, and it was obviously costly. She kept throwing a shy smile at Danny, but he hadn't seemed to notice yet. She bore no resemblance to the older ladies, though, and Marian wondered who she was. Perhaps she was the bride at the wedding Danny talked of attending, because she recalled no mention of any other woman living in his home. Yet the woman seemed to hang on every word Danny uttered tonight.

Marian narrowed her eyes on the woman, deciding she

must be a neighbor as a blush suddenly colored her cheeks and her fan fluttered artfully before her face. Danny hadn't mentioned who was actually getting married, but she was getting a suspicious feeling about this gathering. She shook it away, determined not to let her imagination run away with itself.

But how was she to return the ring to Danny with so many loitering about him tonight? Did she dare to try, or should she wait until morning?

She glanced behind her toward the entry door. No one seemed to have heard her knock, and it was so dark out here now that no one could even see her if they came outside.

Marian could prowl around the manor house and remain completely undetected if she was careful. She was loath to interrupt so happy an evening, but the ring must be returned one way or another. She backed away from the window and, once beyond the pool of light spilling out, she skirted the house, looking for a way in.

An unlatched window was often the most forgotten entry point, second to an unlocked door. If she could find one open close by, she could sneak in, find Danny's study, and leave his ring on his desk. Assuming he *had* a desk.

Or a better idea might be to find his bedchamber instead and leave it on his pillow. Given the number of guest lurking about, it was unlikely he or any member of the family might venture upstairs soon. At least then he would be the one to find the ring and he might never know she'd had it.

Deciding the latter was the better option, she circled the house, testing windows and doors all the way round. The only way in ended up being via a door on the back side of the very room where everyone was gathered.

She was grateful for the easy access, but equally annoyed

by it. Hadn't Danny learned anything from their time together? He ought to be more careful, even here. The side door stood open to let in the night air, with no one even guarding it.

She moved away from that doorway and crouched down beside a marble statue, out of sight of anyone who might decide to take a breath of fresh night air. But after half an hour, no one came out and Marian stood tall again. Why would anyone like them imagine someone like her was watching? They must all believe themselves protected by their wealth and servants, though Marian had seen only the one in the room with them so far.

She moved closer to hear the conversation, grateful that she was uniquely skilled at moving about unobserved when she wanted to.

Given the talk of politics going on, she reasoned she'd have to wait a little longer, and used the time to discreetly study the layout and contents of the chamber. There were deep-cushioned chairs, tables, and settees and even a pianoforte, and beyond that, two separate doors leading deeper into the house. But where they might go, Marian couldn't immediately tell.

The other rooms had been so dark that she'd learned nothing of their contents or purpose when she'd looked for an unlocked window. Which way she should go once inside was not at all clear.

She glanced back at the people in the room with Danny and noticed the butler had vanished.

Her chance to enter came five minutes later when the butler reappeared, and dinner was announced. There was a lot of milling about and conversation as they headed for the door.

Eventually they shuffled from the room, Danny taking the arm of the young woman and the others, talking loudly to each other.

The butler went with them, and knowing this might be her only chance, Marian slipped inside, only to duck behind the nearest large piece of furniture, listening as footsteps returned in a hurry.

The butler closed the previously open door and locked it as well. But he never saw her, and he left again.

When the room was silent at last, Marian got to her feet and looked around her. She was inside a brightly lit square room filled with riches beyond her wildest dreams.

Her uncle would want her to steal anything of value she could carry if he knew where she was tonight. But everything looked so perfect and in their right places that she wasn't even tempted.

She headed instead for the doorway no one had yet used. Marian entered a long moonlit corridor, with velvet curtains hanging at every window and dozens of paintings on the opposite wall. Carved busts interspersed between the portraits, creating a palace-like atmosphere. She moved slowly, quietly, glancing left and right and behind her repeatedly, ready as ever to hide herself at a moment's notice if need be.

She encountered no one in the long hall, or until she reached the far doorway. Then she heard footsteps headed her way and hid herself quick smart. But no one appeared, and she took a risk to look out again.

This long hall seemed to connect to an area under a grand staircase that went up and up and up. Someone heavy footed was moving around on the other side of it, out of her immediate line of sight.

She held to her place, assured she was sufficiently hidden for now...

But then Danny appeared, his expression angry as he raced across the marble floor, headed back toward the room where she'd first seen him tonight.

Knowing time was of the essence, she retraced her steps, too, determined to meet up with him there. She would give him the ring back and go on her way immediately.

But when she arrived in the room, her gentleman was bent over a chair, backside facing her, tossing pillows and small knee rugs aside. "Please be here now. Where is it? Damn it."

Marian admired the unique view of her handsome gent, but then remembered what she was here for. There was no time for gawking. She cleared her throat to get his attention, rather than shout out his name.

"I'll be right there," he called, probably mistaking Marian for someone else so she tried again. He turned slightly, "Did you see a ring lying about anywhere about this room? I looked earlier, but no luck then. I was hoping to be wrong."

"Yes, I have it," she answered as she slipped the ring from her finger.

"Thank you!" he cried, sagging before he spun about to face Marian at last.

His mouth dropped open though when he spotted her standing across the room.

But before he could close it or even speak, light footsteps rushed along the hall toward them.

Marian darted for the closest hiding place, behind a velvet curtain so she wasn't seen and made certain her toes were not peeking out too. She made her breathing even and soft, all the while trying to hear what was going on out there.

"Danny, really. Your guests are waiting for you," a woman chided, her voice aged and weary.

"I know that, Granny. Please distract them for a little longer," he urged.

"What are you looking for?"

"Nothing. Nothing now."

"Darling, I must warn you that your mother hinted to Mr. Wilson that you intend to make a match, and they both have assumed it will be to Amy. They are waiting for you to make the grand announcement."

Marian gaped. Danny was the one getting married. He'd never told her that. Her fingers closed around the precious bauble, and she felt the sting of acute disappointment. So the ring was intended for someone else?

There was a prolonged silence on the other side of the curtain, and then Danny said softly, "Mother should not have shared that bit of news."

"Well, you should have known better than to confide in your mother at all. It's her dearest wish that you'd settle down and you know how she feels about Amy," the other woman said. "She won't wait another five years for you to get around to the business of actually tying the knot. She'll force the issue this week, no doubt, and have a date set for the summer. She has always believed you were fated to wed Amy. But I warned you years ago that she's not the one for you."

"And I told you to stop sticking your nose into my love life, Granny," he said, almost growling his response.

"Love?" the old woman crocked. "I think not. Convenience is more like it in Amy's case."

Marian winced to hear that Danny did not love the woman he planned to marry. She'd thought better of him, but then again, one night together did not make them more than passing acquaintances.

It also sounded like his mother was a more difficult woman to control than he'd confessed to last night, too.

When the silence out there continued, Marian risked a peek to see if they'd gone. Danny stood with his back to his old granny, blocking Marian's view of her and most of the room. His attention was locked on Marian and the curtain she hid behind.

She risked a quick smile, and his eyes flared wide for a moment. But then his gaze narrowed, and he turned his back on her abruptly.

"Granny, there will be no proposal tonight," he said, his voice determined yet muffled as he moved away. "I will make my offer in my own time and not before so many witnesses."

Marian shrank behind the curtain, fighting a grin at his announcement that he would not be forced into a proposal.

"Well, that is a relief," Granny gushed.

"You can rejoin the guests," he ordered, and when Marian risked another peek, she discovered he'd moved to the door, taking the older lady with him. "I'll be along in a moment."

"But we must discuss this further. What will you say tonight to put the Wilsons off?"

"Probably something that will upset Mother. She was wrong to allude to any match," he said. "I will deal with her tomorrow. I trust that is convenient to you, too."

"It will be, of course," Granny promised.

Marian scrunched up her nose at the odd formality of his tone. That didn't match the passionate laughing man she'd spent the night with. Danny had seemed more impulsive and friendlier away from here. Far warmer, too. Perhaps it was his family's choice to be that way.

She peeked out again in time to see Danny steer the old woman out the door by the elbow.

The old lady would be gone any moment, and then Marian would finally be alone with Danny again. She smoothed her hair as best she could and then chided herself for being vain about her appearance. Clearly, he intended to marry someone far more perfect than Marian had ever seen.

Now she'd seen Danny at home among his family, she saw the mistake she'd made, assuming they had anything in common. He was no carefree man who would ever flaunt society rules to do as he pleased. And tonight was the night when he was supposed to charm a proper young woman. The ring was always meant for his bride.

But she still had the ring in her possession, in her hand. She just needed to pass it over, put it directly in his palm, and go on her merry way again.

Marian squared her shoulders and prepared to step out from behind the curtain and complete her reason for coming here.

But suddenly there was some sort of commotion, and when she looked out, the old lady was lying prone on the floor, Danny bent over her.

He shook the old lady by the shoulder, and then shook her again, "Gran. Granny. *Granny!*"

The old woman had taken some sort of turn and didn't immediately answer him. She moaned, and that led to Danny's renewed cries for her to wake up.

Marian had to get out of this room, and now, before anyone heard his cries of distress!

It was also clear that she had lost the chance to be alone

with Danny, thanks to the old lady's turn. She placed the ring down on the cushion of the nearest chair and scurried for the back door as fast as her legs could carry her.

But once at the door, she was beset by concern. She really ought to wait and speak to Danny, about the matter of the ring and his granny. She fled back to the curtain to hide behind again as Danny's voice became louder and utterly panicked now.

Servants would come soon to investigate the disturbance.

She could be discovered if she stayed too close to the commotion.

And a servant might find the ring before he did…

And if they were dishonest, they might not give it to him.

Marian darted out, snatched back the ring from the cushion and clutched it against her breast. But then the old lady roused enough to moan.

However, it sounded like *go go*.

Marian peeked in her direction—and their eyes met, hers and Granny's.

The old lady seemed utterly unsurprised that a woman was hiding behind a curtain, and it was curious she wasn't raising any alarm, either.

The lady waved her hand about in the air behind Danny's back as he tried to sit her up, large gestures that seemed to urge Marian to flee into the long gallery.

"I'm taking you upstairs," Danny announced, preparing to lift the old woman in his arms.

"No," she protested, refusing his assistance. "I'm alright. I'm fine right here. Go. Go."

"Are you sure?"

"Indeed, yes. Fit as a fiddle in just a moment. Go."

"Granny, you just fainted and you're sitting on the floor,"

Danny exclaimed, trying to capture her still waving hands. "I'm not going to leave you. Did you hit your head when you fell? This is hardly dignified."

"Oh, oh. Well, that's nothing new," Granny told him as Marian took a few tentative steps toward the hall, even while keeping an eye on them both.

Granny slowly nodded as Marian took another step toward the hall.

Danny didn't seem to notice and sat back on his heels. "How often are you fainting?"

"That is none of your business, young man," she snapped.

When Danny started to turn to look in Marian's direction, the old lady's hand shot out to keep his attention on her. But she resumed gesturing Marian out of the room with her finger. She then pointed up, and Marian understood her message, or thought she did. There was a better way to escape upstairs.

What was Marian to do? Obey the old woman?

She might have to, because there seemed to be no other choice right now, since she could hear dozens of footsteps rushing toward this room.

Marian rushed into the dark hall and shut the door softly behind her. She could not afford to be seen or get caught up in any concern over the old woman's health. It was not her business to know why the lady had fainted.

It would be best now if she left the ring on Danny's pillow and simply vanished into the night without speaking with him at all. He knew she had come, and it shouldn't be too hard for Danny to discover she'd returned his possession.

His chamber was probably the largest and should be easy enough to find.

Marian found the main staircase and climbed it silently,

encountering no one. They were all too busy rushing to the drawing room. She checked room after room, discovering untold riches in each, until she finally found the only masculine bedchamber and the half-empty trunks she recognized from the prior night.

Marian shut the door behind her and leaned against it, catching her breath for a moment. She glanced around at the chamber, astonished by the mess. Danny must have been searching for the ring everywhere, and still had been until he had seen her.

She went to his bed and placed it upon his pillow.

The ring glinted in the fire's light, and she steeled herself to leave it there. The bauble was never meant to be hers. It would belong to someone called Amy. A perfectly proper young woman who would become Danny's bride one day soon.

But for a few hours, Marian had pretended it *might* have been her ring. She'd indulged more than once in the foolish fantasy on the road that her handsome gentleman from the inn had fallen madly in love with her and swept her off her feet with a grand promise to marry her. He'd, of course, offered her a world beyond anything she'd ever known, too, and safety in his arms. She'd even taken an hour to consider her answer, but of course it had been a resounding *yes*.

If such a proposal had ever been real, she would have lived in this grand house with a family of women about her and with more wealth at her disposal than she could ever hope to spend. But it was not the money or power that appealed to her—it was the family.

If she was part of this family, she would always have someone to talk to when she was scared or uncertain. There had been many times when she'd needed someone of her own sex for advice, and there would be more in the years to come. She'd love to have a granny who mocked those full of their own self-importance, and a mother who told her how she must behave in proper society.

She stood up abruptly from the bed with no idea she'd even dared to sit down upon it. She'd done what she came to do, although it seemed harder than she'd expected to leave the jewel and Danny behind.

Danny had seen her with the ring in her hand, and though she probably owed him an apology about having it, what could it matter if she never apologized? He was with his family now and the woman he'd intended to make his wife.

There was no chance for them to know each other beyond their one night together.

She gulped. In all her years, she'd never once felt any compulsion to linger near one of their victims or regret her misdeeds this much, or at all.

Marian did not want to leave a man who had been nothing but kind to her, but she must. She twirled the ring on her finger—and then stared at her hand in horror. What was she doing, putting the blasted ring back on her finger, and when had she even done so?

She took it off again, threw it back at the pillow, but she missed, and the ring sailed onto the floor instead to disappear under the headboard.

Marian raised her eyes to the ceiling, annoyed by her dreadfully poor aim.

But then the door handle rattled behind her and, not knowing who it might be, Marian dived under the bed before she was spotted again. Her hand, as if by magic, grabbed hold of the ring, and she slid it onto her finger for safekeeping once more.

Chapter Six

MARIAN WAS in his house and had his ring on her finger. The woman who'd shared his bed last night had followed him home. He was shocked by her audacity and glad about it, too. He wouldn't have to chase her half-way cross the countryside now.

If the house wasn't swarming with guests tonight, he'd have chased after her, caught her in his arms, and kissed her witless in gratitude. If Granny had not fainted when she had, he might already have the ring back in his possession.

But he could not leave Granny to the servants' care while she was feeling poorly or abandon all the guests Mother had unexpectedly invited to join them for dinner.

When he glanced over his shoulder, Marian seemed no longer in the drawing room behind the curtains, though he could hardly go over there to check. If she had gone, she could be anywhere in the house by now, or perhaps she had fled outside again.

She had better not have gone away, and if she'd stayed, she'd better not have touched one thing that didn't belong to her—which amounted to everything.

Granny moaned, and Daniel glanced down at her in alarm. This wasn't the first night Granny had taken a turn in front of him, but she'd sworn she was no longer afflicted by her mysterious malady. The last time was a year ago, in London. He'd thought her wholly well again.

He eased granny up to stand and put his arm around her back to support her.

"I'm fine," she promised.

"No, you're not," he whispered, but gestured for the servants to go, keeping hold of her to make sure she was steady. "I've got you."

The old lady pushed him away, straightened her gown, and squared her shoulders. "I said I was fine, young man," she insisted.

Danny frowned at her as he drew back. Whatever had caused her to faint seemed to no longer affect her. Just like all the other times she'd made a rapid recovery. She seemed so completely normal now that it was odd. "No, you are *not* fine."

Granny merely smiled. "Shall we go back to your guests?"

"Don't be ridiculous," he said, leading her to the long chaise and forcing her to sit down. He left her to glance behind the curtains, pretending to check the lock on the door, but Marian was not there anymore.

He returned to perch on a footstool at Granny's feet and heaved a sigh.

Granny nudged him. "What are you looking for over there behind the curtain?"

"I thought I felt a draft and checked to see if the door was locked," he lied, but that assurance only made her smile wider. "You fainted. Why this time?"

She tried to stand up, but he put his hand on her shoulder lightly, forcing her to remain where she was. "Answer me. How bad is it?"

"I'm fine," she promised, knocking his hand aside with more force than he expected.

"I don't believe you." He shook his head and kept his

hands in his lap. "I will send for Mr. Kimble in the morning."

"No."

"But granny—"

"I don't need that scoundrel pawing at me," she hissed.

"I assure you, John Kimble has never pawed at his patients," he promised. "He's a man of science, and he was never much of a cad in his younger days, anyway."

John Kimble was about Daniel's age; they'd gone off to London together years ago. But he was a much younger man than granny was used to consulting with about her health, and she held his youth and, in her mind, inexperience, against him still. But he'd been tending to the villagers for years, and would be the first one to admit if he was out of his depth with a patient. If Kimble didn't know what to do for Granny, he'd write to a respected mentor to ask their opinion. "I'll send for him tomorrow."

Granny climbed to her feet, scowling. "You will do no such thing, young man. Besides, you were leaving tomorrow, were you not?"

"I'm not sure I have to go now," he drawled. Marian was here or had been until a few minutes ago.

"Well, either way, tomorrow will be a busy day if you are in earnest about proposing to anyone."

"Of course, he will propose," Mother said, revealing her presence behind them. "And Kimble will be sent for. Mother has been having quite a few spells of late."

Granny instantly stiffened, and Daniel reached for her hand, "Please, Gran, see Kimble just this once," he whispered. "Don't fight me over one silly little thing. I couldn't possibly do without you in the weeks ahead," he begged. "You promised to dance at my wedding, remember?"

"I promised to dance at your wedding when it was to your one true love," she countered pointedly.

"Scarsdale must join his guests now, Mother," Mama announced, clapping her hands. "I won't have the Wilsons slighted under my roof. Perhaps you ought to retire to bed."

Granny narrowed her eyes on mama. "They haven't enough imagination to realize their company is always unwanted and I'll not leave Danny to face them alone."

Granny was not a particular fan of Amy Wilson and her father, believing them unimaginative and dull company. Her father could drone on a bit about his estate, and in the past, Daniel *had* tried to avoid his neighbor when he was at home. Of course, now it would be impossible to avoid the man. He would have to learn to talk about his estate in equally boring detail, too.

He squared his shoulders. "Yes, very well," Daniel agreed.

Marian and the retrieval of his ring would have to wait a few more hours, most likely. She was sure not to wander off very far. Not after coming all this way. He held out his arm to his granny and forced her to accept his support for the walk to the dining room.

Both Mr. Wilson and Amy smiled as they all entered the room together. "I trust nothing is amiss."

Mother went to Amy's side and whispered something in her ear. Amy nodded and offered Daniel a warm smile. "Isn't it wonderful we're all together again? It has been much too long, hasn't it?"

Daniel nodded as he led his granny to her chair beside an older bachelor neighbor. "Forgive our absence. A matter of business for the estate arose unexpectedly that required my immediate attention."

"I'm sure your poor mother has had her fill of estate

matters to last a lifetime," Mr. Wilson said. "Now that you've returned, she will leave important decisions for you."

He frowned as he adjusted Granny's chair for her. "Mother has done exceedingly well in my absence."

Wilson pursed his lips momentarily at his assurance. "A lady should concern herself with the smooth running of a household."

"I certainly do," Amy said, laughing, throwing a smile of great fondness toward her father, even though he was maligning others of her sex.

Daniel resumed his seat and glanced down the length of the table, wondering how Mother bore such criticism so stoically. But she said nothing, revealed nothing of her innermost thoughts on the current subject, as Mr. Wilson turned the conversation to local concerns. After half a minute, Daniel glanced at the door and then remembered he had to sit still for such conversations now.

He tried to keep his mind firmly on the conversation, but his eyes strayed to his mother at her end of the table. Mama had managed the estate well in his absence these past years, probably better than he could have. That ought not to be overlooked or dismissed by anyone of sense.

Daniel had never once doubted her abilities to take charge while he'd been away. But now he was home, things would have to change. She would have less need to concern herself with the running of the estate, and even less to do with the management of the household once he married.

He wondered if she could give it all up as easily as everyone, including him, assumed she must.

Daniel signaled the servants to serve and turned to Amy. "How is the summer house construction coming along?"

Amy laughed abruptly and then blushed. "It is long

finished, my lord. I've spent many afternoons with Papa there, watching the sun set over the pond and reading to him."

"Sounds charming. I shall have to construct one here someday, so you might read to us, too."

Granny gagged.

"Although nothing beats our grotto in the heat of summer," he said, covering the noise with his remark.

"I cannot believe you would go there still," Amy shuddered. "So dark and damp and unfashionable."

Daniel had seen Amy's reaction to the grotto firsthand long ago. At the time, he'd laughed at her fear of the darkness and shadows. Her overreaction, as it had seemed to be then.

It was only truly dark if the candles were unlit. It was damp because it was fed by a hot spring that constantly replenished the pool. But it was wondrous to swim there all alone or with friends. To forget your troubles in a long, luxurious soak in the warm parts of the pool.

He pushed his food around his plate. "That is the way of grottos. There's no danger there, and it's hardly unfashionable. The Duke of Exeter was telling me only last month he wishes he had one just like it."

Amy smiled somewhat nervously at that bit of gossip and then looked down the table toward his mother. "My lady, will you be attending services tomorrow?" she asked, changing the subject entirely to something he hardly cared about.

"Unfortunately, she is needed here tomorrow," he answered for his mother quickly. Given Granny's fainting spell, Daniel would prefer Mother remain at home while Kimble examined Granny.

Granny wouldn't like him putting his foot down about

taking care of her health, but someone had to look after her if she wouldn't do it herself.

"Oh, but of course, you must have so much to catch up on, too, and many changes you want made now that you are back to take charge," Amy said with a shy smile thrown in his direction. "I'm dying to hear your news too, my lord. How have you spent your time in London for all these years?"

Well, he couldn't answer that honestly. He'd never win Amy's hand in marriage if he confessed to a tenth of the things he'd done in London and beyond. But everyone was looking at him now, and he squirmed as he searched his mind for the least scandalous bit of news he could relate.

He glanced down the table, noting Mother's arrested expression, and Granny's barely hidden smirk. He cleared his throat several times as he realized he would probably have to lie a lot as a prospective husband. "I attended the theater and several important balls this past season."

"And weddings, too," Granny added. "Don't forget the society weddings. Tell her about that last one. Quite the scandalous affair from beginning to end, I heard."

The last one? Daniel was losing track of all the marriages made among his friends. Probably the fault of all the wine he'd consumed at the wedding breakfasts as he watched another friend buckle under the weight of responsibility. They'd blurred one into the other after a while.

Because he wouldn't like to confuse the couples, he decided that a change in subject of his own was in order.

He wanted to learn more about Amy and what she had been doing these past years buried in the country. If they were going to marry, he needed to know who she'd become, learn more of her interests and favorite pastimes, as well.

"Oh! I'll have you know, I happened upon that book you

said you wanted," he said to her, grinning.

Amy frowned slowly. "I don't recall any…"

He reminded her of the title he'd memorized long ago. Not by choice, but because Amy's friend had the book and desperately wanted a copy of her own. "I thought we might read it together."

"Oh, that book," she said, and then winced. "I'm so sorry. Papa found me a copy the very next time he went to town, years ago now."

"I'd do anything to see my daughter made happier," Mr. Wilson threw out with a pointed look in Daniel's direction. "As soon as I heard about the book she wanted, I went right out to buy it for her. You'd do well to follow my example, son."

"Oh, yes well, of course," he said, disappointed that the second step in his plan to get closer to Amy had come undone so easily. The first, of course, was to give her the promise ring when he proposed. The second was the book he'd scoured all of London to find just before he'd begun his journey home. But he was five years too late delivering it to do him any good.

"Hmm. I admit it was a discussion of some time ago. I'm not surprised you couldn't wait. Do you enjoy having your own copy of the story?"

"I do indeed. I've even memorized my favorite passages. But it was exceedingly kind of you to remember my interest, and I thank you for thinking of me while you were away," she mumbled, reaching to lay her hand over his and pat it.

Daniel inclined his head and then glanced across the table. He blinked when Granny discreetly mopped her brow. Did she look a little flushed now, too?

"Perhaps tonight, we could find something else to read

together?" Amy suggested as she squeezed his fingers.

"Yes, I'm sure we could," he said, glancing at Granny again and growing even more worried about her pallor. He withdrew his hand to his lap, gaze returning to his grandmother.

Perhaps the evening should end early for her sake. Granny would not retire on her own while they had guests. He'd probably have to force her to go upstairs as well.

But not in front of witnesses. She'd never forgive him for making a scene in front of the Wilsons and their other neighbors. "Another time, though," he added, and then stifled a yawn. "Forgive me, everyone."

"Of course you're probably tired from the fresh country air," Amy murmured. "Papa always complains of fatigue whenever he returns from his travels. London is such a long way to travel from," she said a little wistfully. "I've always wondered what kept you there?"

What had kept him in London? The noisy, dirty, overcrowded city was full of excitement and scandal. His life there was all the things Daniel had ever loved. And all things he couldn't admit to Amy until after they were married. "It's hard to explain."

Amy folded her hands in her lap primly. "I think I should love to see London one day."

"My dear, you would not like London," Mr. Wilson told Amy in a firm tone that brooked no opposition as he cut into their conversation. He immediately turned back to Mama and started telling her about the size of his herd.

Wilson was an overbearing brute still, it seemed. When he and Amy married, she wouldn't have to do what her father said anymore. He smiled at Amy. "Well, perhaps we could sit together by your pond one day soon and you can recite the book while I follow along in mine instead. London will always be there waiting to be visited."

He made small talk with another guest, discussing local politics and keeping an eye on Granny. Mr. Wilson had to join in and was quite a vocal proponent of landowner rights. But their discussion touched on nothing terribly personal, nor did it involve Amy…and of course, Wilson boasted proudly that his estate was thriving and the best in the district.

There was a long, awkward pause after that pronouncement. One where Daniel couldn't think of a single thing more to say. He was surprised by how ill at ease he was with their old friends and neighbors. He'd known the Wilson's all his life and never had so much trouble talking to any of them in the past.

But he'd never met with them with the intention of proposing to Amy Wilson firmly in the back of his mind, either. Before, he hadn't cared too much about what he said or who he offended, because he'd always planned to return to London soon.

Now that he was staying in the country, he was weighing every word he uttered to stay on Mr. Wilson's good side. And he might need to do this until the wedding day arrived.

After that, he would be himself again, he supposed, or an approximation of what he thought a good husband and landowner should be. He had intended to remain here in the country for as many months as was needed to become a husband, and a father, so he'd likely have lots of time to practice not ruffling his wife's feathers.

But without the ring, his plans, his confidence in his decision to propose to Amy Wilson, had evaporated into thin air.

He glanced toward the distant doorway. Seeing Marian standing in his formal drawing room with a ridiculously radiant smile on her face had ruined all his carefully made plans for his homecoming.

She was an unwanted distraction. A reminder of his former self and a complication he hadn't ever expected. But her smile had lightened his mood considerably from the dread that had besieged him after losing the ring and attempting to make small talk with his old friends in the drawing room earlier.

Amy turned her attention to Mother, and everyone carried on as if nothing was lacking on his part. He sat observing everyone. Amy and her father must surely be waiting for the proposal Mother had alluded to Daniel making tonight, given the way they kept smiling at him.

He yawned and then apologized again. "Forgive me, it's been a long day."

"Indeed, traveling from London directly to here is quite a feat of endurance," Wilson agreed.

Daniel nodded, but raised a brow when Mother met his gaze. He'd not made a direct journey anywhere in his entire life. Mother knew he dawdled everywhere, but clearly, she'd not informed the Wilsons of that flaw in his character for some reason.

But the mention of fatigue after his journey had the desired effect, as Granny yawned, too. Even Amy claimed fatigue, and it was soon decided to end the evening sooner than Danny had dared hoped. There were no complaints about parting ways so early on either side of the table.

That was the only outcome that was going his way today.

His neighbors said good night and wished him a pleasant

stay, as if he was to leave again as he normally would have. Mr. Wilson wished him a good night, too, and then linked Amy's arm through his, leaving Daniel to escort Granny and Mother to the top of the front steps to wave the last pair off in their carriage.

Daniel turned to Granny as soon as the carriage was underway. "Upstairs with you."

"Yes, I believe I'd prefer that," she said, with far too much enthusiasm for an early night.

Daniel looked around. "Mother, might we…?"

But Mother was already walking away, her head bowed, and her steps hurried as she disappeared down the hall leading to the housekeeper's rooms.

"She's disappointed in me," he said with a surprise.

"Have courage. The worst is yet to come," she said cryptically.

To his surprise, Granny allowed him to assist her up the stairs and along to the doorway of her bedchamber. He opened the door and stood back to allow her to enter.

Granny patted his cheek. "I've missed my favorite grandson."

"I'm your only grandson," he reminded her with a fond laugh. "And I've missed you, too, but you ought not to distract me when I'm trying to make a good impression on the Wilsons."

"They ought to be worried about impressing *you*. They don't even know the real you, just the version your mother talks about to them. She'd have them believe you were a philanthropist and a saint next."

"Hardly, although I gave money to those in need recently," he said, thinking of Marian lying asleep in his bed at the inn last night. Her hair tossed across his pillow and her lips slightly parted, her ample bosom rising and falling in sleep in his arms.

He glanced toward the staircase guiltily. Could Marian still be here somewhere? Close by? He wondered if she'd try to steal from him again, or was she after more money in exchange for the ring?

The companion Mother had hired for granny was waiting to attend her in her bedchamber, and Daniel bid them both a restful night. "We'll talk more tomorrow," he promised.

"Daniel," Granny called.

He turned back.

"You ought to go directly to bed now, too. I think you'll need all your strength for the coming days."

"Proposing shouldn't be that hard." He smiled. "Good night."

He headed down the hall but nearly missed a step when he saw that Mother was standing outside his chambers, waiting for him. He had not expected to see Mama again tonight, given the speed of her earlier disappearance.

He stalked down the hall, anticipating a series of complaints made against him. "Did you need to speak to me?"

"She's fine."

"She's not fine if she's fainting all over the place," he chided.

"But never mind my mother tonight. She ought to be thinking of you and making a good impression, not drawing unnecessary attention to herself. She always creates drama where none exists," Mother said with a heavy frown for Granny's distant doorway.

Daniel glanced over his shoulder at Granny's closed door, too. "Is she really all right?"

"Of course, she is," Mother promised. "You ought to worry about yourself more, and Amy."

He didn't want to think about Amy right now. Granny's health was more important to him. "About her turns. When was the last one?" he asked, unwilling to be distracted from his worry over his aging relative to talk about his impending marriage.

Mother pursed her lips. "Oh, some time ago, but it wasn't at all serious then either."

"We'll see what Kimble has to say."

"She won't see him," Mother warned.

"She must, especially if she wants to live long enough to meet my heir one day."

"So, you are serious about that," Mother said, crossing her arms over her chest.

"Indeed. I've come home to make a marriage with Amy Wilson, as I told you earlier."

"Are you sure you know what marriage entails?"

No, but he nodded quickly. "Of course I do, and as she's the young woman you prefer, I assume you must be happy with my decision," he said.

Mother frowned, though. "Promise me you're not marrying to please only me. It has been my dearest wish for her to join our family, but she's a gently bred young woman. I care about Amy and would not want to see her hurt when your attention inevitably wanders."

Although offended by that remark, Daniel forced out a laugh. "It's time, and she's the right choice, as you've claimed all along."

Her eyes narrowed on him. "What about love and passion? What if you don't find them with her?"

"What makes you think I won't?" he said, folding his

arms over his chest now, too. This was perhaps the most bizarre conversation to have with his own mother. "Are you trying to make me doubt my decision?"

"I know you and this is sudden, even for you," Mother said flatly. "Marriage is forever or until death do us part. I find it hard to believe you've suddenly changed your ways. I've heard all about your antics in London and…"

"And?"

She wet her lips. "You don't seem changed by your decision."

Daniel laughed again, "You judge me by my lack of enthusiasm tonight? I'm tired, that is all. I promise that by tomorrow morning you'll see the new, more attentive me."

Her eyes narrowed slightly. "You should have tried to keep her here."

"I was worried about Granny," he insisted.

"Mother and her tricks! Very well. Tomorrow you will propose to Amy," mother demanded.

Daniel gulped. "Of course. I'll bid you good night now, mother."

"Goodnight Scarsdale."

He turned away and headed into his own chambers.

He stepped into his room and immediately noticed a difference. He'd left quite a mess behind in his search for the promise ring, and it appeared his valet had disobeyed his orders and cleaned up after him already.

He shook his head…and a glint of light under the bed caught his eye. Puzzled, he sank down low and got on his hands and knees.

"It's only me," the darkness whispered to him.

He drew back, relieved beyond measure to recognize that voice. "Marian, what the devil are you doing under my bed?"

Chapter Seven

"Well, I didn't think it right to sit on top of it without asking you for permission first," Marian joked, scrambling out from under the bed and dusting herself off. She had been waiting under the bed for some time. The valet had taken a long time to finish his tidying up, after a great deal of sighing and many complaints muttered about his employer's lack of care for his possessions. "This is a handsome room. A far cry from the inferior comforts offered by that inn."

Danny drew closer. "I feared I would never to see you again."

Marian grinned. "You're pleased to see me."

"Yes, no," he said and then huffed. "I just meant; you should be miles away by now. Safe."

"Oh, well, I wouldn't be here if circumstances hadn't required a change of plan. I came to give you this," she said, holding out her hand even while attempting to remove his promise ring from her finger. It seemed to be stuck there again. "I'm sorry. It keeps sliding onto my finger," she joked again as she finally wrenched the jewelry free. Although her finger hurt, she held it out to him with a smile.

"Thank God," he said. "You've no idea how much I missed that ring tonight. I'm in your debt."

"Nonsense," Marian chided, setting her hand upon his chest. "What are friends for?"

He smiled and then glanced down at her fingers. "About

that. You must know. That is to say…I am overjoyed to see you…"

"Danny, I'm certain your mother would not be pleased to learn you've a lightskirt hiding in your room on your first night back," his granny chided as she slipped into the room, even while grinning from ear to ear. "Thankfully, I've arrived in the nick of time."

Marian glanced around him at the old woman. "You signaled for me to flee upstairs."

Danny gaped. "She did what? Why?"

"Yes. Indeed, I did," Granny said to him. "I commend her ability to take direction, for I wish to speak with the young lady on a matter of great urgency."

"What could you possibly have to say to my… my…friend?"

Granny pointed at her. "I wanted by what right she wears your promise ring when you had vowed to only give it to a woman you loved."

"I promised to give it to the woman I *married*, Granny," Danny corrected. "And Marian has it without permission."

"Looks to me like she is loath to give it back, too," the old woman said, grinning from ear to ear again.

Marian glanced down—and cursed out loud as she discovered the ring was back on her finger yet again.

Danny grabbed her hand. "Give me that," he demanded.

"I told you, it keeps appearing on my finger," Marian said, so furious with herself and the ring that she slapped it onto his palm.

The moment their skin touched; a shock of remembrance flooded her senses. His warmth, gentleness, and kindness. His unique scent made her shiver, too. The wonderful evening before, when he'd held her in his arms, was the best night of her life. She hadn't wanted it to end, but he'd been a man of high morals…even if he *had* snuck away at dawn without a word of goodbye.

It was inappropriate to wish he'd been otherwise, given his granny was in the room and he planned to marry. But Marian's instinct to throw herself into his arms had returned with a vengeance.

She quashed the thought of doing just that. She did not belong here with him.

Danny turned to look over his shoulder at Granny, but he kept a gentle hold of her hand. "Granny, I thought you were resting."

"Who needs rest when things are finally getting interesting around here?" She pulled up a chair and sat, eyes alight, as if they were performing for her benefit. "Tell me where you two met?"

Danny shook his head. "I don't know this woman."

Marian winced at the claim and wrenched her hand free of his grip. The ring was still in her possession, and she threw it back at him. Unfortunately, it bounced off his chest, and she caught it in midair.

"Patience, my dear," the old lady said, patting a nearby chair. She turned to Danny. "My dear boy, when will you learn it's impossible to hide anything from me? I am a master at spotting a secret liaison. You two have indulged in an affair recently."

Since the question was asked of Danny, Marian was spared the need to answer the old woman herself because she was curious about how Danny would explain their association. Not that she was ashamed of herself or filled with regret about spending a night sleeping in his arms. Nothing of any great import had happened. Just a passionate kiss and a sharing of confidences during the night.

Marian was a woman with honest desires, and Danny was a man she'd found highly attractive.

Danny, though, was not at all forthcoming about how they met and after watching him stutter and make no sense, she turned to the old lady. "How are you feeling now?"

"Vexed," Granny said, but then she smiled brightly. "He's not always so slow, but he'll catch on soon enough. The promise ring looks like it was made for your finger."

Marian held up her hand, which now had the ring on it gain. She sighed. "It's the prettiest ring ever."

"Sh… She. I gave her…her to…to…" Danny stammered out through clenched teeth as he stared at her and the ring on her finger.

"My young friend took it from him first," Marian said.

"So, which is the truth?" Granny asked, looking at them with a slight smile. "Given or stolen?"

"I want to return it." Marian yanked the ring off her finger at last and held it out to the old woman. "Please take it from me."

"With pleasure, my dear," Granny promised, and Marian pried her fingers apart so it fell into the old lady's palm.

"Well, that's it then," Daniel approached the old lady, apparently master of his own tongue again, and held out his hand. "I have the ring back and that's the end of the matter, right?"

"Absolutely," Marian agreed wholeheartedly, catching his eye. The sooner she was away from that accursed ring, and Danny, the better.

"Not quite the end," the old lady said as she put the ring into her bodice. "The ring stays with me for now."

"But you gave it to me," Danny protested.

"That was when I thought you could make the right choice for your bride. I have my doubts now."

"Granny, don't do this."

"It is done, my dear boy," the old lady warned. "The ring always belonged to me."

Danny fumed and pouted in silence, but eventually turned away from them both. She could hear him muttering to himself. Words that made no sense to her.

Whatever Marian had thought she'd seen in Danny's character at the inn, some mysterious symmetry of feeling or companionship, must have only been a figment of her imagination. He was someone else entirely here. No longer the confidant man who had wished to save her.

"Well, I did what I came here to do, and I'll be on my way again," she told them both. "Do excuse me."

"Wh… Where are you going?" Daniel asked through gritted teeth, snapping around to face her again.

"Anywhere but here," Marian answered, but then remembered to curtsy to the old lady, who, despite her odd behavior, seemed a good-natured soul and worthy of respect. "Goodbye, madam."

"It's not goodbye. You are not going anywhere at this time of night, young lady. Is she, Danny?" Granny exclaimed, rising. "We can at least offer her a bed for one night, and a satisfying meal, too. After all, she returned my ring to me. Such a good deed deserves a reward of some sort, too. Perhaps funds."

"She already has all my coin to continue her journey," Danny ground out. "She has to go now and get as far away as possible."

"Yes, well, it's been lovely," Marian promised,

embarrassed by his curt response. She hadn't asked him to leave the money beside the bed or to leave the ring behind. "Goodbye, sir, and I'm sorry for bothering you yesterday. All the best to you and your mother, too."

"Oh, so my grandson told you all about us, did he? Did he also mention he's finally ready to tie the knot and wed?" the old woman asked, one brow raised.

"I did not tell her anything," he promised.

"I figured it out," Marian threw out. "But only after I arrived and saw him with that young woman in the drawing room. She's beautiful."

"With a great dowry, too," the old woman murmured. "It must have been difficult for you to see them together after coming all this way to meet him again. You have my sympathy, my dear. The heart wants what the heart wants. I suppose you met at an inn and shared a bed there?" Granny asked, looking at her grandson with brows raised high.

When Danny winced, Granny's eyes filled with mirth. "I thought so."

Oh, she was a clever old duck, this granny of his. She must keep him on his toes. Could he keep any secrets from her at all?

Marian was enjoying his discomfort, though she probably shouldn't admit to that. If he really was to marry, then she ought not remain. Marian could not remain one night or even one more hour in this place. He had to be good now, proper. Become a husband and cause his future wife no embarrassment.

"I'll see you out," Danny said suddenly, stepping close. His fingers closed about her upper arm, and she didn't resist the urge to lean toward him.

"Wouldn't being seen with a beautiful young woman, and

alone in the upper halls, cause something of a scandal?" Granny asked with a knowing smile. "Better I show her to the nearest exit than you do it, dear boy. You might be tempted to keep her, judging by the way you're holding her so possessively."

Marian shook off his grip and hurried toward the door. When she turned back, the old lady had the ring on her fingertip, holding it out. Marian's body swayed back toward the ring, and she cursed, fighting to resist the lure of its particular temptation.

"Goodbye," she said through gritted teeth and hurried out the door.

Steps followed her out into the hall. "I'm sure it's for the best that she goes," Granny said loudly behind her.

"Yes, it's for the best," Daniel answered before a door slammed closed behind her.

When she turned, the old lady was rushing toward her. "Now, my dear. Never mind about his poor welcome tonight. I'm sure he's happy to see you, just afraid to show it. You and I are going to have that conversation we're both longing for," she said.

Marian shook her head. "No. I am leaving."

"No. No. You're not in any sort of trouble with me, my dear," the old woman promised. "Quite the opposite, in fact. I simply must know what compelled you to sneak into my grandson's home to return the ring, and at this late hour."

"I knocked and no-one answered," she confessed. "I found an open door and was trying to return the ring when you came in."

"They tend to hang thieves first and ask questions later around here, I'm afraid. My grandson is rather important and my daughter. Well, enough said about her for now."

"Of course he is important," she said, looking around. Thick carpet on the floors, works of art on every wall.

Granny stared at her and then smiled wider. "You don't know who he is, do you?"

"He's Danny."

The old lady laughed softly. "I'll explain the rest later, I think."

The woman was barmy. Marian had returned the ring and should feel good about it. Except that she didn't. Her finger felt oddly bare. "I just felt I should give it back to him in person."

The old lady studied her long and hard until Marian squirmed. "Is that all it was?"

"What other reason could there be?"

"You mentioned an associate took my ring, and it seemed to me like you might be in some sort of trouble over returning it," Granny said. "No sensible young woman sneaks into a manor house like this if they've any self-preservation. A rogue is in residence, my dear. You risked your reputation, your very freedom for him."

"A rogue about to marry."

"So, what are you doing here, so obviously far from your usual haunts and at such an hour? I suspect you have fallen in love with my grandson after one night, and have come to change his mind about this foolish marriage he intends to make?"

"No," Marian promised. "Absolutely not. I've no designs on your grandson. None whatsoever."

"So, it's the other thing. A pity. A great pity, indeed, because you're much more to my grandson's taste than the other lady he considers," the woman said, and then clucked her tongue. "Come along, my dear. I'll see if I can stir the kitchen to provide for some tea and biscuits for your supper, then I'll find you a bed for the night."

The old lady didn't wait to see if Marian agreed. She just turned and left her standing in the middle of the hallway. When Marian heard a noise behind her, she pursued the old lady into another chamber that smelled of fragrance and overflowed with every knickknack and fabric imaginable.

Marian fairly goggled to see so many riches at hand as she looked round in wonder.

"Clear a space to sit. I think there's a chair behind you, under those old gowns," the old lady said.

Marian discovered an upholstered chair under three ball gowns and a pair of shawls. She didn't know where to put the gowns so they wouldn't be wrinkled, so she set them across her lap as she took a seat.

The old lady gave the bell a few vigorous tugs and then turned to face Marian again. "Let me help you."

She did not move to take the dresses, though. Marian narrowed her eyes at the old woman. "What do you want in return?"

"Nothing," the old lady said with a careless shrug.

"People who say they want nothing are always liars," Marian told her.

The old woman huffed. "I actually agree with you on that score. You are wise to be so suspicious. Very well. What I want is your conversation. I'm starved for excitement here, as you can plainly see by the company my family keeps. It's been very dull in the countryside these last few years."

Marian wasn't sure she believed the woman. "You have your daughter and grandson for entertainment."

"I've the capacity to hear more than just their endless bickering and complaints," the old woman said with a gentle smile. "I daresay my grandson hadn't time to tell you all about us. Stay with me for a while. Hide from your problems here. I'll even pay you for your trouble."

Marian narrowed her eyes at the mention of money. "How much?"

"The current companion earns six shillings a quarter."

She wouldn't get far away on six shillings when it was time to run again. "I'm worth more than your first offer."

"You are a very bold young lady," the old woman said, beaming as if she was pleased by that.

"You're the one who wants my stories," Marian countered, shrugging, but she was enjoying herself, haggling over nothing of any real value. "Triple. Each month I stay. Paid in advance."

"Highway robbery," the old woman cried. "Double and a story every day."

Marian raised a brow. "Bedtime stories?"

"Any time I like stories, young lady," the old woman countered, wagging her finger. "And I'll provide you with a new wardrobe, too."

New clothes could be sold later. Marian was no grand lady to need very much, anyway. But she knew how to spin a yarn out of nothing. It had been a tool she'd used many times to make new friends whom she'd later robbed.

Marian pretended to think about it, but it was easy to conclude she would be wise to stay here for the moment. There was clearly room, and it was unlikely she'd have to spend any time with Danny if she was the old lady's companion and he was off courting that other woman.

After a while, Crossman would stop looking for her, if he even was, and then she could go her way without constantly looking over her shoulder. Crossman would never dream she'd take employment in the home of their last victim. "Agreed."

The old lady beamed.

"What shall I call you?"

"Yes, I suppose introductions are overdue. Mrs. Cora Nolan. And you are Marian…?"

"Trill, of nowhere in particular."

"Are you a vagabond?"

"I like to see fresh places," Marian assured her.

"Because you're always running from the law?" Mrs. Nolan asked with one brow high.

"Nothing so dire. I've hurt no one," she promised. Not that her former associates, as she now must think of them, were as careful with the people they robbed.

"You take what does not belong to you, my dear," Mrs. Nolan reminded her. "That can hurt the people you've never met yet, too."

Marian glanced down, filled with chagrin because the old lady was correct. Crossman had taught her not to dwell on the past, things she could not change, and there was no way she could ever repay the people she stole from now other than to never steal again.

A silence fell over them until a young man appeared at the door carrying a tea tray. "Tea and biscuits for you, Granny," he said, and then looked around and spotted Marian.

Marian had seen this fellow at the inn, and in Danny's chambers tonight, and wondered if he'd recognize her.

His eyes widened, and he glanced over at Granny with alarm clear in his expression. He wet his lips. "Forgive me, Mrs. Nolan. I was not aware you had company."

"Now you are," Mrs. Nolan said, smiling at him. "Have you met my new friend?"

"Not formally." The fellow gulped. "Might I speak with you in private, Mrs. Nolan?"

"You may whisper in my ear," she said, and then cocked her head to one side.

The young man gave Marian a severe frown and then leaned down to whisper in the old woman's ear. His confidences went on for quite some time, but the old woman's features never changed to anger. She merely nodded.

When the fellow eventually stepped back, he appeared rather smug.

"You can go," Mrs. Nolan announced.

Marian got to her feet.

"No, not you, Miss Trill. Sit down, my dear," the woman turned to the servant. "Sunday, you are dismissed, but have your mother attend me."

"Surely I should—"

"No. No. It's all right," Mrs. Nolan assured him. "My new friend will stay with us for a long while as my honored guest."

The young man choked but was waved off and scurried from the room.

"His name is Sunday?"

"My grandson's valet, and indeed, it is the name he was christened with," Mrs. Nolan said, then leaned on one bejeweled hand to study Marian. *Her* ring glittered among them now. "That is beside the point, really."

She wet her lips and tried not to think about the ring she'd given back. "What did he say about me?"

"Nothing I had not concluded myself after seeing you and my grandson together."

Marian exhaled. She wasn't ashamed to have been in Danny's arms, or his bed last night. It had been an impulsive and satisfactory transaction. She had not intended to seek him out again if not for the ring taunting her from across the room. If her life hadn't been threatened, if she'd not fallen asleep, and if Danny had bothered to say goodbye at the inn, their paths would never have crossed a second time.

She sat back down, wondering if the valet would cause her trouble later.

Granny sat up straight again. "Now, let's talk about you."

"What sort of story would you like tonight?"

"No story tonight, but we really must decide what you're wearing tomorrow. That is quite an ancient dress, isn't it, and utterly unsuitable for your new position? I require my companions to dress with a certain flair."

"I haven't anything better," she whispered.

"But you will," she said as an older servant hurried into the room. She stopped dead when she saw the old lady and Marian together. "So, it's true. You found a replacement for the girl already."

"Not exactly, Mrs. Paul. This is Miss Marian Trill," Mrs. Nolan stated, winking. "The woman my grandson is smitten with."

Marian choked at the suggestion.

The other woman blinked. "I see."

"She'll be staying with us until the wedding, at least," Mrs. Nolan announced bluntly. "She'll need help with dressing each day and a long bath tonight or tomorrow to wash away the past. That new girl my daughter foolishly hired to be my companion can become Miss Trill's personal maid," Mrs. Nolan decided, smiling Marian's way.

Marian squirmed. "I can look after myself."

"But why should a lady have to?" Mrs. Nolan said. "A proper lady requires a high degree of pampering."

"I'm not—"

"Silence, my dear."

"It will be done, madam," the lady said, and looked Marian up and down with a critical eye. "I think she'd suit bolder colors. No pastels for this one."

"I quite agree," the old woman said. "Perhaps something in yellow for the day and emerald satin for the night."

"You've just the gowns, then, if you'll permit them altered," Mrs. Paul suggested as she walked into an adjoining room.

When she returned, her arms were full of bright fabric, orange, ruby red and a stunning shade of blue.

Marian sat up a little straighter as the housekeeper laid them out on a bed. Her palms damp from anticipation and possessiveness.

The woman showed her the lovely bold orange. A round gown that Marian craved at first sight.

"I think this should fit almost perfectly," the housekeeper promised. "Stand up."

Bemused, Marian stood as the gown was held against her and shown to the older woman.

"Yes, that's the one for tomorrow's introductions," Mrs. Nolan said, tapping her hips. "Now something with more flare for dinner."

The maid went back into the other room and returned with a green satin gown. It seemed heavy and appeared studded with glittering beads. She glanced at the old woman, who was wearing a jewel shade of blue herself tonight. "You have so many beautiful gowns."

"Yes, of course I do. I'm old and throw away nothing of

beauty. But so many of my gowns are wasted in the countryside unless you're willing to stand out."

Marian frowned. "Why would you not want to stand out?"

"The audience disapproves." Mrs. Nolan shook her head. "My dear, I've much to teach you about the demands made on a proper lady, it's not at all the life it seems."

Marian wasn't sure she needed to know more, but she could humor the old woman for a few days. After all, her stay was only temporary. "Are you sure about this?"

"Never once have I doubted my instincts about young people. That's how I chose Mr. Nolan to marry, and why I encouraged my daughter to fall for his good friend. I saw the same spark in him I see between you and my grandson tonight."

"It's just lust," Marian refuted quietly. "It happens all the time."

The old lady laughed. "My grandson never stutters in front of others unless he's around a woman he really cares about. Just as I don't swoon unless there's a good reason to dust off my old acting skills to cause a distraction."

Marian narrowed her eyes, suspicion dawning. "Was it all an act?"

"If you stay, you might find out," Mrs. Nolan teased. "Mrs. Paul, put my new companion in the room across the hall for convenience's sake. I'll inform my daughter of my new hire myself in the morning."

"She won't like it," Mrs. Paul warned Granny.

"She never accepts change easily, but she will not disobey her mother," Mrs. Nolan promised. "As for my grandson, well, we will see what she does to his plans when temptation remains so close to hand."

Marian blushed, though she was surprised she even could. Granny must be daft to want her to tempt her grandson away from making a proper match.

But none of that changed Marian's decision to stay. She had the promise of payment, new gowns to wear and safety for the time being. Provided Crossman never looked for her here, Marian would be extremely comfortable indeed.

Her eyes settled on the sparkle of gems across the old lady's fingers, and she heaved a sigh. She'd fallen in with wealthy people, and wealthy people rarely had any sense.

A bit of flattery and a few tall tales could see Marian walk out of this place with more than Mrs. Nolan intended to give in the end. She would probably not even have to steal it. Mrs. Nolan was too much like her grandson. Being too kind and too generous to a stranger would be her undoing, as it had been to him.

"If you'll come with me, Miss Trill. I'll show you to your new room," Mrs. Paul murmured, gesturing Marian toward the door. "Mrs. Nolan needs her rest. I'll arrange your bath for the morning."

Chapter Eight

Daniel froze with one foot in midair, halfway up the stone staircase as he heard women talking.

"Now that is something I have trouble believing actually happened," Granny exclaimed loudly. "Did you really spend a night on the roof of the queen's carriage inside a trunk?"

Daniel put his foot down as Marian answered, "Well, I couldn't avoid it. The queen's men were sleeping all around me, and inside the carriage, too. I recall it was an oddly comfortable night, sleeping on her gowns inside the trunk."

"So young to be so daring. However did you escape?"

"Someone brought bread for their breakfast, and they all scurried after it," Marian said, laughing. "I climbed down unobserved while they were stuffing their mouths but with nothing to show for my long night spent in captivity except for one lone garment in hand. I slipped out through the broken window I'd come in through and fled. Unfortunately, I couldn't wear what I'd taken in the end. The garment was ten sizes too big for me and it made no sense to keep it."

Granny laughed uproariously. "Now that I can believe. There's not much of you, is there?"

"I'm still hoping I'll grow taller one day," Marian said, with a good-natured laugh.

"I always hoped for that too, but it never happened to me," Granny confessed.

Daniel didn't think there was anything wrong with a

woman of short stature. Marian more than made up for any lack of height with her bold personality, the same way his granny and mother did.

The conversation died down and Daniel continued on a few more steps and peeked through the open door cautiously. Marian was sitting in his drawing room, sipping tea, and she seemed to be sorting through embroidery threads spread across her lap. She offered an assortment of colors to Granny to choose from.

It was clear Marian had improved her wardrobe considerably from the day they met. At first glance, one might think she'd always belonged in a grand house wearing her pretty orange grown, but he also thought he recognized what she wore. Hadn't that gown once belonged to his granny?

He should have known better than to trust Granny to keep her word and show Marian the way out the door and off the estate this morning. But he was better prepared to deal with the problem of Marian once and for all. She should not still be here.

He forced himself to move forward, eyes locked on Marian's pretty face, flushed from laughter, and tried to find something to dislike in her manner. Unfortunately for him, she was still so damn appealing that he found himself tongue-tied again. Something that embarrassed him still.

Her blonde hair shone in the morning light, and her soft pink lips were entirely too kissable.

He buried that thought deep as he stepped into the room. He could not kiss Marian here, or anywhere.

Granny spoke first. "My darling boy. I'm so glad you're back. You'll never believe who's come to visit. It's my old friend's daughter, Miss Marian Trill, from Portishead."

His step faltered a little and his tongue became unstuck. "Is that right? Portishead?"

"Oh yes, I had no time to tell you when you first came home that we've been corresponding for some months now. I said to Marian that since her parents have passed on, God rest their souls, she could come stay here as my new companion. It's not what she's used to, of course, but I'm sure she'll settle in easily enough. Isn't it wonderful?"

Marian didn't so much as blink at all the lies spilling from Granny's mouth. But he did. Several times. And his tongue froze over any sort of immediate response to her, too.

He closed his eyes briefly. Counting random numbers in his head until his throat relaxed. Marian could not remain as a companion here. Granny would take her everywhere, including to the upcoming celebration for his marriage to Amy!

He wet his lips and forced his tongue to cooperate as he spoke with greater focus. "I don't believe you need a companion."

"Oh, I certainly do. You don't understand how often I'm bored here," Granny told him, admiring her unfinished embroidery and then showing it to Marian. "Your mother will be much too busy with the wedding to keep me company. You know how she prefers me to keep my nose out of the estate business, and your affairs. I've let her run things as she sees fit, of course, but I have time to devote to our young friend. I want to do this."

"My marriage is not anyone's business but mine," he protested, pointing out the first of her inaccuracies. "And I don't think you're as bored as you say you are."

"I may as well be alone for the way your mother is always rushing hither and yon trying to please that foolish girl,"

Granny grumbled. "Now, Miss Marian Trill, I have the pleasure of presenting my grandson, Jeremy Daniel Clifton Wallace, Earl of Scarsdale."

Marian seemed taken aback by the introduction and gulped. "A pleasure, *my lord*?"

He nodded sharply. There was a reason he'd not told Marian of his title. Now, she would be my lording him as everyone else did. "How do you do?"

"Very well, thank you," she said demurely, a frown marring her brow as she turned her gaze on Granny. Her frown only became more pronounced.

Granny nodded enthusiastically, but then looked past him to the open door at his back. "Ah, there they are, Lady Scarsdale. We were all wondering where you were."

Daniel spun about. Mother stood behind him with Amy and an unfamiliar maid by her side, and mother did not look happy to see him, not that that was unusual at all.

He bowed to them all as they entered the drawing room. Daniel offered Amy a few extra words of greeting and then offered her a seat. Amy's maid headed for a hard wooden chair some distance away by the door.

Mother remained on her feet longer, frowning at the unfamiliar face in the room. However, she had too many years of experience to show any great surprise over the sudden arrival of one of Granny's friends and turned to sit, lips pursed tight.

Daniel sought to smooth things over in advance. "How are you today, Mama?"

"Very well, thank you, and all the better for having so many special guests, Lord Scarsdale," she said, gesturing to Amy.

Amy blushed.

Thankfully, Granny performed the introductions between Mother, Amy, and Marian, the latter of whom uttered a softly voiced "how do you do" and then fell blessedly silent.

Daniel caught Amy's gaze a few times and smiled, but was aware of everyone's eyes on him. "Where are you coming from this morning?"

"The orangery. Your mother and I were just talking about the exciting new plans you have for the estate," Amy answered.

Daniel glanced at his mother immediately. Since he'd mentioned no such plans, he was taken completely by surprise and did not know what to say in response. "My plans? Yes, indeed."

Mother smiled slightly. "They are impressive, as all the other improvements have been. I cannot wait to see them completed."

"Yes, terribly exciting changes," he muttered, frowning still. Why was mother suddenly crediting him with the improvements she made to the estate?

And what was Mama doing to the place now, and why hadn't she bothered to inform him already? This was hardly the time to embark on any new project at the same time as the expense of a wedding was in their future. Daniel wanted to focus on Amy and finding the right moment to propose to her.

Although now he had to get the ring back from Granny, instead of from Marian. Granny had refused his request last night for no good reason.

He stared at Granny, but she kept her attention on her embroidery and whispering with Marian. If that ring was in his pocket right now, he could propose to Amy and set his own plans in motion.

Yet with Marian still here and his family in the room, of course, he could not propose to Amy even if he had the ring.

He would have to steal Amy away to talk to her without everyone knowing he was doing so. Not that they wouldn't know what he wanted to speak to her about in private.

The clock out in the hall chimed. "I'm afraid I must return home to my father now," Amy said, pouting a little.

Daniel glanced at the clock on the mantle and cursed. Had he known Amy was on the estate, he would have sought her out sooner. But without his pocket watch, he had lost track of the time. "Oh, no. So soon?"

"Yes, I'm afraid so. Papa normally comes with me every morning to be of service to your poor mother, but he was detained at home by his steward at the last minute and sent his regrets. I must be home to take luncheon with him."

"I hope nothing is wrong at home?"

"I'm sure it's nothing at all serious," Amy murmured with a wave of her hand. "Estate business, no doubt."

"I'm sure you've no need to worry about that sort of thing," Granny murmured. "Your father worries enough about our two estates as it is. He must be exhausted. Do hurry home."

Daniel winced, but the criticism flew entirely over Amy's head, and she curtsied and excused herself, bid him remain where he was and let her maid escort her from the room.

Daniel watched Amy go. Their time together was all too brief today, and had not advanced his cause. He would have to make sure he was informed of when she came to call in the future.

He turned to look at Mother once more, one brow raised. "I've heard nothing of any substantial changes being made to the estate since my return. What the devil are you up to now?"

"The estate must adapt to new discoveries to aid propagation," Mama told him. "It's not important that you know every minor detail as soon as you arrive home."

"Well, Amy seems to think I know everything already."

"Well, you will eventually. I'm trying to teach her my way of doing things. The girl has little understanding of cultivation yet, though I have high hopes that once away from her father, her proper education can begin." Mother scowled and turned her attention to Granny and Marian. "What I want to know is, who's this woman?"

"This," Granny said, gesturing to Marian, "is my new companion."

"You already have a companion, hired at great expense, and I recall no carriage arriving this morning." Mother turned her eyes on him. "When did the young lady arrive?"

"Yesterday," Granny said with a smile for Marian. "Late, while we were all at dinner."

Mother turned a stony gaze his way. "I suppose this is your doing?"

"I'm as surprised as you are," Daniel promised.

"Good, then she can be easily sent back again," Mother said, glaring at her mother.

"I'll not allow Miss Marian Trill to be sent away," Granny declared, scowling right back at Mama.

"Now wait a moment," Daniel protested, getting to his feet. "It's just a misunderstanding."

Marian put a restraining hand on Granny's arm. "It's all right. I'm happy to go."

Mother's lips pursed tightly, and she frowned. "Did you say Miss Marian *Trill*?"

"Yes, my dear."

"Trill, as in the Trills of *Clayborne Street, Portishead?*" Mama asked, appearing to recognize the name.

"Indeed, that's the very family," Granny promised with a pleased smile. "Old friends. You remember how fond I was of all of them?"

"You were fond of everyone, deserving or not," Mother counted, eyes narrowing dangerously on Marian. She looked her up and down and finally nodded. "Welcome to Hammersley Lodge, Miss Trill. It's a pleasure to have you visit."

"Thank you, my lady," Marian replied, lowering her eyes demurely as if she was some inexperienced debutant out to make a good impression on a high-ranking lady. "It's a pleasure to be here."

"Yes, it is. I trust your journey from Portishead was not too fatiguing," Mother murmured with more politeness.

"A little, but that is common after any long journey," Marian replied with a self-deprecating smile. She looked about her; eyes filled with wonder. "It's a far cry from home, but I'll do my best not to cause you any embarrassment and hope that you will forgive my awe of my surroundings."

"Mistakes are understandable, my dear," Granny assured.

"I'd be grateful for any guidance you can offer," Marian said, keeping her eyes lowered.

Daniel wasn't fooled, though. He could see from his position that she was studying Mother closely. Deferring to her wishes without appearing to be fawning and suggesting a wish to be guided by her, too, was bound to win her over. It was a subtle art this woman employed to slip below a man's guard and make him feel important. Clearly Marian employed it with women, too.

Mother nodded decisively. "Just as it should be."

"Marian, dear. Would you be a lamb and fetch my shawl from the morning room? I believe I left the yellow one on my chair. I'm feeling a distinct draft from the open door, but I'm loath to close it and deny everyone the view."

"Yes, of course," Marian replied and hurried away.

"Charming girl," Granny said to Mother as soon as Marian was out of the room. "A little rough about the edges, but a month here with us will smooth those blemishes out."

"I'm not so sure I will have the time to tutor her in the social graces," Mother answered, frowning at the door that Marian had vanished through. "The last girl you dragged home for deportment lessons was more trouble than I expected."

"Never you worry over Marian, daughter. This one is different and willing to learn, unlike the last. She's a keen eye and intellect. I'll take on the chore of keeping an eye on her and educating the girl myself," Granny promised. "I did it for you and look how that turned out."

"Yes, and that should worry everyone. But I have more pressing concerns on my mind today," Mother said, and then turned to him. "Well?"

Daniel raked his hand through his hair. He could hardly believe Mother would allow Marian to remain with so little fuss. "Well, what, Mother?"

"Are you going to follow Amy home to the Wilson estate to ask her father to let you marry her?"

"Yes, I might, if given half the chance," he snapped, glaring at Granny.

"There's no need to take that tone. I'm not preventing you from proposing," she replied.

"But you won't give me back the promise ring I want to give her."

"No. Not just yet," Granny said with a sweet smile that belied her stubborn nature. "You can propose without it, you know. In fact, with the right woman, even words are largely unnecessary."

"It would be the same with the ring and the words," Daniel grumbled when he saw her pleasure in his discomfort.

It amused Granny that a woman he'd spent a night with had followed him home, unaware of his title. The fact that his family had known hers once was beside the point. Mother had just accepted the acquaintance of a thief in their midst. She would be furious about it when she found out.

Marian seemed perfectly content to go along with the deception Granny had embarked on. And why wouldn't she? Living in a grand manor house, wearing pretty dresses, had to be a vast step up from what she was used to elsewhere. She needed a place to hide from her former associates, too, and here was infinitely safer. He would have to keep an eye on her and make sure she stole nothing, without drawing attention to what he was doing.

He looked between the pair, at his mother who didn't question the timing of the arrival of Granny's new companion enough, at Granny's smug smile, and shuddered. Now was not the time to ask what game Granny was playing with them all.

A tap sounded on the door, and the butler appeared. "Mr. John Kimble and Miss Gabriella Kimble."

Daniel rose to his feet and hurried toward the door to welcome his old friend to the estate. John Kimble was of similar age and looked to be in good health. "My dear friend."

"My Lord Scarsdale," Kimble said, bowing slightly. "I was so pleased to learn you had finally come home again."

"I am glad to be home." Daniel turned to the young woman at Kimble's side and nodded. "Miss Kimble. I barely recognized you. You've grown so much."

"I should hope I've changed, my lord," Gabby Kimble leaned a little toward him. "It's been five years since we last saw each other."

"That is true, but it feels like just yesterday poor Kimble had to rescue you from that tree branch you were stuck on," he murmured, bowing to her. "And how is Claws these days?"

Claws had been a stray and wild kitten, made into a surly housebound pet. Gabby's cat had caused all sorts of trouble for her when he was here last, and for John, too, who had frequently needed to rescue the little beast from disasters of its own making.

"It's Felix now, and he is still an avid adventurer," Gabby confessed, grinning. "I love him to distraction still."

"Let's hope one day he just lays there and gets fat instead of into trouble," Daniel suggested.

"I doubt that. Too much like his owner to hope for a change of temper now," Kimble teased, earning him a discreet elbow in the ribs from Gabby. Daniel laughed at the pair and turned around to find Marian had returned to the room.

He performed the introductions between his old friends and Marian, introducing her as Granny's new companion.

They all seemed delighted to meet each other, and Gabby and Marian sat down, side by side, obviously interested in becoming better acquainted.

Daniel took John Kimble aside as soon as he could.

"You're looking well despite being stuck in the countryside with only your ward and the sick for company."

"Gabby and the concerns of our small village keep me on my toes," Kimble said, laughing softly. "She's like a sister to me now. Annoying but adorable."

"I don't have the faintest notion of what that's like, but siblings always looked difficult to me."

"I let her have her head most of the time, caution her when she's being led astray. Your mother has been a vastly steadying influence. I'm gratified she took an interest in the girl a few years ago."

"I hadn't heard about that," he said, folding his arms across his chest and staring across the room to where the ladies were now settled together and ignoring him.

His attention invariably caught on the smile on Marian's lips, and he wondered about her wanting to be here. She'd met none of them before, and she appeared to fit in smoothly with his mother and grandmother so far, but he worried about her influence on Gabby Kimble. "I always imagined my mother would be too involved in the estate to worry about anything else."

"She was indeed a few years back. But Gabby was invited to call once a week and has learned a great deal about household management from her," Kimble explained. "It was a relief to have Gabby off my hands for a little while each week. Each time she returned, I felt she'd grown in confidence and was much wiser for the visit."

Danny laughed. "Is that so?"

"Yes, indeed, which is why she's off to London next season. Your mother has offered to help bring her out, and I will take every offer of help I can get." Kimble grinned and then slapped Daniel's shoulder. "So, you're back? For how long this time?"

"Forever."

"What? No!"

"Yes," Daniel said, as he lowered his chin slightly. "I'm home to stay, and marry, too."

"So that pretty girl over there is merely pretending to be your grandmother's companion? The cheek of you."

"No, not her," he blurted quickly. "I will marry Miss Wilson."

Kimble spun to face him. "You cannot be serious?"

"But I am. It's time," Daniel insisted.

"To marry, maybe, but surely not her," Kimble said, a look of dismay on his face. He wiped it away quickly.

Daniel sighed. "Say what's on your mind, sir."

"I fear you'll be miserable," Kimble promised.

"I'm sure every prospective husband fears that in the beginning. It's just nerves about losing one's freedom."

"It's what remains of a man's common sense screaming out for rescue, I believe." Kimble met his gaze. "Amy Wilson is proud and manipulative. She'll run roughshod over you as soon as you put a ring on her finger."

Daniel reared back from the assault on Amy's character. "Why would you imagine such a thing?"

"Because I know her better than you. Amy Wilson has two vastly different sides, but once you make her a countess, I bet only one will remain. She's not the woman for you," Kimble warned, scowling.

"Well, I think you're wrong," Daniel said stubbornly. "What has she ever done to you to make you say such things?"

"Nothing to me directly, but I hear much that worries

me. She's sharp with the servants at Wilson Hall, miserly with her charity to the poor. She kept a young boy to fetch her things, and he never had a full night's sleep or a word of gratitude in all his years in her employ."

"Surely she only does what her father expects of her," Daniel suggested, remembering Mother saying Amy's father had limited her understanding of many things.

"Yes, and that's what worries me."

"What do you mean?"

"I mean, Wilson is always sticking his nose into how your estate is run, belittling your mother to all and sundry behind her back. Thinks he should have been asked to run the estate in your absence and tries to undermine her confidence."

"Wilson was a great friend to my father for many years. I'm sure he's just concerned that I was not here to run the estate myself."

"He's not a friend now. Last year, I heard him say he resold grain he bought from this estate for quite a lot more than he paid your mother for it."

"Profit is good business," Daniel said slowly, dismayed by what he'd learned today.

"And that was after advising her to sell to him on the cheap because the market was glutted," he warned. "Gabby tells me your mother's expression when she heard what he'd done could have frozen Hell over. She quite lost her temper after he was gone."

"Mother never loses her temper," he said. "Well, only with me."

"Well, she did that day, and then carried on as if it hadn't happened. Welcoming Wilson back to the estate out of misplaced fondness for Amy was a mistake he'll take advantage of again and again."

Daniel inhaled. Leaving Mother to run the estate hadn't seemed problematic from the distance of a few hundred miles. But now, he wondered if he ought to have done so. He did not like to hear that she'd been duped by their neighbor. He'd have to learn more about that, after Kimble had gone. "Would you care for a drink, sir?"

"I'm here to see your granny, remember? Your mother's message said she had taken another turn."

"Yes, she fainted. Or seemed to," Daniel explained.

"It could be merely the thrill of your return. I know how fond of you she is. But if she permits, I'd like to listen to her heart. A friend sent me a new apparatus for that sort of thing."

"Do you ever miss London?"

"Of course, and perhaps when Gabby is safely married off, I'll revisit some of our favorite old haunts with you once more. I expect it has changed very much since my time there."

"It has," Daniel agreed, "but in other ways, it remains exactly the same."

"Balls, parties," Kimble murmured.

"Scandals, mayhem, disorderly conduct," he answered, laughing. "And that's just by me."

"I can't wait to hear all your news then," Kimble said. "It's been much too long since we've talked."

"Most of your old friends have married," he warned.

"Ah, so that's why you've come home with your tail between your legs." Kimble laughed. "Did the woman you want turn you down?"

"Yes, but she turned down everyone else too, so I don't take it personally." Daniel sighed. "I'm just so tired of it all."

"Tired of what?"

"Chasing women. Looking and never getting to keep one for long enough," he drawled. He'd never quite put it that way before, and certainly not to a male acquaintance. But he'd known Kimble all his life. They'd gone to London together, but Kimble had not been keen to stay once he'd been saddled with a ward.

Daniel's dissatisfaction with his time in London had increased over the years since. Once the excitement of the first few years wore off, the thrill of the chase too, it just never seemed to come back fully. "Perhaps I'm just lonely."

"We're all lonely. We can only choose our diversions wisely and hope for the best," Kimble offered.

"As ever the optimist," Daniel murmured.

"Pragmatic," Kimble countered. "Trust in fate and everything will work out in the long run, I'm sure."

Fate had dropped the most imperfect woman into his lap the night before he'd intended to propose to another more proper lady. He'd a nagging feeling that fate was also laughing at him for desiring the wrong one still. He shook off that feeling. "What of you," he asked. "Anyone special in your life?"

"In this place?" Kimble laughed. "You must be joking. The most appealing woman I've seen in years is that lovely thing sitting beside your grandmother."

"Her companion," he reminded Kimble.

"Yes, we were introduced," Kimble replied. "I don't suppose she's a dowry?"

"I wouldn't think so," Daniel warned. "Not that I know much about her, really."

Kimble looked toward the women. "She's not from these parts, is she? Where did Mrs. Nolan find her?"

"Why?"

"You're not the only one who gets lonely," Kimble said with a deprecating smile.

"You know Grandmama. She has friends everywhere."

"Well then, if she's approved by Mrs. Nolan, I truly must get to know more about the lovely lady. It seems Gabby likes her already. That's good enough for me."

Daniel turned to look at Kimble in shock as he realized the man intended to pursue Marian. *Romantically.*

The idea of that left a distinctly sour taste in his mouth. "I need that drink now."

"I'll come with you. Or perhaps I shouldn't," Kimble whispered. "Miss Trill might like my conversation more than you do."

Daniel reached out, grabbed Kimble by the upper arm, and towed him toward the study. "You're coming with me. Ladies do excuse us," he said more loudly as his eyes fell on Marian again.

Marian Trill was lovely, exciting, and unexpected, but she was not the woman for John Kimble or him.

Chapter Nine

Marian had never arranged flowers before, but she was doing her best because Mrs. Nolan had asked her to try her hand at it. She said it was something proper ladies always excelled at. Since Marian was pretending to be one, she ought to know something about it.

She fussed with placing the hot house blooms in the crystal vase and turned the flowers outward, hoping it didn't look too underwhelming. She'd chosen the brightest booms for her arrangement, although all the others in the room, done by Lady Scarsdale and Miss Amy Wilson, were more sedate.

"Very refreshing," Mrs. Nolan murmured to her approvingly. "Put that one on the table by the window, across the room."

Marian did as requested, placing the vase in the center of a highly polished walnut side table beside a large, comfortable armchair.

And then she glanced out the open window.

Lady Scarsdale and Miss Wilson were outside together still, basking in the cool afternoon breeze and happy with each other's company. Marian would have liked to enjoy the breeze too, but Granny had not been invited to join them, and so she couldn't go out either. Not that she wanted to spend time in Miss Wilson's company. She seemed rather silly and more than a little full of her own importance.

Mrs. Nolan was much better company. She was a woman of vast experience, and she seemed ready to share her knowledge with Marian on almost every topic under the sun. But she was constantly digging for information about Marian's murky past, and that made her uncomfortable because she knew so little of it.

"Wherever did Mrs. Nolan find her new companion? I was completely taken aback to see a new face in your drawing room earlier," Amy whispered, though the sound traveled well enough to Marian's ears.

"She's a connection from Portishead," Lady Scarsdale answered dismissively.

"She seems so out of place here," Amy replied. "Lost."

"Yes, I suppose she might feel that way. Everyone is at first. It's been years since we've seen her, and I imagine my mother felt obligated to offer the girl a position when she learned her father had passed away," Lady Scarsdale finished, repeating the tale Mrs. Nolan had spouted earlier. "She's no one of any great importance, I assure you."

"I had already assumed that," Amy murmured. "Shall we have more tea, my lady?"

Marian scowled and fussed with the flowers angrily. All this family ever did was eat and drink tea and gossip about each other. Granny had been sharing tidbits about Amy Wilson for hours, and the more she heard, the less reason she had to be impressed by the pampered fool.

Marian also knew enough about the other woman's many vaunted accomplishments to know she couldn't possibly compete, and shouldn't even try. But what sort of woman waited years for a proposal from a man, an earl, who had abandoned a fancy place like this and the woman everyone knew waited to marry him?

Not that Marian wanted Danny—Lord Scarsdale—for herself.

Living here just these few days was as dull as Granny had claimed it to be so far. No one dropped by except for the Wilsons and Kimbles, and the family hadn't ventured beyond the borders of the estate. No wonder Granny begged Marian to stay to tell her stories. She'd been trapped here for years and must be rather desperate for excitement in any form.

The pair, Lady Scarsdale and Miss Wilson, continued sipping tea and eating little cakes as she watched, and Marian feared they might continue there for hours more. They were content with each other as if they were mother and daughter already. Honestly, she didn't know how Lady Scarsdale could be so blind.

It was so clear that Lady Scarsdale was fonder of Miss Wilson than Miss Wilson was of the countess. The affection and consideration weren't returned in equal measure by Miss Wilson.

There was no one thing she could put her finger on that suggested a ruse or scam underway by the young woman, though. She seemed the sort who expected love and praise but gave none out. But if one wished to gain all of this, a title and untold wealth, along with Danny as a husband, then Marian could understand Amy's motivations.

Not that anyone should need to feign delight at having Danny court them. Titled or not, wealthy or not, he was a very appealing man to look at. Funny and of largely sober habits, he was a man who knew how to love and respect the wishes of women. Though obviously he was a disappointment to his mother—which many young men often were.

She turned back to Mrs. Nolan to ask about the source

of the strife between mother and son, only to discover the older woman gone from the room. Marian cursed softly. Granny was always doing that. Disappearing without warning. No wonder past companions had never stayed in her position long. She was a difficult woman to keep up with.

"I wonder what is keeping your son from joining us," Amy murmured. "He said he would be right back."

"I'm sure he'll be along at any moment now," Lady Scarsdale answered, and then her foot tapped beneath her gown.

Marian shook her head. Danny drove his mother to distraction without even trying very hard. Even from here, she could sense the tension in the lady was increasing because of the lack of marriage proposal and his absence.

Yet if he was truly in earnest about marrying Amy Wilson, surely, he ought to be trying harder to court the young woman. It was obvious his mother wouldn't stand in his way, though his granny just might.

Marian would rather not bear witness to his proposal, and after a few minutes of indecision, turned away from the gossiping ladies and went looking for Mrs. Nolan instead.

There was no sign of Mrs. Nolan in any of the lower rooms, and Marian hurried up the main staircase toward the woman's bedchamber, hoping to find her resting there despite the early hour.

The old woman had said she didn't normally sleep during the day, but Marian was coming to realize the old woman lied as routinely as Marian had once stolen.

As she raised a hand to the door, she heard Danny talking within the room and froze with her knuckles inches from striking the wood.

"This is a bad idea, Granny," Scarsdale said. "Mama will throw a fit once she learns the truth."

"You leave my daughter to me. I told her everything she needs to know about Marian for now. Besides, your mother is more astute than you give her credit for. Look how well she does, ignoring Amy and her meddling father."

"I don't want Mama lying to anyone about anything," Scarsdale complained. "What's this about Mr. Wilson meddling, though?"

"He's always coming round, making snide comments about your absence, and attempting to undermine her confidence and authority over the servants. I think he's been trying to take over these past years. All because everyone knows you'll marry his daughter, and you'd need his blessing for the match. My daughter has worked diligently to keep this place running while you've been thoroughly enjoying yourself in London."

"I know that. The ledgers tell me she has done extremely well without me. I've no complaints."

"You ought to tell her you're proud of her," Granny suggested. "Before it's too late."

"Mother has never been comfortable with compliments from me," Danny complained. "I wouldn't know what to say that would please her."

"Reminds me of someone else we both know," Granny mused.

"Amy is always flattered by praise."

"Of course she is. Everyone has complimented Amy Wilson on her looks, her manners, and her great many accomplishments. I meant you should offer compliments to the *other* lady in need of a little flattery," Granny said with a soft laugh. "Practice on Marian."

"I wouldn't like her to get the wrong impression."

"You can't just ignore her, or do you want your mother to suspect there is something going on between you? She's pretty, and you are a virile young man. And there still is something between you both. I know what you're thinking when you look at her, and what she hopes for most when your eyes meet. You're wondering if you can do your duty and continue an affair, but that would not be wise," Granny cautioned. "She deserves better. Marian, I mean."

"For the last time, nothing serious happened between us," he protested. "But tell me why you've spread so elaborate a tale about Marian coming from Portishead."

"She does," Granny said.

"Yes, but why say you know her family? I've never heard of them before."

"You'd have to ask your mother about that."

"Mother dislikes discussing the past," Daniel grumbled. "If I ask her, she'd tell me it's not important, like she always does."

"It's not really so farfetched that we know each other. I've merely embellished the tale a little to explain how Marian came to be here. We've helped many acquaintances from Portishead, even those of low rank, like her family. Are you ashamed of such connections?"

"You know I don't care about that or the money you spend helping your old friends," he said, with an ominous tone. "Lower classes. Upper classes. We're all the same when our clothes come off."

"I taught you well," Granny said, sounding proud of her grandson. "I did once know a gentleman in Portishead with the last name of Trill very well. Never intimately, of course. My heart, as you know, was claimed at an early age. But

Trill…clever fellow, very handsome, utter degenerate. You would have liked him the moment you met."

"You cannot suggest to anyone that Marian has a relative like that," he protested.

"But every family has a black sheep, my dear boy. He was probably her grandfather, or even her old uncle. We would have to visit Portishead again to be certain."

"Her grandfather?"

"Well, the Mr. Trill I knew was older than I, and he had a pair of sons who might be about the right age to be Marian's father," Granny replied.

"I'm sure that family would be overjoyed to know you're all too willing to foist an orphan upon them without proof of a connection," Danny growled.

"I did not say I know the sons. They were much younger than I to be of interest to me. But they grew to be men when I lived in Portishead. One was to be married, though I never received a wedding invitation."

"I think it's risky to claim any such connection could exist," he warned.

"Miss Wilson will hardly bother to check Marian's credentials for being my companion when her lifelong ambition has always been to become a bride and your countess."

"And what happens after we are married?" Scarsdale asked. "The five of us have to live with that lie under the same roof forever."

"I should hardly think it will cause you a problem, since I shall only be here until the day you tie the knot," Granny said. "I'll head back to Portishead at last, where I belong."

"What?" Danny protested.

"I will have no reason to stay, my dear boy. I came to

help your mother when you were born and returned because your father passed so soon after. I didn't want her to be alone with her grief, and my stay has lasted much longer than I ever intended. But soon she'll have her hands full with a daughter-in-law and adjusting to her new role as dowager countess. Then there will be babies on her lap. Seeing me lingering about will only cause her more agitation than happiness."

"That is simply not true. But what about Marian? Mother doesn't need a companion."

"Of course, she doesn't need a companion, and she certainly cannot have mine. No, I'll take Marian away with me, and I will find out if my suspicions are correct."

"What suspicions?"

"That my suspicions about her parentage isn't an exaggeration at all. There is something oddly familiar about Marian's face that nags at my memory. I'm sure once I return to Portishead, everything will become clearer."

"Does she want to leave with you? Have you told her your plans for her future?"

"Not in so many words, but I have mentioned a longing for Portishead, and she seemed quite keen to hear more of my old home and haunts."

"Portishead has surely changed in the years since you were there last."

"Change is good for the soul. So is the excitement of a new adventure. I feel young again with Marian about. Besides, I'm much too old to just sit in a chair and wait for your children to come into the world like your mother has. I like Marian, and she seems to like me. She's amenable to a little deception and an adventure or two. Imagine the mischief we could get into together far from here."

"I'm trying not to," Scarsdale said, sounding pained.

"Don't fret about the pair of us, my dear boy," Granny murmured. "Soon you'll have a wife and all the children you could ever need to worry about. I'm sure Amy will accommodate your desire for offspring from the very first night you are man and wife. I'll take Marian away with me, and perhaps I can find her a nice rich husband, too."

"No, absolutely not," Danny exclaimed loudly. "You will not play matchmaker for Marian Trill to any of our acquaintances."

"Everyone needs someone to love, my dear boy. Especially a girl like Marian Trill. Trust me, she'll be happier without your fleeting affection."

"It's not as if I have a choice now," Scarsdale argued. "I can't unmake my decision to marry at this point."

"That is true, I'm afraid. You are committed now to another lady, even without proposing yet, and poor Marian must forever wonder what might have been between you both. So will you."

"You go too far, Mrs. Nolan," Danny said, sounding rather angry now.

"And you, my dear boy, have your head stuck in the sand," Granny quipped back. "Think carefully about what I said tonight."

There was a long pause, and then there were heavy footsteps headed toward Marian.

She flattened herself against the wall as the door was flung open. Danny emerged and stalked away, his shoulders tense, his hands balled into fists by his sides as he disappeared into his own chamber and slammed the door behind him.

He never even noticed her.

"You can come in now, Marian," Granny called out.

Marian hurried inside and shut the door behind her, then she turned and faced the old lady warily. Granny was more insightful and devious than she'd first seemed. It sounded like she was deliberately trying to sabotage her grandson's marriage plans by promoting Marian as an alternative. But he was an earl, indecently wealthy, and otherwise engaged. If he asked, Marian could never marry him. His mother wouldn't stand for it.

"I'm glad you heard all that," Granny said. "I dislike repeating myself."

Marian decided not to address or try to deny her being drawn to Danny the way the old lady claimed. She focused on the lie. "You don't know me or my family," she said firmly.

"Come and sit beside me, gel," the old lady demanded.

Marian did as asked. "You never met me before three days ago."

"That is true," Granny said, and then reached to capture her face by the chin. "But I recognize this face, or some other version of it. Where do you think you came from? Under a hedgerow? You've not shared a great deal about your past and present situation for good reason, but I can easily guess what was left out. You are alone, and never once mentioned any family or friends. Do you want to tell me about the trouble you're in now?"

Marian stilled. How much should she tell the old woman? If she said too much, she'd either hang or be immediately sent away. People did not trust thieves for a good reason.

"I won't betray you," Granny said as her hand fell away.

Marian raised her chin. "I don't really know where I come from, and it doesn't matter."

"It does matter," Granny disagreed.

Marian waved her hand about and shrugged. "I have only vague recollections of my father's shop."

"A shop?" The old lady's eyes came alight. "What do you remember about the shop? What was in there? What did he sell?"

"I remember people coming and going at all hours."

"He was prosperous?"

"No," she drawled, recalling the hunger and uncertainty she always associated with her earliest memories. "We were not well off. The shop was dusty, I used to draw patterns on the floorboards and got smacked for it. But there was colored glass above the front door and at the window. I used to lie on the floor and watch the pretty lights dance over me. But it often felt like I was there alone for hours."

The old lady nodded. "Do you remember your parents' faces at all?"

"Nothing of my mother or any other woman. My father was dark-haired and angry." Marian wet her lips. "He was always arguing with the people who came to his shop."

"Arguing, or was he bartering instead? Discussing the price of goods he sold and bought, perhaps?"

"I really couldn't say," she admitted. It pained her that she knew so little about her origins now. "Why?"

Granny shook her head. "Just an idea. Were there any other relatives or people you recall from your past?"

There had been just one, but now she was not so sure about her connection to Uncle Crossman, either. "I might have had an uncle."

"Ah, good. Now we have somewhere to turn our attention. Tell me about him."

Uncle never spoke about himself. "I barely knew him and have not seen him for some time. We became separated."

The old lady nodded. "And why did that happen? The separation, as you call it."

Uncle Crossman was a thief, dishonest about the truth and likely not related to Marian. Plus, his associates, fellow thieves she'd thought were allies, wanted to get rid of her. She had no desire to discuss her past or them, and every instinct inside her suggested that if she ever met them again, they would only lie about her origins. "I cannot say," she lied.

The old lady patted her hand suddenly. "We'll find out the truth together. My grandson has contacts and the funds to pay for a proper search for your actual relations."

"Please don't go to any trouble on my behalf," Marian said. "Or expense."

"My dear, if you wanted to impose, my grandson could be putty in your hands." Granny searched her face. "But you won't ask him for help again, will you? You'll be miserable, and he'll be even more so without understanding why."

Marian wet her lips and looked down at her gloved fingers. Beneath the new soft leather were the rough hands of a poor girl, brought up in a world so completely different from this. Danny might have helped her for one night, but asking him for more was utterly out of the question, now she knew more about him.

"His life won't be miserable. Miss Wilson seems exactly the sort of woman who should be his bride. Beautiful, accomplished, a credit to her family."

"I completely disagree with you on that score, but I refuse to argue more today. But just think of all the fun we could have together. All of us living happily here, and in

London together, too. I can already see my daughter approves of you."

Marian shook her head. "She would throw me out if she knew the truth of who I really am."

"Who said she hasn't guessed yet? She sees a great deal more than she lets on about. My daughter is an intelligent woman who knows how her son behaves beyond these grounds. Provided she doesn't see any fresh scandal with her own eyes, she will most likely ignore a past one."

Marian stared back at the old woman in astonishment at that statement. Clearly, she was delusional. "I should let you rest."

"Nonsense, my dear. There is no time to rest for the wicked. We're expecting company soon. We must refresh our attire and return downstairs to the drawing room."

"Who is coming?"

"That physician friend of his, and his ward. I've no need for doctoring, but the man's ward is a treasure. I'm sure you two will have lots to talk about again today."

That was all Marian needed. Another person to lie to. So much for making a fresh start. Her entire new existence was being bound by lies and none of them were her making. "If I must."

"You must," the old woman assured her.

"You really didn't faint yesterday?"

"I did not faint."

"But you did swoon," Marian countered, having seen that with her own eyes. "Why?"

"Well, swooning is an entirely different matter. Seeing your face at the window gave me quite the start, I must say. I thought I was seeing a ghost of an old friend there at first."

"Why didn't you tell anyone about me? At the window and later?"

"And have them think me mad and seeing ghosts, too?" granny said, and then shuddered. "That is the last thing my grandson needs, given his intentions."

"Yes, his intentions." Marian sighed. "Is it wise for me to remain here? I mean…she, the woman he will marry, will notice me. I don't want to get in the way."

"You would do me a great favor if you could."

She wanted Marian to stop her grandson's wedding. "No."

"Always so difficult, the young. You remind me of my old life. The life I'm almost forbidden to speak of now. Back before my daughter married up and became a countess. It's not enough for me to enjoy garden parties and drink fine wine and believe there's nothing more to life. I know what's out there. What we all are missing out on. But here, the endless days of dull regularity prevail. I imagine you don't have any experience with that existence."

"No, not really. Each new day has always been a complete surprise, and no two were every repeated."

"I understand that not every woman can come from a good family or a steady situation. My brother and uncles were all rogues and thieves."

"Thieves?"

"Cutthroats and pirates on one side, scoundrels on the other. Of course, it's not the done thing to talk about such things in esteemed company. I'm sure Miss Wilson knows none of it still, even after all these years. She hears only what brings her pleasure and ignores the rest."

"Wouldn't Danny have told her about your family long ago, or now perhaps he can in the future?"

"It will not be that sort of marriage, my dear. The sharing of confidences is rare in the aristocracy. No, they marry for money and power, and couples hardly speak to each other, with some exceptions."

"Is that what he's doing? Marrying for power and wealth?" she asked.

"Gracious, no. He's marrying for convenience and to please his poor mother. My grandson has always been a bit of a rogue, takes after my side of the family, I'm proud to say. His mother, however, has painted him a gentleman as refined as his father was to our nearest neighbors. Proper, studious, and kindhearted."

"He *is* kindhearted," Marian protested.

"With an eye for the scandalous ladies, too, don't forget," she murmured. "His father was cut from a vastly different cloth, but the boy lost him when he was young. He fell in with the wrong crowd at first in London, of course, and by then his taste was set. His current circle of acquaintances is better mannered than the former, and far more important. Distinguished rogues, every last one. Though Danny has never harbored grand ambition or fame, much to his mother's disappointment."

"I see," Marian said slowly. "That still doesn't explain why you want me to stay so badly."

The old lady smiled. "You're here to prove my theory that a rogue's taste in women never really changes. Especially not on the cusp of making a proper match. If you stay, you'll be amply compensated."

Marian met the old woman's gaze directly. "And if I don't?"

"Then I'm afraid you will make the acquaintance of the local magistrate and explain how you came to have my promise ring in your possession," Granny said with a deadly smile. "I know what you're *really* doing here, Miss Trill. You're the honey before the sting to come. I will not allow you to rob my grandson when your family finally catch up with you."

"No one is coming to rob you," Marian swore, but then gulped. "If they come at all, it will be to punish me for betraying them by protecting Danny from their ambush."

"Ah—at last, a grain of truth," Granny said, almost purring with satisfaction. "It's just as I thought. You do fancy him."

Marian laughed softly. "Well, do you blame me? He is very handsome."

"Not at all, my dear, I've always hoped he'd find someone just like you. Someone who saw the good in him and appreciated the wicked, too. That is not Amy Wilson, I assure you."

"It could be," Marian suggested, but deep down, she hoped that was not the case. Danny deserved so much more than either of them could give him.

Chapter Ten

It was always a difficult day when Mother and Granny sat out in the garden together. Granny liked to sip champagne under the sun and Mother always disapproved of that sort of thing. Add in a neighbor mother wanted to impress, and an almost lover he was trying not to notice, and that meant Daniel couldn't relax.

He was constantly dreading someone's slip of the tongue while he was trying to get to know Amy again.

Granny's bawdy laughter and Marian's softer chuckles kept drawing his attention away from his important conversation with Amy Wilson.

The flowing champagne had loosened Granny's tongue a great deal today. She was gregarious, loud, and teasing of all and sundry, even the servants who were waiting on her. Her ribald conversation was embarrassing mother, but not Marian.

"When I was a young woman, there were gentlemen lined up to dance with me every night," Granny whispered to Marian. "I could have had my pick, but I chose my Edmund. He was the most handsome fellow, the most prone to laughter. I tell you it's better to laugh together than never at all."

Granny and Edmund Noble had met at seventeen at the theater and fallen madly and instantly in love. However, Edmund had been impressed to join the navy shortly after he'd proposed and never returned to marry her. He was taken by the tides of war at sea too soon, leaving Granny utterly heartbroken. It was only later, when her delicate condition was impossible to deny, that she found out he'd come from one of the richest families in the next county.

Granny had been given enough hush money by his family to make the scandal of their bastard child go away, but she had already taken his family name to lend respectability to her young daughter's existence.

Those early days she spoke of so fondly were a somewhat delicate subject in front of Mama and others. Granny had trod the boards as an actress in her youth at a rather scandalous dockside theater, to support herself and her child. She'd been quite famous at one time and had had her share of wealthy protectors in the early years. Not exactly the past that Mother, now a respectable countess, ever wanted others to be reminded of.

"Have you met my horse?" he said to Amy to turn her attention from Granny. "I got lucky when I went to Tattersalls last year. Outbid even the Marquess of Wharton for the animal."

"He's an important man, isn't he? The marquess is often mentioned in the papers."

"Indeed, yes he is," he said, pleased she was keeping abreast of the current news of high society. "I am fortunate to call him a good friend, and his wife, too."

"Wasn't she the one who engaged in trade?" Granny called out loudly. "I'm keen to meet a woman like that, a no-nonsense kind of gel, and her cousins, too. Remarkable that they all married so well."

"Their business was to offer elocution lessons to

gentlemen," he assured Amy when she frowned. "Dancing practice and improving conversational skills."

Granny arched her brow. "So, what did *you* go there for, young man? You dance very well and no one of any sense could find fault with your conversation."

Daniel clenched his jaw. She knew full well that his visit to the Hillcrest Academy had been a ruse to speak with a pretty girl, because he'd told her so, to make her laugh. Of course, that pretty girl could be married by now, or maybe not, to Lord Sullivan, a new friend of his. "My stutter returned."

Granny gave him a long, disbelieving look. "You haven't stuttered in years around a pretty girl."

Well, she knew he had stuttered recently, because she'd heard him lose his words recently, and in front of Marian no less. "I suspect I was overly tired and, after realizing that, it went away of its own accord," he promised.

"What were you doing in London to be so tired?" Amy asked, wide-eyed and curious. Amy could never know of the life he'd led in London. Since those days were behind him now, he'd rather not discuss them either.

"Attempting to keep up with my friends is a full-time occupation," he said with an awkward wince. "The social season can be exhausting. But I am glad that is all behind me now and I'm home."

"The rigors of the social season in London are something you will need to gird your loins for, my dear," Granny said to Marian. "You'll utterly enjoy it if I have my way."

Amy's eyes flicked to him, and then to Granny as she frowned. "I didn't imagine we'd be going to London. Do you think I'll like it, Mrs. Nolan?"

"Going to London is not essential," he blurted, because

he never intended to take Amy there. His friends might be indiscreet and embarrass him. Amy might even meet some ladies he'd previously engaged in affairs with, too.

"Well, I don't know about you," Granny said. "Every woman should have a season, so she might find the right husband. Danny intends to remain in the country with you. The place is full of scandals and deceit, and affairs abound everywhere anyway."

"Oh," Amy said, and her lips pinched tight together as she looked at him.

"It's not as bad as Granny makes out," Daniel promised.

"No, I'm sure it's not so bad now, since you stayed there for so many years," Granny replied and hid a grin.

"I just think a quiet country life has much to recommend it after all," Daniel assured Amy. "There's no reason to go to London ever again, really."

"There's the theater," Marian murmured. "I've heard wonderful stories about Drury Lane performances and eating ices and amusements that last all night long."

Given Marian had hardly spoken a word all morning, he was taken aback momentarily by her wistful tone. She was interested in visiting London. He thought she would enjoy it more than Amy ever could. She'd revel in the attention she'd receive, and the amusements to be found there, even those held in less-than-proper surroundings.

If she was ever to go, Granny would prepare her well for London's scandalous society, but who would protect her from scoundrels? She didn't have her uncle anymore. He wondered if her travels had actually taken her to the great city already, but he shouldn't ask her about that right now. He was supposed to be ignoring Marian.

"You must have gone to the races too," she added. "How exciting that must have been!"

"Yes, I've gone with my friends more than once and had a great deal of fun. We're a large group and make a merry day and night of it when we go."

"It sounds marvelous to live in a city that is as lively at night as it is in the day," Marian exclaimed, suddenly more like herself than she had been in days. "All that noise and bustle constantly around you."

"It certainly can be wonderful if your horse comes in first at the races. You win a small fortune," he admitted, grinning back at her. "When your and your friend's horses are neck and neck, well, we can become quite competitive. There's also riding in Hyde Park and attending the pleasure gardens, too."

"You visited the scandalous pleasure gardens?" Amy asked, interrupting his and Marian's conversation. She looked rather shocked.

"Well, yes," he admitted. "But it wasn't only me that went."

"I only ever went there once," Marian said with a sigh. "It was so crowded I could barely move. I'm sure I stepped on a dozen toes because I just had to see absolutely everything."

"When were you there?" he couldn't help but ask. "Perhaps we bumped into each other and never knew."

"We might have, but I think I would have remembered you," Marian promised.

Amy cleared her throat, and Daniel quickly spun back to face her, horrified he'd become distracted by his grandmother's companion again. He had to think of her that way and *only* that way. As someone to be polite to in passing. Someone he didn't want to know more about.

He turned his back on Marian, and smiled at Amy. "I

think you'd like London," he told her, although why he lied, he didn't quite know. Amy would hate London. The crowds, the scandals, the way he reveled in the wickedness to be found there.

"What I really long for is a ball to be held here again," Amy said, looking around. "It's been years since the last one. Do you remember the fun we had dancing together?"

Fun? Danny remembered the torture of it. He'd only just come of age, and Mama had decided that everyone in the district had to know he had reached his majority. The way he'd been stared at, fawned upon by the unmarried women of the district, and the matrons with unwed daughters, had made him sweat profusely after the first few passes had been made at him.

The ball had gone on until dawn, but after three hours, Daniel had escaped out a window and spent the night drinking with the old gardener, stationed down by the grotto to keep the revelers out of there.

"It was a grand occasion," Mother murmured, lifting her head finally from her knitting. "My only regret was that my late husband had not survived his ailments to see you and my son dance together, Amy. Such elegance, such grace."

"Thank you," Amy said, a flush of color now upon her pale cheeks as she looked over at Daniel and smiled.

Daniel squirmed as he recalled it had not been so perfect a dance together as everyone seemed to believe. His hands had been sweaty in his gloves, and he'd felt as if a thousand eyes were on him all night. Including Amy's, which were lit so brightly in triumph as she'd gazed upon those watching them dance together.

He couldn't wait until their set had ended, and he could

escape her. From that moment on, Mother kept suggesting he choose Amy to be his wife and make babies with her.

Was it any wonder he'd been in terror of becoming leg-shackled for so long? Right now, he was being revisited by those same panicked feelings as he looked at Amy's pleased smile again, and Mother nodding.

If they held a ball, he would be required to dance with Amy. And at such a ball, he would never once dance with Marian, who he thought would be great fun to partner in a set or two.

He shifted in his chair and sought not to think about all the pleasures in life he was denying himself now as a duty-bound, almost-engaged man. There were many losses, and all his favorites, too. Drinking, wagering, attending outlandish amusements and having a jolly fun time as a bachelor.

But most of all, he would miss engaging in harmless flirtations with other women.

He struggled to keep his eyes from Marian as that staid and dull future he'd planned truly sank into his brain. It would be an enormous loss of his freedom and satisfaction in life to wed. Any woman, especially a pretty companion of his granny's, was utterly off limits already. He would never share his bed with anyone but Amy ever again, either.

He tried to focus his attention on Amy and tried to feel something more for the woman than just admiration and respect. She was the perfect lady in every sense of the word. Elegant, well-informed, an accomplished musician and painter of watercolors. Trained to run a large household like him and be satisfied with country life.

But she was utterly boring.

She hadn't revealed a spontaneous bone in her body yet and certainly had not when she was younger. He could have accurately predicted her response to almost any question put to her at once. She still deferred to Mother, eager to stay on her good side when she ought to be worried about what *he* thought of her, and what he might want from a wife instead.

It occurred to him that if they had any chance to grow closer in marriage, they would have to find interests in common. He did not think he could bear a dull, predictable marriage like some fellow lords had.

Not that his friends had had an easy time courting their future brides. The newly wed Whartons tempers still clashed. She, the new Lady Wharton, sided with the Dowager Marchioness of Wharton often against her husband.

But Sylvia differed from Amy…she was a matchmaker and something of a diplomat. She had brought about an understanding and peace between the Marquess of Wharton and his mother. They were back on friendlier terms thanks to Sylvia's timely intervention.

Her cousin Eugenia Hillcrest had married the easiest of men. A man destined to become a duke. They did not fight exactly, but it was easy to see they were deeply passionate about each other, and their opinions, too.

And Aurora Hillcrest and her most persistent suitor, Lord Sullivan? Time would tell how that match went. Given that Aurora had no desire to marry anyone the last time he'd seen her, had been violently opposed to the idea of marriage to Lord Sullivan, he was not sure there would be constant harmony between the pair out of wedlock, either. Though perhaps they had reached an accord at last over their love for each other and found an acceptable compromise. He certainly hoped he'd been of some help there.

Yet, Amy and he were not in the same situation.

How would they live as man and wife? Would they learn

to desire each other or meet only under the covers at night for as long as it took to get his heir and spare? The latter was not what he hoped for between them. He'd always enjoyed prolonged lovemaking. A night spent holding a woman close, with laughter and conversation interspersed with kisses, and with no thought for tomorrow or the consequences.

He looked across at Marian. That was how their night together would have ended had he not been coming home to marry Amy.

But now, days after that brief interlude and beside her opposite, his current choice for a bride…he could not forget that Marian had needed him and likely still did.

Amy did not. Not really.

But thanks to Mother's excitement over his intentions to marry, Amy was waiting for his proposal. He could not be of much help to Marian when he was newly engaged or married.

"What do you think, my lord?"

He looked at Amy and around, realizing he'd been woolgathering, and discovered everyone was staring at him. "I'm sorry, my mind wandered. Must be the heat of the day. What were you saying?"

Amy looked vastly displeased by his inattention.

"An excess of heat can make you drowsy," Mother suggested. "Perhaps you should take a stroll about the grounds with Amy, my lord."

Daniel withheld a groan but stood. It was to be expected that Mother would try to speed up his proposal. To refuse a stroll with Amy would be rude, so he offered his arm.

"Marian can accompany you to ensure propriety is

maintained if you like," Granny offered, gesturing to Marian with a bland expression, as if she'd not said the most blasphemous thing possible.

"That will not be necessary," Daniel said, curtly. "We will remain in full view at all times."

Marian looked down at her gloved fingers, clearly as uncomfortable as he was about the suggestion of her chaperoning them.

Daniel led Amy away along the path, but made sure they could still be seen. He dug a finger under his cravat, attempting to loosen it. "It's a warmer day than I expected it to be."

"Yes, the days have been warm, but many are in the countryside. Father says when he was in London as a young man, he hardly ever saw the sun or felt warm."

"The brief glimpse of stars is a fine compensation at night," Daniel told her, not that he ever really looked up to notice if he could see the stars. "After a while, you become accustomed to the lack of sun."

"That must be why you're so pale now," she murmured.

He rubbed his jaw. "A few weeks in the saddle roaming the estate and I'll be tanned again."

"I did not say the pallor didn't suit you," she promised, and took a deep breath. "You're as handsome as you were the last time we met. Very much like your father must have been at that age."

"Is that right?" Daniel released Amy so she could pick up her skirts for the walk up a short flight of steps. "I hardly remember him."

"One only has to look at his painting in the master suite to be reminded," she suggested with a tight smile.

But Daniel's hackles rose. Had Amy been in the master

bedchamber while he'd been gone? Invaded the privacy of *his* bedchamber without his permission? Mother had gone too far this time if she knew. He and Amy were not even engaged!

The chamber should have been locked unless servants were cleaning it.

He worked to subdue his temper, but it wasn't easy. "What were you doing in the master suite?"

"Oh, your mother had a bee in her bonnet about cleaning it in readiness for your return a few weeks ago. She wanted to take your father's picture down, but I assured her you would want it to stay hanging over the mantle."

Daniel had always wanted the picture of his father removed from the wall overlooking his bed and placed in the long gallery, beside his ancestors. But Mother had insisted it remain private. They'd argued over who was master here at the time. And because she wouldn't cede to his authority over the portrait and a dozen other inconsequential things, he'd left the estate yet again in a huff one day and stayed away for a good many years after. "I will take it down."

Amy stopped and stared at him. "Oh, but why?"

"Because I do not want to be reminded of how I will age every time I wake in that chamber," he announced.

That wasn't the whole reason. Seeing his father as soon as he opened his eyes every day made him miss the man all the more. The father he'd hardly had the time to know. A man much respected and whose memory was almost worshipped by everyone else.

Amy fixed her gaze on the path ahead. "Well, if you want my opinion, I think it should stay right where it is to remind you of all you could be."

"It comes down today," he said, but looking at her with

genuine interest to see how she might respond to him exerting his authority. He would not let any wife of his countermand his orders the way Mother had done so often.

"He was very handsome, and you look more and more like him every day," Amy promised, and then laughed. "I still remember when you first got those horrible spots on your nose."

"Those days are far behind me," he said, annoyed she was talking about his appearance at fourteen. He thought he'd aged well. No longer lanky and awkward. No spots at all to mar his skin. He was certainly not the young man she had grown up beside.

He'd been shy once, and the loss of his father so young had made him an object of pity, no doubt. Not to mention that horrible stammer he'd developed around pretty girls when he'd finally discovered they existed. But he was a man now, with all the maturity that came with age and experience in the world. He rarely stuttered…except around Marian, it seemed.

"I'm glad," she admitted, looking up at him cautiously. "It's gratifying to have you by my side again."

They had completed a half circuit and kept in full view of their chaperones the whole time, but he knew nothing more about Amy than he'd always known—she was opinionated and always interested in knowing what his family would do.

But even after such a short walk, he was keen to have it over and done with.

He led her back to the outdoor seating and was relieved when she left his side to immediately return to Mother and whisper in her ear.

He noted Marian was gone.

He tried not to show his interest in where she might have

disappeared to, but Granny caught his eye and grinned slyly at him. "My companion went to fetch something for me from inside."

"Very good," he said, as if he didn't care.

He stood around in the baking sun for a moment longer and then decided he'd done enough courtship for one day.

So, he excused himself and returned inside, claiming estate business took him away when there was nothing at all pressing for him to do.

The manor was blessedly cool, and there were no servants in sight to report his lack of decorum to his mother later, so he threw off his coat and launched himself onto the long chaise. "Bollocks."

He heard the distinct sound of a woman snicker, and he sat up to look around.

Marian was halfway up a ladder beside the door he'd come in through, a scrap of paper in her hand and a confused expression on her face.

He frowned. "What the devil are you doing up there?"

"Granny wanted a particular book."

"What book is it?"

"I'm not sure I know. It's written in Latin, and I can't find anything that matches her description."

Daniel groaned and went to hold the ladder. "Come down."

"I'll just be a moment longer," Marian promised.

"I said come down at once."

"Oh, very well. You don't have cause to be cross with me. I'm just trying to do my job as Granny's companion," she promised.

He snatched the paper from her the minute her feet

touched the floor, read the words neatly printed out, and then crushed it into a ball. "That's not a book title."

"What is it?"

"It's a message for me."

"Do you read Latin?"

"Yes, so I know you were sent on a fool's errand."

"Why would Granny do that?"

"Because when I want to escape company, I almost always come to the library to hide. It's the last place anyone expects me to go."

Marian looked confused. "What did the note say?"

He gulped. It had read *kiss her, you fool.* "I'd rather not say."

Marian rubbed her brow hard. "Well, be that way. Do excuse me, my lord? I am expected back."

Daniel caught her arm when she moved away, though. "Is something the matter?"

"A headache, but it's nothing for you to worry about," she blurted.

"Too much sun and champagne, perhaps," he said softly, raising a hand to brush a damp lock of hair back from her flushed face.

Marian's breath caught as she tracked his touch, and he allowed his hand to skim across her cheek, touch her shoulder, and come to a stop against her gloved fingers. Their fingers teased softly against each other's, but they did not become entwined. "Or is it the tedium of being proper?"

"I've no idea what you mean," she promised.

"I believe you do." Daniel drew in a deep lungful of her scent and smiled at how much easier it was to be alone with someone like her. Someone he desired. Someone he wasn't trying to impress. "Drink some plain water and go sit in a dark, quiet room for twenty minutes at least. It will help tremendously."

"I can't. I'm expected back with a book that doesn't exist," Marian said, wide-eyed and staring at his lips.

Daniel smiled and then studied the books on the shelf behind Marian's head. He wanted to kiss her that very moment, but the anticipation heating the air between them was just as good.

He pulled a book from the shelf. "Give her this one instead," he murmured, holding it out to her. "It's more suitable for the occasion."

Marian held it against her chest. "What is it about?"

"Birdwatching for enthusiasts new to the sport," he answered with a wry grin.

Marian frowned. "But Mrs. Nolan told me she doesn't like birds."

"Well, I don't like Granny to meddle in my love life, and yet she persists," he explained.

"Is that what she was doing with that note?"

He moved closer to Marian, drawn to her expression of honest confusion. He stared down at her upturned face and slightly parted lips and knew he wanted something other than a wedding. Yes, he wanted to kiss Marian rather badly, but of course she would forever be denied to him. "She tried, but…I don't need suggestions like that at the moment."

Marian's eyes glowed with sudden understanding and regret, and she slowly slid along the shelving away from him, her eyes full of sympathy. "Thank you for the book, my lord."

"Thank you, Marian, for not understanding any Latin," he said, wondering what might have happened between them if Marian ever discovered what Granny had suggested he do with her.

Chapter Eleven

MARIAN DID her best not to watch Danny and Amy walking about the garden a second time that day, but it was impossible not to when all Lady Scarsdale and Mrs. Nolan did was draw attention to what they might be saying to each other.

And especially what they were *not* doing at this point in their courtship.

"He should have taken up her hand by now," Granny said, casting a sideways glance at Marian.

"He's being respectful," Lady Scarsdale replied, while her fingers continued to knit whatever she was making.

"Do we expect this match made in this century?"

"Yes, of course we do." Lady Scarsdale put down the knitting and exhaled. "Nothing would make me happier than seeing my son finally settle down with the right woman."

"Join us to molder in the countryside, you mean? Can't you see he's already restless?"

Lady Scarsdale pursed her lips as she studied her son. "I think he will eventually learn to enjoy the slower pace of life found in the countryside."

"I think he'll go out of his mind with boredom within three weeks of the wedding night," Granny countered with a shake of her head.

"You are wrong about that. Amy is just what he needs.

She's always been a calming influence on him," Lady Scarsdale promised.

"Yes, her conversation is so calm and predictable she always puts me to sleep," Granny muttered softly, and Marian tried not to laugh at her observation.

The pair—mother and daughter—held wildly different opinions on how Danny's courtship should have progressed by this point. Granny thought it much too slow, given their long acquaintance, and Lady Scarsdale felt it was proceeding as it should be.

Lady Scarsdale summoned a servant to pour another glass of champagne for her mother.

"Miss Trill could use a top up," Mrs. Nolan suggested.

Marian demurred. Her headache had receded even without Danny's suggestion that she take to a quiet corner to rest for the afternoon. "No, thank you."

"What's the matter? Has the champagne gone to your head?"

Marian smiled. "Not at all. But I'm sure I need to keep my wits about me when I'm around you."

Mrs. Nolan chortled and nudged the book Danny had sent out to her a little farther away until it fell off the table.

Marian scrambled to pick it up and dusted it off carefully. Books were expensive and exceedingly rare in her life, and since she was interested in birds, she opened the copy. She could read well enough, but this slender volume was mostly filled with engravings of bird life in the region.

Lady Scarsdale nodded approvingly at her and then turned back to her mother, "It seems there is some hope for the girl after all. She's already resisting your subtle corruptions and has a mind willing to be improved by reading."

"Subtle? That doesn't sound like me. Besides, I've no intention of wasting my time trying to mold the girl in my image," Granny said, chuckling. "She's daring enough, but also has a wise and sensible head on her shoulders. Imagine what she could do in London," Granny murmured. "The gentlemen would line up to dance with her for her beauty alone, but they would stay for her wit. She could have her pick of one or all."

"Until they see me dance or feel my clumsy feet crush their poor toes," Marian threw out, blushing because she'd meant to hold her tongue around the countess.

Lady Scarsdale turned to look at her directly. "One can always learn to dance properly, Miss Trill."

"Yes, Lady Scarsdale. I would hope I'm not a lost cause if I had proper instruction."

"I believe there's hope for anyone to make a good match. Take my son, for example. I was sure I would have to wait another ten years for him to remember his duty and choose a bride, but he's at last come to his senses."

"Have you always hoped he'd marry Miss Wilson?" Marian dared ask, already believing she knew the answer.

But Lady Scarsdale shook her head. "I always hoped he'd find someone compatible, but in all his years in London, he gave no sign of forming a lasting attachment to any woman he met there."

Mrs. Nolan leaned forward. "So, if he had met someone else first, you'd forgive him for not marrying Amy Wilson?"

"At this stage, that is highly unlikely," Lady Scarsdale said, and then turned to look at Mrs. Nolan, eyes widening. "Has he said anything to you that suggests otherwise?"

"No. No," Mrs. Nolan promised, leaning back in her

chair. "But I will still hope for a love match for the boy until my very last breath."

Marian kept her gaze fixed on her book and pretended to read. Marriages among the aristocracy seemed to be a cold, practical business. Openly discussed as if that was completely normal, too.

"Mother, do you know if Scarsdale returned with a special license to marry Amy?"

Mrs. Nolan shook her head. "He did not, to my knowledge."

"Then the marriage will take place in a month," Lady Scarsdale said, with great satisfaction. "That gives me time to prepare."

"Or more than a month," Mrs. Nolan argued. "And by the look of his progress, it will be another day before we hear of a proposal taking place."

Marian looked around to see Danny and his future bride begin another arc around their position. Keeping in full view and doing nothing particularly romantic to her prejudiced eye. "They seem pleased with each other's company at least," Marian said for want of something to say to add to the conversation. "Where will they be married?"

"There is a chapel near the Wilsons' estate grounds where all the members of her family have married," Mrs. Nolan told her.

"A wedding in the estate chapel would be my preference," Lady Scarsdale argued. "That is where the late Lord Scarsdale and I were married, and his father before him, too."

"That is your tradition," Mrs. Nolan said. "I recall hearing Miss Wilson exclaim she wanted to follow in her own family footsteps when she wed."

That brought on a deepening of Lady Scarsdale's near

perpetual look of concern, but it was replaced with a determined expression. "I'm sure my son will honor his father and make a marriage in the estate chapel."

"He might if she gives him any say in the matter," Mrs. Nolan murmured darkly, as if she suspected he would not. "Miss Wilson has strong opinions and is almost as stubborn as you. She'll probably wear her mother's wedding gown to honor her on their special day, even though yours is far more suitable for a future countess."

Marian had attended only one country wedding and was feeling uncomfortable sitting around discussing an event that was still only a dream. Danny had to actually propose to his neighbor for any wedding preparations to start, surely.

"It will be a grand event no matter where, and no matter what Miss Wilson wears, I'm sure," she said.

"Yes, I intend for everything to be perfect when my son weds," Lady Scarsdale promised. "I've had it all planned out for years."

"Right down to the flower arrangements and the polishing of the servants' boots," Mrs. Nolan added with a warning nod in Marian's direction. "Where they will take their honeymoon has long been decided, too. She was this way for her own wedding day. Drove me to distraction, as I had nothing at all to do but attend."

Lady Scarsdale seemed a managing sort of woman, and Miss Wilson was much the same. "Was it as wonderful as you hoped?" Marian asked. "Your wedding day, Lady Scarsdale?"

"Yes, as was my marriage," Lady Scarsdale promised, raising her fingertips to her lips. "My husband was everything I wanted in a match. Kind, thoughtful and he loved me to distraction."

"You were luckier than most, I expect," Marian said. "I mean, you were luckier than your son will be."

"Why do you say that?"

"Well, it's clearly not a love match between them, is it?" she said, looking over at the pair who were walking at a distance from each other. "Miss Wilson doesn't act like she's in love with your son. If I were in love with him, I'd not hesitate to show him how I feel every moment."

Lady Scarsdale frowned for quite some time before she replied, "Love *always* takes time."

Marian wasn't sure about that. Love was there from the start, or it wasn't at all. It was something that could never be faked, or if it was, then it would never bring true happiness to either party.

A throat cleared. "Mr. Kimble and Miss Kimble have arrived," the butler announced.

Marian turned to see the family's friends approaching and hastily got to her feet. Mr. Kimble was as handsome as ever, and Miss Kimble was charming in a blue gown and matching pelisse. Her bonnet was adorned with ribbons and wildflowers, and Marian ached for one of her own exactly like it.

"Ah. Mr. Kimble, Miss Kimble, so good of you to come visit us again," Lady Scarsdale said, extending her hand to the younger man.

He kissed the air above her fingers, smiling warmly. "I'm always happy for an excuse to visit you, my lady. Mrs. Nolan. Miss Trill."

"How do you do?" Miss Kimble said, dipping a deep curtsy to them.

"Miss Kimble. How lovely you look in blue," Mrs. Nolan

added. "You and Miss Trill in yellow make quite the pair of exotic birds."

Marian thought Miss Kimble looked more lovely than she ever could. "You're too kind."

Miss Kimble beamed. "I'd never outshine you, Mrs. Nolan."

"Granny, my dear. How many times must I remind you?"

"A dozen more, Mrs. Nolan," Miss Kimble said, then she rushed toward the older woman and kissed her upturned cheek.

"Now, my dear, I have a special treat for you today. I want you and Marian to spend the day together."

"But I'm your companion," Marian reminded her gently.

"Plenty of time for that later. Young people should spend the day together," Mrs. Nolan insisted. "Go off with you both and see what you can find in the garden together. Gabby, be a dear and show her the grotto."

"Yes, madam," Gabby said dutifully.

"No accidentally falling in today," Mr. Kimble murmured, grinning cheekily.

"I only did it the once," Gabby complained. But she grinned back, which seemed to be her favored expression.

Marian had already heard about the grotto and couldn't wait to be shown, anyway. She dipped a curtsy, as the other girl did the same to Lady Scarsdale, and then they turned away together.

They were a few yards away when Gabby spoke again, pointing out parts of the garden and their purpose, and her favorite spots, which Marian had only briefly glimpsed from the upstairs windows. She had seen little at all beyond the front drive the night she'd arrived.

Finally, Gabby paused for breath. "I must warn you; I tend to babble when I'm nervous."

"Why would you be nervous?" Marian asked.

"Well, obviously you are someone important," Gabby claimed.

"I'm really not," Marian promised. She was here to hide, but the lies were piling up and she couldn't tell this girl the truth. Oddly enough, she'd rather tell this woman the facts about herself and know what she really thought about her then. She settled for a version of the truth that wasn't too shocking, "I haven't two shillings to rub together, in fact."

"I don't judge people by their wealth. Mrs. Nolan's friends are always important in some unique way," Gabby insisted. "It's why I was so pleased to speak with you again. I just know we'll become good friends."

Miss Kimble was a fool to want that, but Marian smiled and agreed with the young woman as they walked along. It was pleasant listening to someone her own age, too. The girl had enormous respect for both Lady Scarsdale and Mrs. Nolan, though they were acknowledged to be wildly different creatures.

"Lady Scarsdale says I must learn to curb my tongue before my season begins, but Mrs. Nolan wants me to always speak my mind. It's difficult to know which advice to follow sometimes, isn't it," she said, laughing with good humor.

"I suppose so," Marian agreed, although she'd received little advice from Lady Scarsdale so far. "I hear that you're going to London soon?"

"Yes. Next year. Lady Scarsdale promised to help me prepare for my first season, and I'm determined not to make a fool of myself. Making a good impression is vital when hunting for a husband."

"You're very young to be worried about that yet?"

"I'm old enough to know what I want or don't," Gabby assured her with a merry laugh. "I know how to run a household, deal with merchants, and keep accurate accounts. My cousin's household is insignificant compared to this grand estate, but I pay close attention when I'm here, and Lady Scarsdale is always willing to explain what I don't understand about the challenges of running a larger estate. I'm sure I'll be successful in finding the right husband for me."

"With that attitude, you certainly will be," Marian promised.

"Lady Scarsdale warned me that if I'm too bold, stating what I want too forcefully, I would repel some suitors."

"Obviously, those men wouldn't be the right man for you anyway," Marian mused. "What exactly do you think you want in a man?"

"To have him fall madly in love with me as soon as possible," Gabby said with a giggle and a wink. "Oh, and a title might be nice, too, but that is not a desperate wish."

"I suppose those things are important to some. But why the rush to wed?"

"For my cousin's sake, more than mine," she said, with complete seriousness. "John gave up his life and ambitions when he became my guardian. Taking me in, raising me as a beloved sister. I would repay him poorly if I dragged my feet to the altar. What about you? What do you hope for in a husband?"

"I'm not looking for one," Marian said, in equal seriousness. There wasn't a man for her. Certainly not in this world of grand aristocratic matches.

"Don't be silly. Of course, you are, and men will line up to dance with you next season."

"Next season?" Marian shook her head. "I won't be in London next season."

"Will you be staying here, or will you be gone home by then?"

Marian only smiled at that question because she didn't know where she'd be *tomorrow*, let alone next season. She'd always gone where the winds of chance or her uncle had taken her. It was so odd to have no one to answer to, although she supposed that for now, she answered to Mrs. Nolan. There was no one else to tell her what to do with her life anymore. It was a rather lonely feeling, actually. Being so disconnected from the people she'd always known was something she'd never imagined happening to her.

Marian turned around to look at the distant rooftops and pointed to them. "Is that the nearest village?"

"No, that is Mr. Wilson's estate. Our village is in the other direction. You must have seen it on your way from Portishead."

"I must have been asleep then," she blurted, hiding the fact that she'd come from the other direction. "Where is your home?"

"Between here and the village," Gabby said. "It's quicker to walk there than come by carriage."

It had been remarkably easy to find Danny's home, honestly. He'd given such wonderful descriptions that night at the inn that every turn she'd taken had been the correct one in the end.

Gabby tugged at her sleeve. "What was your home like?"

"Nothing like this," she blurted, looking around. "If you don't mind, I'd rather not talk about that."

"Me too," Gabby agreed, and then smiled. "There's sadness in my past as well."

Marian breathed a sigh of relief that she wouldn't have to explain how she didn't belong here or anywhere. As much as Miss Kimble seemed to like her right now, learning the truth about Marian's past could change that markedly. It was best if they became friends only on a superficial level. The fewer lies she spoke, the less she had to remember later.

"Tell me about your cousin, Mr. Kimble," Marian asked as she looked back at the manor house and the five figures now sitting out on the lawn. Danny and Miss Wilson, she noted, were on opposite sides of the gathering.

"My cousin is a good man, amusing, too. I am hoping he finds a gracious lady to marry when we go to London next year as well."

Did Gabby think of nothing but marriage for everyone around her?

When she went back inside, she ought to think seriously of leaving all this behind her. There were maps in the library, most likely, that could show her parts of the country she'd never imagined.

"It's truly a shame that Lord Scarsdale came back when he did," Gabby said, her lips pursing in distaste.

"What do you mean by that?"

"I mean, she's getting everything she ever wanted without lifting a finger to deserve it. Oh, she's going to be insufferable now."

"Who?"

Gabby took Marian by the arm and led her deeper into the gardens. "Miss Wilson, of course."

"What do you know about that?"

"Her and her plans for the earl? Poor man? Miss Wilson has long claimed their union is written in the stars."

"The stars?"

"This place has been her obsession since she was just a little girl. Knows everything about it and the occupants. I'd not be surprised if she weren't already taking over subtly, you know. You should hear her when Lady Scarsdale is not around. Quite dreadful."

"What does she say?"

"It's subtle, but over time she hasn't painted a flattering picture of the woman we both respect," Gabby warned. "She's bound to the past. Dull and unaware of her own deficiencies as a countess and a widow. I tried to tell my cousin about her criticisms and slights once, but he's deaf to that sort of thing. Says it's none of my business or that I'm imagining things. I so hoped he'd speak to Scarsdale about her. They were good friends once."

"I see," Marian said, looking back over her shoulder at the countess. They were too far away from the manor terrace now to see anyone, and she spun back to Gabby. "Lady Scarsdale adores Miss Wilson."

"That is true, unfortunately," Gabby whispered. "Despite my cousin's warning, I tried to say something about it to her once. But Lady Scarsdale won't hear a bad word said against Miss Wilson from anyone, least of all me. Miss Wilson found out, too, and I ended up on the outs for six months. All because I tried to do the right thing. It taught me a valuable lesson. Do not cross Miss Wilson, at least until after my season."

"What about Mrs. Nolan? I cannot believe she'd be so blind or enjoy hearing the countess maligned."

"Oh, Granny's a completely different story. That's what

she wants me to call her, but Lady Scarsdale insists I do not. Granny tried to talk to her daughter about Miss Wilson, but they argued so much it was horrible," Gabby warned. "I hope that Lord Scarsdale sees through Miss Wilson's false affection on this visit and long before it's too late."

But Danny would propose soon, and then it would be the end of everything. The end of his happiness? And his mother's, too, perhaps.

That did not sit well with Marian. The family had been nothing but kind to her so far.

It was on the tip of her tongue to pledge to help reveal Amy Wilson's nasty side. But what good would that do if Danny were determined to marry the woman? She'd only be sowing further discord.

Danny would not thank her for interfering with his love life, either.

He could become furious with her, in fact, and have her thrown out before she was ready to go. He already had plenty of reasons to be cross with her. Not for following him home to return the stolen ring, but for staying.

She'd promised she'd be no trouble for him and his family. Marian never went back on her word.

"We should go back," Marian murmured. "Mrs. Nolan might need me."

"Not yet. We've arrived at the grotto. Come and see," Gabby whispered, pushing through a veil of weeping willow to reveal a dark tunnel. "Don't be scared. The dark only lasts a little way in."

Marian had good eyesight and followed Gabby into the short tunnel. She put her hands out to each side of her and discovered rough brickwork.

"There's a turn here," Gabby said, fingers reaching back for her hand.

Marian gripped her fingers tightly, and they walked into a dazzling chamber together. She looked up and found windows of glass above her head.

"Careful or you'll get a wet hem," Gabby warned.

Marian lowered her gaze to the ground and saw water immediately before her.

"It starts shallow but drops deep almost immediately," she told her.

When Gabby stepped aside, Marian got a better look at the large chamber they were standing in.

"Someone built this?" she said in awe as she spun in circles. The walls were studded with quartz stones and the light from overhead hit them to dance over the lapping water. There were flagstones around the edge of the pool and stone benches to sit upon.

"The late Lord Scarsdale had it built for his first wife, although I understand she never came here often."

"It must have cost a fortune," Marian whispered.

"The spring was always here," Gabby told her as she removed her bonnet. "Lord Scarsdale just built over and around it to add privacy. Each summer they open the grotto so the village families can enjoy it, too."

"So, Miss Wilson uses the pool?"

"Of course not. If she had her way, this place would be torn down, and the spring destroyed."

"Why would she want to do that?"

"Because she's a fool and without a generous bone in her body. She'll never allow the common folk so much liberty on the estate when she becomes countess." Miss Kimble kicked her slippers off. "We must enjoy it while we can."

"What are you doing?"

"Taking a dip?"

"But you promised not to get wet," Marian reminded her.

"No. I promised not to fall in by accident. Swimming is another matter entirely."

"But we're expected back," Marian argued, glancing back at the entrance to the grotto.

"No, we're not," Gabby promised. "The only reason Mrs. Nolan suggested I show you the pool was for us to do this."

"She never said that."

"Well, of course not," Gabby agreed. "She almost always says the opposite of what she means."

"But Lady Scarsdale might disapprove,"

"If she did, she would have said so before we left. Come on, Miss Marian Trill," Gabby complained. "You're wasting precious time."

Gabby finished undressing down to her shift. Before she could pull that over her head, Marian whispered, "What if someone comes?"

"There's already a maid guarding the door. Mrs. Nolan wouldn't let anyone surprise us here."

With that, the other woman tossed aside her chemise and walked into the shallow part of the pool, completely naked. "There's cloth in that trunk behind you to dry off with later," she added before she suddenly jumped into the water, disappearing completely under the surface.

Marian didn't waste any more time worrying about being caught. She stripped off her new gown and hurried into the warm water for a quick dip.

Chapter Twelve

DANIEL WAS ALMOST ready to roar with frustration. First, he couldn't seem to make conversation with Amy Wilson for more than a few minutes without wanting to walk away, because second, whatever Marian was doing and saying seemed much more interesting.

"More tea?"

"Yes, thank you," he murmured.

Amy cast him a shy smile. "It's always a pleasure being at Hammersley Lodge."

"Yes, it is."

Marian kept laughing at something John Kimble said to her, and he found himself tensing all over. He wanted to go over there and tell his old friend to stop flirting with her.

It wasn't Kimble's fault that he could sit in the sun with his ward and Marian, her new friend, and make the pair laugh uproariously. Amy preferred the shade and was not inclined to laugh at anything he said so far. He was stuck sitting next to Amy for the rest of his life, too. Short of making a fuss to rearrange the furniture and everyone around him today, there were no other vacant chairs that he could move to.

"Cake?"

"Yes, please, unless you want the last piece."

Amy demurred. "I've eaten far too much today already."

One slice of cake might be considered enough for Amy,

but Marian and Gabby were indulging in a third slice each and laughing about ruining their figures because it was so good. Neither young lady seemed concerned about overstuffing themselves. Not like Amy constantly seemed to be. His future wife was also as stiff as a board, even in informal settings like this.

There was no slouching or leaning toward him when they spoke. It was like talking to an automaton doll. She had so little animation in her expression, he idly wondered what she'd do if he stuck a pin in her leg.

Kimble suddenly threw his hands up in the air and bellowed out a laugh, and Marian leaned back in her chair from him, grinning too, before leaning toward him to speak so quietly, Daniel couldn't hear the exchange.

He gritted his teeth as Kimble laughed at whatever it had been, though, and Daniel reached for the last piece of cake on the plate. "All the more for me," he murmured, taking a savage bite.

"A gentleman will always look better with a few extra pounds than a lady," Amy confessed to him in a low tone. "But women should always abstain for the sake of their health."

Daniel wasn't sure he agreed with that sentiment. Slender women had never much appealed to him before. He'd always preferred curvy women like Marian, though once upon a time, he was sure Amy had possessed some meat on her bones. He glanced sideways at her now. She was rather thin and narrow. Apparently, she'd been abstaining from every second slice of cake the whole time he'd been gone from the district.

Suddenly, Marian excused herself and headed toward them.

As she reached him, their eyes met briefly. A stab of satisfaction at her being so close brought an immediate smile to his lips. But then she continued on toward the manor and disappeared inside without saying a word.

Daniel gulped and turned back to find Amy watching him through narrowed eyes, and the last piece of cake stuck to the back of his throat so badly, he had to reach for his wine to wash it down.

As he looked up, he saw Kimble was studying the manor now, and watching the door Marian had disappeared through. But then his ward said something to him, and he laughed, and Kimble's attention returned to his cousin finally.

But for the next ten minutes, Kimble kept glancing over his shoulder at the manor.

Kimble was definitely interested in Marian.

The thought gave Daniel no joy and more than a little worry. Though, why wouldn't Kimble reveal his interest when Daniel had declared he had none in the woman himself? Kimble was a bachelor. Handsome enough to please any lady who caught his eye, and he had money—or had, the last time they'd spoken of their situations—to afford a mistress or a wife.

But could Daniel allow an attachment to grow between them without warning Kimble about Marian's past as a thief? He would not like to tarnish her reputation. Marian fit in well in their small society, and he hoped fervently that she had reformed enough since becoming his grandmother's companion that she posed no danger to anyone.

Perhaps it would be better to warn Marian instead not to encourage Kimble. Yes, that was what he should do and immediately.

Daniel made up a credible excuse to leave Amy's side to return to his study. Going to his study first should not make it appear that he was following Marian.

Once inside, he changed direction and prowled around the lower rooms for her until he spotted Marian hurrying back down the main staircase. Her cheeks were pink, and she was out of breath, but did not see him until the very last minute.

When she did, her face lit up with joy and anticipation, reminiscent of their first encounter. In one hand, she held two parasols that obviously belonged to his granny, and she lifted them up to show him. "Were you seeking an escape from the heat like I was?"

"No. I need a word with you," he answered, grabbing her by the arm and towing her into the nearest chamber. He shut the door behind them and leaned on it. "What have you told Kimble and his ward about yourself?"

Her brow furrowed. "Not much. Why?"

"Because I want to remind you that you can't go around claiming that your family came from Portishead when they probably never did," he told her, folding his arms over his chest to glare down on her.

"I never made up that story," Marian complained. "I was told I came from Portishead and, according to Granny, my family might have been in business there. She seems to believe she knows more about my family, too."

"So, just to be clear, you will continue to lie about who you are to everyone?" Daniel asked.

"Yes. I don't know *who* I am anymore," she said. "What else do you want me to say?"

"Nothing. Maybe hint that Granny's memory cannot be relied upon on the matter of your family."

"I won't speak ill of your grandmother for any reason. But I do remember a shop," Marian said. She looked up at him, but her gaze was unfocused. "Glassware and silver sparkling in the morning light, and colored glass panels painting patterns on the hardwood floorboards. Granny seemed to think that memory is an important connection to have made." Her eyes regained their focus on Daniel. "Why are you worrying so much about *me* when you haven't proposed to Miss Wilson yet?"

"That is none of your business. When are you leaving?"

"As soon as I can," she promised, biting her bottom lip as she glanced down at the ground. "But your granny has spun so complicated a tale about my being here that if I leave with no hint of where I'm going, it might raise more questions and suspicions about who I really am."

Daniel groaned. She had a point.

Marian looked up at him. "I'll do my best to stick to Granny's story, especially around your friends. Do you really mind so much my staying here?"

"Yes, I do, in fact. You're a difficult woman to have underfoot. Much too pretty," he complained, and when her face light up, he shook his head. "And you'll be gone soon, so it hardly matters if you're a distraction to my plans."

Her face lowered again. "Yes, but you're a distraction to mine as well," she murmured, and then winced. "I'd best hurry back to Miss Kimble before your granny sends someone to look for me. That would draw attention."

Granny would probably send Kimble. Daniel gritted his teeth. "Yes, you need to go."

"I'm going," she said, pulling a face. "And you better go back to wooing Miss Wilson, before she becomes any colder."

"What do you mean by that?"

"Well, it's clear she's not hanging off your every word. I haven't heard her laugh once today, and you're usually so funny and charming. You always make me smile."

"But not in the way Kimble does for you today. *He's* hanging off *your* every word today. What are you whispering to him? No. Don't tell me. I'm sure you're aware of how your talented tongue attracts all men—you're like honey to a bee."

Her frown returned. "You ought to be too busy with Miss Wilson to notice anything I do or say."

"Hard not to notice you when you do all you can to be noticed by everyone," Daniel complained bitterly. "Perhaps you could moderate your laughter."

Her lips parted a full minute before she asked, "My laughter suddenly irritates you?"

"Yes," Daniel complained, though as soon as the omission was out of his mouth, he regretted saying so. It wasn't true. He loved when Marian laughed with *him*. He dropped his head, crowding Marian and forcing her to look into his eyes. Hers were wide and pretty green, and her pink lips parted slightly. "Perhaps you should sit beside my grandmother for a while and be her paid companion, as you are supposed to be."

"Is a paid companion not supposed to enjoy herself? Must she be dull and invisible?"

"Something like that," he said, unable to look away from her tempting lips. "You have never been dull or invisible to me, though."

Marian's fingers caught the button on his waistcoat and a slow smile twisted her lips. "Is there anything else I can do for you today, my lord?"

"I think it would not be wise to encourage Kimble's conversation."

Marian's jaw dropped, and she stepped away from him. "He was talking to me about his ward."

"His eyes linger upon you the most," Daniel complained, deciding he might as well get it all off his chest now while he had a chance to speak bluntly. "He fancies you."

"That is ridiculous," she quipped, folding her arms across her chest. Which only made her full bosom more obvious and appealing.

He prowled after her. "I know what I see when I look at you," Daniel insisted. "A luscious beauty within arm's reach. Kimble is not looking at you like he does his ward, but as a woman he'd like to take to bed."

Marian punched her hands on her hips. "Are you jealous?"

Yes! "Men like Kimble never change their ways. He'll use you and discard you like every other scoundrel you've ever met must have done," he warned.

Her lower lip trembled. "The way you did?"

He gritted his teeth, fighting his own regrets about Marian. "If anything serious had ever happened between us, I would have. But nothing *did* happen between us."

"Just a harmless, meaningless kiss that took my breath away," she said, shrugging away the event, but he could easily see his words had upset her. She took a deep breath and let it out slowly. "Perhaps this time it will be a lady using a scoundrel for a change," she said, lifting her chin high again.

"If you encourage my friend, there will be hell to pay," Daniel began, but he was distracted by the defiant narrowing of her gaze.

"Is that right? What will you do to me?"

He looked her up and down slowly. Marian was a luscious woman, blessed with an adventurous spirit and, until now, unencumbered by the rules of proper society. Had things been different, he would have bedded her without a shadow of a doubt. He could still take her over his knee, or the nearest desk, if she provoked him well enough.

If she ever wanted a husband when she went to London, someone with wealth and good looks, she could have one with just snapping her fingers, and there was nothing Daniel could do to stop her. But here, now, he couldn't abide the idea. Especially if they were his friend, Kimble.

Kimble, who didn't know the real Marian and never could, was blinded by her pretty face and the lies Granny had woven around Marian's reputation to make her fit the mold of a proper lady. Beguiled by Marian's bright laugher and wit, the way Daniel had been at first. Kimble, buried in the dull countryside for so long, wouldn't stand a chance if she encouraged the poor fellow.

Yet if Daniel couldn't have her, why should he begrudge her a beau?

Daniel shook his head. He should not imagine Marian's future after she left him, or picture her as a wife, but he couldn't get the unpleasant image out of his mind and heart.

Getting Marian away from the estate, sending her somewhere safe from her former associates, ought to become his priority for everyone's sake.

But he liked knowing where she was, seeing her smile, and knowing that her former friends hadn't found her yet.

Still, watching her charm, an old friend burned more than it ever should. He ought not to notice that her nose crinkled when she laughed without any ladylike restraint, or that she bit her lip when she was listening intently to what he had to say.

Daniel struggled to resist that persistent, knowing smile of hers every time they were together.

He inched closer to Marian, pulse speeding up. Imagining of those pert lips pressed against another man's felt wrong. They should only be touching *his*—and he lowered his head to steal a kiss.

Marian must have sensed his thoughts, because she moved away from him before he even touched her.

"I'll do my best to moderate my laughter to a level you'll never notice, my lord."

Daniel straightened immediately. He'd been rebuffed. "Thank you," he said, as much for her promise as her rejection. At least one of them had all the restraint needed to keep him faithful to his future bride.

"As for Mr. Kimble…if he has any intentions, only time will tell. As long as he remains respectful, I can't see the problem in speaking to him whenever he comes to call, especially when your mother is watching me so closely all the time."

With that, she turned up her nose and spun on her heel, before striding for the open terrace doors.

He watched Marian flee outside with a glad but heavy heart. He'd no right to take his frustration out on her. It wasn't her fault he was having second thoughts about marrying Amy. But if she wasn't always around, he wouldn't be constantly comparing the two women and finding his choice so lacking.

Daniel followed after Marian a few steps and would have gone all the way outside…had he not heard the unmistakable sound of a throat clearing directly behind him.

Daniel turned.

Mother.

He ran a hand through his hair, "Yes, Mama?"

"What are you doing in here? I thought to find you in your study still."

"Was there something you needed me for?" he asked, hoping Mama had arrived too late to see him with Marian, and especially when he'd tried to kiss the woman.

"You've a woman out there to be charmed into marrying you, but you're consorting with Mother's companion in the library instead," she complained.

Daniel groaned.

"We talked, Mother, about the books," he explained, trying not to sound too defensive as he pointed around them. "Now, since we are alone, I wish to have a conversation with you about these plans you're making in my name," he said.

"They can wait until after Miss Wilson has accepted your proposal," Mother insisted.

"I'm not proposing today," he announced, moving closer to the door to look at what Marian was doing now. She was sitting by Granny's side and looking forlorn. He'd a fear his words might spur her to encourage Kimble to pursue her, but it seemed she'd heeded his warnings.

"You will escort Miss Wilson to cut some flowers for me then," Mother said as she caught him by the arm and dragged him outside against his will.

He didn't exactly resist. But Mother was stronger than she appeared. "Miss Wilson, here is my son to accompany you to the greenhouse at last."

"Ah, wonderful," Amy said as she stood and crossed the lawn to join Daniel. "We will go now?"

Feeling distinctly uncomfortable with the blatant

maneuvering, Daniel kept his gaze fixed on Amy to keep from seeing Marian's reaction.

No one offered to accompany them, and he looked back with longing when everyone began to laugh again. Everyone seemed amused by something Kimble had said, all except for Marian, that was. She was watching him leave her in the sun, looking lovelier than ever.

He gritted his teeth and faced the front as he continued to walk beside Amy, determined to put Marian from his mind once and for all. He gulped, though.

The greenhouse was some distance from everyone else, and that they could be entirely alone when they got there. Mother had set him up to propose to Amy in the greenhouse.

Daniel immediately looked around for a servant to act as a chaperone.

He crooked his finger at the first maid he saw, the one who had been serving as Granny's companion when he had first arrived home and beckoned her to join them.

The maid was delighted to leave the weeding of a garden bed to others and go along with them to cut flowers.

Amy cleared her throat, akin to how his mother always did. "I think your grandmother is finally softening toward me."

He frowned. "Is that right?"

"It was her idea for us to cut flowers together," Amy said proudly.

Daniel nearly groaned. So, Granny had given up trying to thwart his plans and was not attempting to hurry them along? Yet, Granny had been against this match all along. She did not like Amy?

He cursed under his breath. It felt like a betrayal.

Oblivious to Daniel's train of thought, Amy continued

talking at him. "I've done all I can to win her favor, of course, these past years, but she's never been an easy woman to please, has she?"

"I don't know about that," he countered. "Granny just likes to have fun."

Amy wound her arm through his without warning, so they had to walk close together. "How much longer do you think she'll stay?"

Daniel glanced down, startled by the odd question. "What do you mean, stay?"

"I mean, she still talks of Portishead with such fondness that I've always expected she'd go back," Amy whispered, which put her face much closer to his shoulder than he cared for.

"She has a lot of friends there," Daniel said, attempting to release the woman clinging to him like a vine.

Yet Amy could not be budged, because she seemed to have more words to whisper to him. "And the Trills? Funny name. I had no idea a connection existed or how fond she was of Miss Marian. It's all so curious and odd that she never discussed the woman, or her corresponding with Marian."

Daniel frowned. Was Amy really so accustomed to knowing everyone's business? "Who my grandmother writes to is her own business."

"You are correct, of course. But I'm sure your mother was taken by complete surprise by Miss Trill's unexpected arrival. There was such an unseemly rush to have a guest chamber made ready," Amy said, looking to him for confirmation that he knew more than he did. "Were you surprised, Jeremy?"

For a moment, Daniel didn't understand that Amy was referring to him by his actual first name. Jeremy was a name that Daniel had never cared to use very often since it was his father's, too.

"Yes, but not at all concerned about her act of charity toward someone in need who was dear to her," he said, framing Marian's arrival in such a way that aligned with the story going round. "My grandmother has a vast number of friendships, and she has always made herself at home here."

"That is true. She is quite unorthodox about the acquaintances she keeps. It's little wonder your mother disapproves. I wonder, given your grandmother's strong fondness for Portishead, that if you made the suggestion, she might want to take herself on a holiday there soon. She could take Miss Trill along with her to keep her company were she to stay. I'm sure she'd never be lonely."

Daniel decided not to tell Amy about Granny's intention to leave as soon as he married. He knew Granny hadn't warmed to Amy at all, and that was why she was planning to go. Daniel hoped to change her mind. "My grandmother has always been free to come and go as she pleases."

"You are so generous to your family." Amy winced. "It is such a pity that she has never made as much an effort to fit in."

"Yes," Daniel said slowly. He believed his grandmother had enlivened the district with her wit and charm and an odd assortment of friends coming to stay over the years. He didn't want her to fit in. To become silent and unobtrusive. She encouraged discussion of current ideas and challenged the attitudes of everyone she met. That was not something to ever complain about, yet Amy clearly saw it as a flaw in her character rather than a benefit.

He glanced over his shoulder as the maid cleared her throat repeatedly. The maid's brow had risen high as she looked at them and he managed to disentangle himself from Amy's grip. "You'll find the greenhouse you want in that direction, my lord," she whispered.

"We know that, you silly girl! Do not interrupt your betters again," Amy snapped at the maid, and then drew in a breath and smiled up at Daniel. "This is the site for the new greenhouse, I believe."

Daniel nodded, taking it all in. The lightning-fast change of Amy's mood, her lashing out at the maid, who was only doing what she was supposed to do as a chaperone. "Ah yes. The new greenhouse. Thank you for the reminder."

They were in an open patch of lawn, surrounded by low plantings and not much else. He studied the spot carefully. A good place for a new greenhouse…if he'd thought he ever needed another one.

"It is nice to have you here to make good on your promises, but it will be a shame for me to see another beautiful patch of lawn torn up so close to the manor," Amy murmured. "You'll see the new greenhouse from the morning room windows every single day. Are you certain it would not be better placed somewhere else? Perhaps nearer the grotto, where water can be sourced more easily."

"Only if you made holes for pipes in the grotto walls," Daniel mused.

"My father says that would be considerably easier and cheaper than carting water from the existing well."

"Does he now?" Daniel mused, unimpressed that Amy and her father had designs to ruin the grotto his father had designed and enjoyed. It was Daniel's favorite part of the estate.

Mother had yet to discuss her plans, and for him to approve the expense of it, but he was certain she would have considered every alternative position for a new greenhouse. Changing the grotto would never have been an option.

They walked on a little more and then ducked inside the greenhouse together. The greenhouse was occupied by the gardeners at present, watering plants and moving them about. It was utter chaos inside.

Yet Amy forged ahead, ordering servants out of her way, leaving Daniel to follow. It was clear to see they'd come at the absolute worst time to pick flowers for the house.

That didn't seem to bother Amy one little bit, as she picked up shears to cut the blooms. The gardeners nodded to him as they backed away from Miss Wilson. Amy cut a flower on one bush and then continued on with the same bush, handing them back to him one by one.

The head gardener's face turned a mottled red as the cutting continued. "Not so many from that one!" he cried out in alarm.

"It's for the countess," Amy chided, and continued to snip nearly all the buds off one rose bush to finish off her bouquet, neglecting to see one perfect bud fall to the ground.

Daniel stooped to pick it up and, as he straightened, he caught the gardener's exchanging looks of anger as Amy moved to the next bush.

"I think that will do for the flowers," Daniel announced.

"But I'm not done yet," Amy told him.

The gardeners muttered amongst themselves as she cut another bloom.

"That is enough," Daniel said, snatching the shears from Amy's hands.

"The decorating of the house is women's work," she chided, trying to take the shears back.

"The estate, and house, are *mine*," he countered. "So are the flowers."

Faced with his unexpected opposition, Amy pouted.

Daniel hardly ever noticed the flowers adorning the house anyway, but mother did like them. He urged Miss Wilson and the maid to leave the greenhouse ahead of him, and then turned back to the older men. "I'm so sorry."

"Those blooms had been saved especially for Mrs. Nolan's birthday," the head gardener informed him. "They were to make a special bouquet for her birthday celebration dinner."

"Miss Wilson must not have known."

"Begging your pardon, my lord. That is not true. Miss Wilson was with the countess when the request was made weeks ago," the gardener grumbled sourly. "If you'll excuse me, my lord, I'd best see what can be salvaged."

Daniel frowned. Amy had deliberately cut flowers meant for a special occasion mother had planned. "Do what you can, and I'm sure it will be enough for the birthday dinner."

Daniel walked outside slowly, twirling the stem of a single rosebud between his fingers, deep in thought. The surprise for Granny's coming birthday was something he'd not heard about yet, but it was lessened now by Miss Wilson's forgetfulness, or had it been done in spite? Amy had been enthusiastic with her cutting from just those bushes.

When Daniel reached Amy again, he discovered the maid he'd brought along as chaperone, and the flowers just cut, appeared to be gone.

But that meant he was left alone with Amy again. Her eyes dropped to the bloom in his hand. She squared her shoulders then and smiled warmly at him.

Daniel gulped.

She must imagine him about to propose—but he was

even further away from that moment, given all she'd said and done today.

He dug his finger under his neckcloth to loosen it as she drew closer to him. It might have been the perfect moment for romance—secluded, and him with a single blood-red rose to offer a future bride.

Instead, he said, "I trust you can find your way back, Miss Wilson."

Her brow furrowed. "Of course, but aren't you coming with me?"

"No, there's something here that requires my immediate attention. An emergency."

"An emergency? I should stay and help?" Amy asked, almost pleading for him to say yes.

"No. That won't be necessary. As you said, I should involve myself more with the running of the estate from now on," he said firmly.

The maid suddenly reappeared, noticed the bloom in his hand, and rushed toward him.

"There it is," she said, reaching for the bloom. "I feared I'd dropped one somewhere in the garden."

"Yes, you did," he said, handing it to the maid with a flourish.

Daniel caught Amy's glare at the maid, and it was long enough to make the young woman recoil. "I'd best take this back inside with the rest, my lord. Thank you for saving it for me."

Daniel nodded. "Miss Wilson will be returning to my mother now."

"Very good, my lord. Shall I escort her there for you?"

Amy's eyes narrowed dangerously on him. "That isn't necessary."

"No, no. The maid is right. You are a guest here, Miss Wilson. I should hate for you to become lost in the shrubbery," he murmured, watching the first signs of a temper Amy Wilson had ever shown him. He knew she'd have one somewhere, of course. Everyone got angry.

He turned his attention to the maid. "If you don't mind, could you inform everyone that I won't be back until after supper?"

Amy's smile faded. "I can tell them, my lord. Will I see you tomorrow?"

"Perhaps," he said, refusing to commit himself. Amy's behavior today had given him a lot to think about, as had his own growing reservations. He'd engaged in two arguments today, one with Marian and now with Amy, and there was only one he truly regretted.

Which begged the question, did he really want to marry Amy Wilson, when he only cared if Marian would forgive him?

Chapter Thirteen

"AND THIS CHEST contains what remains of my wedding trousseau," Lady Scarsdale announced to Marian and Gabby with a fond smile as she opened a large but shabby trunk at her feet.

Gabby had expressed an interest in seeing it when they'd returned from the grotto yesterday. And upon her return visit today, the lady had been eager to show off the treasure chest of wonders to them both immediately.

They were in the countess' bedchamber, surrounded by more riches than Marian had never dreamed existed. Lady Scarsdale's bedchamber was large and so feminine that Marian had instantly coveted it for herself, even if she felt unworthy of setting foot in here.

Mrs. Nolan had chosen to remain downstairs in case Miss Wilson finally arrived. No one could understand what might be keeping the woman today when she was usually so punctual.

Marian was glad for whatever reason kept her absent from the manor. Now that she was fully aware of Miss Wilson's disrespect toward Lady Scarsdale, she couldn't help but notice the condescension directed toward the countess when Amy spoke to her.

It was astonishing Lady Scarsdale failed to notice, or perhaps she was accustomed to ignoring any unpleasantness directed at her. Marian was not so inclined or even willing to forgive such rudeness toward a member of Daniel's family.

It had become a habit for Marian to pay attention to every move Lady Scarsdale made in the past few days. She was wise but not terribly talkative, at least not with Marian. The countess had almost single-handedly run the estate for her absent son and done a remarkable job of it, by all accounts. She was incredibly talented and gracious, too. There was much Marian could learn from such a woman just by watching how she behaved around others.

"It's truly beautiful," Gabby gushed, pausing to admire every single garment. "How wonderful you were able to preserve it so well. It looks almost new."

"Thank you. I made it all myself, did all the embroidery without help. The late Lord Scarsdale provided the pearls on the gown I wore on my wedding day."

"How utterly romantic," Gabby gushed again, pointing out to Marian a wealth in pearls stitched into the dress still in the trunk. "What do you say, Miss Trill? Would you wear something like this? An heirloom gown, or would you want to make your own?"

"I…" Marian studied the last dress properly. "It looks too fragile to be worn."

"Nonsense." Lady Scarsdale showed her the full length. The over gown was sheer lace but embroidered heavily from shoulder to hem with seed pearls all over. "I have it aired each year and packed away carefully to avoid wrinkles. It has long been my hope to see it worn again one day."

Marian lifted her hand to touch the sleeve of the garment. The fabric felt like new between her finger but as fragile as it seemed. Obviously, a creation made with love and a reminder of happy times in the countess' life.

"I would want to wear something just like this. Something important. Something made with love by my mother. It would have been a family heirloom that meant the world to me if I had any family left," she whispered, and then smiled. "I've not the skill to sew a gown of my own."

The countess inclined her head—and then she did something that surprised Marian. Lady Scarsdale held the gown against Marian's body, sizing her up.

"It would fit you, I think," she said, looking her up and down, assessing the length and fit across her chest.

Marian held the dress against her carefully and took a few steps toward a mirror as Lady Scarsdale held up the bodice by the shoulders and allowed her to see what she might look like on a wedding day in such a dress.

But Marian's eyes blurred with tears after a single glance at herself. She'd found something she wanted more than gold, a pretty room, more than the promise ring she still coveted for her finger.

She wanted this dress and everything it represented. Hope. Happiness. Love. Family. Forever. A husband who adored her.

But a woman like her could never have such a wealth of treasures.

Marian hastened to return the dress to the countess, overcome by the unwanted emotions assailing her. Yearning had always been in her nature, but her ambitions and dreams had changed markedly since coming to live here. They had grown to be impossible.

"I must return to Mrs. Nolan now." And then she fled, but not to the drawing room, where Mrs. Nolan might see her tears and ask about them. Somewhere she felt safe.

She went to Danny's bedchamber and slipped into his room. He wasn't there, of course, but the smell of his cologne, and knowing he was not far away, comforted her.

She stepped to the side and slid to the floor behind the door in an untidy heap, covering her face as her emotions continued to overwhelm her. She should never have come to this place. Never have followed after a man from a family so obviously far above her.

But she had, and now she knew what was missing from her life, and it hurt so much to know it would be forever denied her. She missed her mother and father, not that she remembered them clearly. She missed the idea of them and the life she could have led had they not died, and her only choice was to go with her uncle, who'd made her a criminal.

If she'd had parents, she might have worn a pretty dress to mark her coming out to society, taken dance lessons like Gabby had, learned to embroider, to play the pianoforte, to mingle with the right sort of people and talk of nothing of importance all day long. To make a lasting good impression wherever she went and be happy, not knowing how lucky she was.

To be missed.

To deserve to wear a gown like Lady Scarsdale had just shown her, when she married a man who she loved with all her heart.

Marian had a lifetime of wants that could never be satisfied in her current situation. She was tainted by a past she'd no say in, and now with no hope of ever being good enough to make a match of the sort Gabby Kimble anticipated.

Marian wiped at her eyes angrily. Angry with herself.

Angry with the world. Angry with Danny, although it wasn't his fault because she had followed him home without an invitation of any sort.

She must put those impossible wants aside and concentrate on what she could have here and now and in the future.

Money.

She could earn it as a companion, or steal it.

Stealing was the only thing she'd ever been any good at. Her one true accomplishment.

She wiped at her eyes one last time and climbed to her feet, chastising herself for her moment of weakness and resolved to stop feeling sorry for herself. She never had been the sort of woman to resort to tears when thwarted. She knew what to do to make her dreams come true. What she always had to do.

She had to steal for her future, and to get out of this place tomorrow with enough money lining her pockets to take her far away from Danny and his proper life.

Living the life of a lady's companion was making her sentimental and weak.

Vulnerable.

She couldn't survive with regrets making her doubt her every action in the years ahead.

Yes, it was time to leave this gilded palace, and for that, she'd need as much coin as she could carry.

She studied the room in front of her and then began a careful, thorough search of every drawer, every book, nook, and cranny where money might be hidden away.

But Danny was as careless here as he had been at the inn where they'd met. She found enough coins littering the bottom of a desk drawer, in waistcoat pockets, even pound notes marking his place inside a book kept beside the bed to take her far away in her own hired coach if she wanted.

Really, a man who flaunts his wealth always deserved to have it taken away from him eventually.

And yet…she put every single coin and pound note back where she found it as she realized it had begun to rain. Reasoning she didn't need it at that very moment when travel in such conditions would be difficult. She could and would steal from Danny when it was the right time, when the weather cleared, and hopefully before it turned for the worst again.

Knowing she could easily have the money she needed solved all her problems.

She would travel all the way to Portishead first, although Crossman might return there one day as well. But she couldn't worry about that now, or him anymore. She would discover if she had any other family left in Portishead and then move on to greener pastures, where no one would know her.

She would then close the book on her past as a thief, her misdeeds, and remake herself into the sort of woman others held in the highest respect.

She had Lady Scarsdale to use as her example of how to behave in society and make a new name for herself. She was not like Miss Kimble, who expected love and romance and a husband to sweep her off her feet.

Not every woman had to marry, or have a family, either. If she was ever lonely, and could afford the expense, she could take in an orphan or two. Save them from a life of petty crime and protect them the way she should have been.

She didn't really need a fancy wedding gown or family or even a husband to turn to when she was frightened or sad.

And then she turned around and found Danny standing in the room with her.

Marian hadn't heard him come in, and her breath caught at the smile that spread across his face. She'd been too lost in her own thoughts and hadn't been paying attention, and that was another sign she was in the wrong place at the wrong time.

She was usually more aware of her surroundings than this. "Excuse me," she said, and went to pass him, but his arm shot out, halting her retreat as she ran into it.

As his fingers closed on her hip, a shiver of excitement raced through her. But he was a temptation she should resist with all her might. He was the reason for her confusion and the unwanted emotions that had besieged her today. He made her want a chance to live a good life and to be his.

When he pulled her close, she fell into his arms with no real resistance. She fought her attraction, desires, but a sigh of relief escaping her lips when she inhaled his scent proved her undoing.

He held her flush against his warm body, and her arms rose to encircle his neck without any decision on her part to do so.

He said nothing at all, but held her gaze as if waiting for her to say something to encourage him or stop him. By his behavior and intense gaze, it was easy to assume what he wanted from her. Passion. Heat and satisfaction. The same rush to intimacy that had occurred that night at the inn before he'd drawn away. Marian had wanted that too, but there were many reasons not to give in to her urges with him anymore.

Good ones.

She couldn't stay with him, and he didn't really want her around. He intended to marry a mean-spirited woman who would ruin his life and incite further division between his family. When he married Amy Wilson, he would probably forget her all too easily.

But couldn't Danny see he had appalling taste in women, herself included? He was hell-bent on making his life one misery after another. Chasing after things he ought to be more cautious of.

"Have you been crying?"

"It's nothing. I stubbed my toe."

He glanced down and nodded. "That can cause a tear or two."

Danny was entirely too trusting. His first question should have been to ask what she was doing in his chambers, but he still had not said a word about that. He should have told her to leave the room immediately for the sake of propriety.

Amy would never dare come to his chambers uninvited, the way Marian had. They were a bad influence on each other, and it had to end now.

Marian rose up on her toes and pressed her lips hard to Danny's. It wasn't a gentle kiss she offered, and it wasn't meant to mean anything beyond goodbye. To bring an end to the way she'd felt about him from the very beginning of their acquaintance.

Before Danny could respond, Marian wrenched away from him and fled the room. Fled him and the regret that was making her choke up with fresh tears and cause her heart to hurt like it never had before.

She ran headlong into a slender form, who grabbed her by the shoulders and held her still.

She looked into Lady Scarsdale's eyes and saw astonishment reflected there. But then the countess glanced behind to the open door to her son's bedchamber, and censure and disappointment soon followed.

Marian couldn't bear to see the loss of respect another moment, and she ran blindly from her too.

She was done for here. Her reputation, what little she'd regained in the last days, vanishing in the blink of an eye. All because of Danny and the way he made her feel.

She never should have gone to warn him at the inn.

Never should have let herself care about him, or anyone else in this place.

If Lady Scarsdale guessed the rest, that she'd met her son before she even arrived here, her time as a companion to Mrs. Nolan was absolutely over, too.

She had to leave tonight, before she was thrown out tomorrow.

Marian fled to her chamber, a large guest room granted to her out of misplaced kindness, and locked the door behind her. She cried tears of frustration and loss, until she could weep no more, and then she pulled herself together again.

Her bag was still under her bed, packed in readiness to flee at a moment's notice, the same as when she'd hidden it there.

She should go now to avoid any later unpleasantness.

But then she glanced down at the pretty dress she was wearing, and her heart sank. She would normally change into something more suitable for the long road before leaving anywhere. She also still had to fetch that money she'd found in Danny's room to take with her.

She had to go back to his chamber for that, most of all.

Marian stripped off the expensive gown and laid it neatly on her bed. When she retrieved her older gown and put it on, her nose wrinkled in distaste at the shabby state of it. It was old and worn and not very flattering, but it was hers.

She compared the two dresses and decided that for now, she would wear the nicer gown over her old one when she left the estate. She would travel as a woman of some affluence and perhaps hire a maid to accompany her, too.

She would keep the dress as a reminder that her greatest mistake was letting someone close to her heart.

Caring about what people thought of her had been a great folly.

She glanced out the window to determine the time of day, only to see the Kimble gig departing, bouncing madly along the front drive with Gabby at the reins and Mr. Kimble holding on to his hat with one hand and the carriage seat with the other.

Marian laughed softly, but tears were only a moment away again. The only real friend she'd ever known, a genuine original in every sense of the word, had already left the estate. Marian regretted not being able to say goodbye to Gabby so very much, but it was probably for the best.

Best for Gabby.

Marian would never see Gabby again and could not even wish her well on her journey toward matrimony next year. She hoped Gabby found someone who could love her as she deserved. Someone who met every one of her requirements in a gentleman. Handsome, kind, wealthy, and perhaps even titled.

Someone a bit like Danny.

She watched Gabby and her guardian drive away until

the carriage finally disappeared from sight. But then another carriage immediately replaced it on the drive, headed toward the manor house at a stately clip. It was a large enough not to mistake the grand conveyance headed their way, pulled by a team of four white horses. It was the Wilsons' carriage coming again.

A keen depression settled upon Marian's shoulders then. Amy Wilson might again be among them for dinner. She couldn't face that woman over the dinner table again, and why should she ever have to? It's not as if anyone but Mrs. Nolan worried if she were absent.

And then, while everyone was at dinner, she could gather up whatever money she would need for her journey and leave.

Satisfied with her decision, she took one last look at her chamber and sat down on the bed. There would be plenty of time to return to Danny's room tonight.

If she timed her leaving just right, she might escape detection by the servants entirely, too.

Marian could be on the road to the next village before the sun was high in the sky tomorrow and long before anyone realized she'd gone.

Time sometimes passed slowly when you were waiting to lighten someone's pockets, but eventually, she judged the sky dark enough for her escapade. She crept out into the hall. As she'd anticipated, there wasn't a soul on the upper floor or anywhere near the master bedchamber. The family should all be downstairs, dining on stuffed pig and drinking wine and laughing together in wait for a proposal while the servants waited on them hand and foot.

She moved along the hall purposefully and let herself into Danny's bedchamber.

It was just as she remembered, empty, a bit untidy, and filled with the scent of his sandalwood cologne. She moved through the room, collecting the coins she'd found earlier in the day and hiding them away in the many pockets of her old gown. But when she got to the desk drawer, she found it was locked, which hadn't been the case last time.

That was a small obstacle to overcome for someone like her. She put her hand to her hair and extracted a hairpin, one of the new wire ones she'd been given by Mrs. Nolan when she'd first arrived. It was not shaped quite right, and she felt a pang of regret as she twisted the object to suit her immediate needs and then went to work on the lock.

It clicked open easily, and she dug beneath Danny's papers to find the money so imperfectly hidden at the bottom of the drawer.

She counted out the notes on the tabletop, one hundred and twenty pounds. More money than she'd ever had in her life, or ever expected to see again, but still not enough for a long and comfortable life. It was merely a drop in the ocean to someone with a thriving estate like this, but Marian felt another unexpected pang of regret. She'd rather stay than have the money.

But that was impossible.

She had to leave before she was forced to pretend the joy she just did not feel. She would be expected to celebrate Danny's engagement along with everyone else when it was finally announced. But she couldn't pretend anymore, because it would wrench out her heart, stab it with knives of regret, and turn her bitter.

No. Leaving was her best course of action.

She stuffed the money between her breasts, under her stays, and closed and locked the drawer again.

Then, with one last look around the room, she headed for the dressing closet, where she suspected a safe might be a hidden that was sure to set Marian up for a comfortable life far from Danny.

Chapter Fourteen

"Where is your companion tonight, Mrs. Nolan," Amy asked as the first course of dinner was laid out before them. "Will she be joining us for dinner?"

Daniel could kiss Amy for asking that question. He'd been wondering what was keeping Marian for the last half hour, but did not wish to single her out for notice. He was missing her smile.

"I'm afraid not. She was to dine in her room tonight," Granny answered after a moment.

"Oh, well," Amy said brightly. "Her loss. This beef is so exquisitely tender."

Daniel's loss, too. Having Marian nearby always made him feel at ease, especially around Amy Wilson.

Daniel turned his head to regard his grandmother. He'd heard nothing of any plans for Marian to be excused from tonight's dinner, and there had been many opportunities for him to be informed. Her absence made him feel incomplete.

After Marian had fled from his chambers earlier that day, he hadn't actually seen her again. Perhaps she was feeling uncomfortable or shy about kissing him, although he couldn't imagine why she would.

The impulsive and reckless kiss between them had come as a surprise but had not been too shocking, though it *had* seemed rather desperate. He was starting to feel the same way about Marian's absence.

Because he wanted another kiss just like it.

He wanted Marian back in his arms again, where she belonged. Marian Trill had become a constant surprise and secret delight of his, and he wished to know all there was to know about her. Steal more time alone together.

He gulped and set his glass of wine aside and tried to devote himself to the contents of his plate. But he ached to know what Marian was doing, eating in her chambers, and found he had little appetite tonight for filling his own stomach. He pushed his plate aside, signaled a servant to take it away and then picked up his wineglass again, but didn't want to drink, either.

He'd hoped that coming home would have ended his reckless pursuit of inappropriate women, but it seemed he remained unchanged in his preferences.

But today it had been Marian who had sought him out, in his own chambers, even after he'd warned her not to flirt with John Kimble or him. It had been a possessive weakness on his part to feel the pinch of jealousy over a rival for her affections and smiles. He'd known he'd behaved badly then… but he'd envied Kimble the right to respond favorably to *his* woman.

His woman?

Yes. That was how he thought of Marian, even now.

After she'd rushed away, he'd regretted that he'd not apologized for being an ass. He could hardly complain about her seeking the attention of another man when he was seeking the hand in marriage of a different woman.

He'd felt some guilt over it all until well after she'd fled. He'd moped, regretting he couldn't pursue Marian to find out what was wrong.

He believed Marian's past as a thief had been left behind

and that she had taken an honest turn with her employment here with Granny. But she hadn't changed her plans. The fact she'd found a way to avoid dinner tonight, when she'd appeared promptly at every prior meal, concerned him.

She was preparing to leave.

Daniel could not let her go yet. She could not leave him to his fate to marry a woman he wasn't at all attracted to half as much as he was to her.

That worried him a lot still.

How that kiss had seemed final between them.

A parting.

Had she already gone?

He glanced at the dark windows and then over at Granny, who seemed unconcerned about not having Marian by her side tonight. As much as he longed to go in search of the paid companion to reassure himself that all was well, he was constrained by the Wilsons' attendance at dinner.

"Have you had much interest in the London town house yet?" Mr. Wilson suddenly enquired.

"What sort of interest could there be in my London town house?"

"Well, my daughter said you had no plan to return to Town," he replied. "I could be persuaded to lease it from you for the right price."

"I'm not leasing the town house. I may not have a pressing need for London at the moment, but of course Mother intends to go to support Miss Kimble in her first season next year."

Amy turned her gaze on Mother. "You are far too generous."

Daniel was taken aback by Amy's disapproval.

Mother clearly heard it, but her expression remained

unchanged as she answered. "I gave my word to help her, and I have high hopes for her making an excellent match," Mother said, patting her lips with a napkin and then setting it aside. "Would you excuse me? There's a matter that requires my attention."

"Might I be of assistance?" Amy asked, half rising from her chair.

"I'm afraid not," Mother answered. "Do continue dinner without me."

With that, Mother exited the room, leaving Amy frowning after her. She seemed vexed by not being needed, too.

Mother's swift exit from the room left him and Granny to entertain the Wilsons. Something he found he no longer wanted to do.

Daniel had groaned to himself when he'd seen them standing in the drawing room too early for dinner, and he'd found himself glancing at the clock all night long so far.

He requested the next course set before them and turned his attention to cleaning the fish off his plate as fast as he could without seeming to do so.

But Wilson took his time picking at the fish, asking questions about his plans for the coming months between mouthfuls, and trying to involve his daughter into the discussion of every single decision Daniel had made.

Mr. Wilson even managed to include his own participation in any plans mentioned.

When Daniel had pictured coming home, and his future married life, it had not been with a view of him and his wife sitting at home or having to explain himself to his father-in-law over every meal.

He had pictured them, Amy and him, as completely

separate from everyone else—and each other, except in matters of any children they might have.

But as he considered it longer, he realized there would be much more overlap. More time spent together with his mother, Granny, and Mr. Wilson, unfortunately. Far more decisions to be made together if they were ever going to rub along satisfactorily.

As the evening progressed, so did the long, awkward pauses between topics. Wilson had not outright asked if Daniel was going to offer for his daughter, but he kept glancing between them every time they spoke to each other. He alternated sighs or approving nods of his head until the last course was taken away.

It was clear Amy's happiness was very much on his mind.

When Granny stood, inviting Amy to join her for tea, Daniel breathed his own sigh of relief and stood too. "Do enjoy yourself ladies," Daniel said, more than ready for the peace of gentlemen in the dining room alone, and a much stronger drink in his hand. "We'll join you both soon.

"Nonsense. Why part at all when there's just the four of us? We should not deprive the women of our company and sensible conversation," Wilson said to him.

"I am always flattered by my grandson's conversation," Granny answered.

Wilson offered Granny his arm and led her away to the drawing room instead of staying here with him.

Amy looked around the room. "I have always enjoyed this dining room. We could remain here together for a while if you like."

No. He quickly headed out of the room, knowing Amy would follow him.

When they entered the drawing room, Wilson whispered

a few words to his daughter, and she smiled and hurried over to sit beside Granny.

Wilson turned for the sideboard to help himself to a glass from the estate's finest whiskey without asking Daniel's leave.

Daniel watched the older man with growing sourness, wondering if he even remembered he was a guest here anymore. Wilson was rather too free with his opinions lately for Daniel's tastes, and helping himself to whatever luxuries surrounded him was almost the last straw.

He stood up abruptly. "You seem to have made yourself at home here, Mr. Wilson."

"Yes, indeed." Wilson turned, catching his eye. "Something is on your mind, son," he murmured, one brow arched.

"No. Just noticing how some things change and others haven't."

The older man frowned severely, and he didn't understand. Wilson had been father's friend but not Daniels. Only Daniel's closest friends should be so free with his whisky.

"Shall we smoke a cigar together on the terrace," Wilson suggested.

"Not tonight."

Wilson had also suggested smoking cigars the first night Daniel had returned home and been disappointed enough at his reluctance to chide Daniel for not living up to his father's reputation as a generous host.

Yet nothing could compel Daniel to take up smoking cigars, for the simple reason that women did not like the smell or the taste of it on his tongue when they kissed him.

He was sure Marian would not.

He suspected Amy would not think to complain about it.

He bit his lip and glanced across at Granny and Amy Wilson and heaved a sigh.

There was no escaping the truth. He was more concerned about what Marian thought of what he did than the woman he had planned to make his wife.

But did he still want that? Marriage? To have and hold one woman forever?

The answer was, of course, a resounding no where Amy was concerned.

He was not even astonished by his own change of heart. Under no circumstances did he want to make an offer for Amy Wilson's hand now they'd spent some time together. He did not want Mr. Wilson to assume a fatherlike role in his life or to have the Wilsons always coming around as they had done all of this week.

They were dull and boring, and he didn't even like them. They had nothing in common, besides being neighbors for the whole of his life.

But he was stuck with them tonight unless he gave them a reason to leave.

There was much he didn't care for about Mr. Wilson, but in his five-year absence he'd forgotten it all. The sly suggestions he had a long way to go before he was deemed fit for his father's title had not been uttered yet, but that sort of comment had been frequent when he'd been younger and afraid of putting a foot wrong.

Granny had never liked Wilson nor warmed to Amy, who seemed never to hold an opinion in opposition to her own father. If he'd married her, he rather thought he'd have been quite miserable.

Thank heavens for Marian showing up in his life when she had. He might have made a grave mistake and not just for his own peace. There was Granny to think of, and Mother too. Mother was used to doing things a certain way, hers, although she had tried to educate Amy to become a countess, to be generous and kind to those of the lower classes, he wasn't sure any of it had stuck.

He rubbed his face, tired of it all.

"Are you weary, Mrs. Nolan," Amy asked of Granny.

Daniel turned to Granny immediately. Yes, Granny must be as tired as he was of the Wilson's company. She would happily help him get rid of them, too. "Are you all right?"

"I'm fine," she replied curtly.

"No. No. I'm quite sure I saw you yawn several times during dinner, too," he insisted.

Amy patted Granny's hand. "You must take better care of your health."

Daniel nodded subtly at Granny, hoping she'd play along. "You were awake quite early this morning."

"Was I?" she answered, frowning at him.

Daniel moved to sit at her side. "Have you forgotten that it was very early for you? You woke me up before the sun rose, too."

Granny blinked. "I usually only ever sleep as long as I need."

"Oh, but you must be as exhausted as I am," Daniel decided, and he yawned too for good measure. "Perhaps an early night would be best for both of us."

Amy started nodding along. "I would hate to keep you."

Granny narrowed her eyes but seemed to have finally understood Daniel's scheme. "Yes, well, I'm sure a good long night's sleep will be just the thing for everyone," she suggested. "I should hate to send our guests home so early, but I fear whatever is keeping your mother will last all night long."

"I'll go and find out what the problem is and then turn in." He glanced over at the Wilsons. "I'm afraid it would be best if…"

"Yes, I suppose we'll see you all again tomorrow," Wilson said with a heavy sigh and also a touch of frustration. "I'm sure you've much to set to order here, now you're finally back in charge."

"Yes indeed," Daniel agreed, though he'd no issues with the way Mother had run the estate in his absence. He would go slowly when lifting the burdens from her shoulders. He'd not like to alienate her, now that he was about to disappoint her so badly, and after all the good she'd done for the family purse.

Wilson went to his daughter and drew her to her feet. Amy seemed suddenly inclined to resist, though. "I could stay and help Lady Scarsdale with whatever has drawn her away, or even help put Mrs. Nolan to bed."

Daniel almost groaned at the implied insult to Granny's competence and put a hand over hers to silence any retort. She was not so doddery she needed assistance for going to bed.

"There's no cause for concern about my grandmother. I'll take care of her."

Amy smiled. "You're so kind to the women of your household."

"Of course I am. I love them with all my heart," he said proudly, and included Marian in that sentiment, too. "There's nothing I wouldn't do to protect my family and ensure they are as happy as can be, living here with me. This estate couldn't function so well without each of us doing our part. I have a lot yet to learn from them still."

Granny gripped his hand a little tighter at his praise, and he was sure she was smiling up at him proudly. But he kept his eyes on Amy, watching her reaction to his statement. Since his return, Amy had made the odd comment that suggested he'd be better off without the women of his family constantly being underfoot. He resented the recurring pattern of subtle disrespect toward them both, but especially toward Granny who was the original *original*, and essential to his happiness.

Amy's smile wavered at his steady glare. "Of course."

"I'm glad you understand," he answered, patting Granny's hand a few more times.

Amy turned to her father, grasped his arm, and turn him toward the door, where a servant stood holding her shawl to keep off the chill of the night on their short journey home.

Daniel walked behind them both to the door. "Oh, before I forget. I didn't get a chance to share the news from Wraxall."

"News?"

"Heard there was some trouble there a few days ago."

Daniel had met Marian at Wraxall. "Oh?"

"A man and a woman were almost apprehended for stealing," Wilson said.

Daniel's stride faltered. "Who were they?"

"Some young fellow and his light-skirt."

"I hadn't heard," Daniel glanced at the other man. "Who told you?"

"An old beggar with a boy, limping past my gate. He was looking for his runaway daughter and asked if I knew someone who matched her description."

Daniel's stomach clenched. "And did you?"

"Of course not."

Daniel tried not to let his relief show, but he was elated by the news. "What did the old man look like?"

"Just an ugly beggar and his grubby son," he said rather dismissively of the pair. "I've little time for conversation with the lower classes."

"I see." Daniel rubbed his jaw. Could it have been Marian's uncle looking for her? "And the young boy? I ask because I wonder if they'll come here next, seeking work?"

"I couldn't say. They were headed away from here though, and good riddance, I say," Wilson said. "He put his hand out, but I refuse to pay for gossip."

"I'm sure you never will, too," Granny muttered, coming to stand beside Daniel again.

Wilson inclined his head and headed for the carriage and helped his daughter inside. Daniel was relieved beyond measure when the carriage door closed behind the Wilsons, and he was free. Free to speak his mind again. Free to criticize his nearest neighbor. "I'd forgotten what a curmudgeon he was."

"He'll never change or understand why charity is so important to those with nothing," Granny answered and turned back inside without waiting for him.

Wilson had reinforced Daniel's decision to never propose marriage to Amy with his lack of compassion and generosity.

Mother and Granny were devoted to sustaining the poorest families from their own pocket and provided seasonal work to many local families. They had never turned away a family in need.

Amy and her father always did, and neither one deserved to become part of Daniel's generous family.

Daniel hurried after Granny, who had returned to the drawing room to sit down again. He poured them both a glass of sherry and then sat beside her and put his feet up.

It was good to be lord of the manor again. To be among good people. Women who were kind and dear to him.

"What was that all about, Danny? The rush to get rid of the Wilsons and using my supposed exhaustion as an excuse?"

"I just wanted it to be us again."

"They didn't like being dismissed," Granny warned.

"I know, but I am no longer concerned with how the Wilsons feel about what I do like I originally was when I came home."

Granny studied him and then chortled with laughter. "Music to my ears, lad. I only wish your mother had been here to see how fast you showed them to the door. Wilson has always been insufferable."

"I'm glad she wasn't here, actually. She'll be disappointed in me again, no doubt," he confided.

"There is nothing new in that, though, is there?"

"No, I suppose not." He took a sip of sherry and decided he needed something stronger. He returned to the sideboard and filled a glass with whiskey instead. The burn down his throat was good and reminded him of all the things he'd missed in London. Being true to himself and his own nature most of all. He'd forgotten how vital that was to his sense of self-worth when he came home. He loosened his cravat and then threw off his coat, too.

He returned to sit down again and undid a few buttons on his waistcoat, too. "I had hoped the years away would have softened her toward me."

"She loves you. Loves us both, but it's not easy for her to

show it. Never has been. She's not at all like the pair of us. If not for the promise ring when she was younger, I think your mother and father might have circled each other for forever, never saying what was in their hearts."

Granny held up the ring, and then offered it to him.

This ring had caused him so much anxiety. "I've always felt I couldn't propose to a woman without it."

"Why, because of your father?"

"No, because of mother, actually." He held up the ring before his eyes. "It's rather plain and not at all the prettiest ring in existence, but it's true. Given with love and received with the same. Father could have given her riches to wear beyond her wildest dreams, but this was enough for mama. A secondhand ring that had once graced your finger. Mother stopped wearing it the day papa died."

"Yes. Her heart was broken. She begged me to take it back to make the pain go away."

"Did it help?"

"You cannot forget the one you love just by giving up a bit of jewelry. The sentiment remains long after the one you love is gone. When your father asked to give her this ring, the ring my Edmund had given me, it was with my blessing. He was a good man, your father. A bit like this ring, too. Not much to look at, but of vast sentimental value. He committed himself fully to your mother despite the difficulties her past presented him with."

"That is what I intended to do," he promised.

Marian had become important to him, perhaps the most important person in his entire life, and he could only imagine offering it to her.

He turned to look at Granny again. "Those stories you told about Marian. Was there any truth to them?"

"There might be. I sensed a distinct familiarity the moment I saw her crouched outside the window of the drawing room, staring up at you as if you were everything she ever wanted and couldn't have. That impression has only grown stronger since she agreed to stay."

Daniel nodded, fighting a blush over Granny's description of Marian at the window. "So, based on your *impressions* of her, you believe you know her family."

"Oh, yes. I knew them very well indeed," Granny insisted. "Why, her grandmother and I were the best of friends for nearly twenty years."

Daniel gaped, shocked to his toes that Granny had kept that nugget of news to herself all this time. "Tell me about her family."

"Well, there's so much to say. Her grandfather owned a shop and bought and sold trinkets and such to anyone who came to call. A very enterprising old rogue. His son, I hate to say, was only fortunate in his looks, not his business acumen. If I recall correctly, the business was struggling when I left Portishead to come here when your father died."

"What happened to him? The wife too? You believe those were her parents?"

"I don't rightly know if they were or not, or what happened to them. I think I heard his wife died soon after a stillbirth, and I think his affairs went downhill soon after that," Granny said with a sad shake of her head. "I could write to the friends I still have there and make inquiries about her inheritance, if you like."

"Her inheritance?"

"The family was once very wealthy and may still have some money set aside for Marian's dowry," Granny confided.

"I should inquire, because it will be useful to have it confirmed for when we go to London next year."

"You don't need to go to London."

"Oh, yes, we do. Since Marian and Gabby got along so well, I don't see why they couldn't experience the season together, under your mother's supervision, of course. It can be a competitive sphere and they'll need a good friend they can rely upon not to steal the other's beau and share secrets with. I should think they would support each other through almost anything."

"Does Marian wish to go? To have a season and a husband?"

"I can't see why she wouldn't," Granny said. "The girl is a beauty and smart and with your mother's help, there is nothing to stop her securing a match with anyone she favors. Now that you've seen sense about our neighbor's daughter, *you* shouldn't waste time either. Or have you changed your mind about marriage entirely?"

"I did not say I wouldn't marry," he assured her. "The time was simply not right, but next time I promise I will do it for the right reasons."

"Good. You deserve to be happy, dear boy."

He was almost happy right now, or would be if Marian showed her face. But the idea of Marian in London without him did not sit easily.

He turned to Granny again. "You really made Marian your companion only because she seemed familiar to you?"

"Well, I've always enjoyed making new friends, as well. So do you, for that matter. In Portishead, I was always the first to know the juiciest gossip and anyone of importance who happened to visit there. But most of my old friends are gone now and hardly anyone unfamiliar comes here. That was until Marian snuck inside and brought so much laughter and joy with her."

Daniel sighed and covered Granny's hand with his. "Are you really so lonely for your old life in Portishead that you want to leave us?"

"Sometimes I am, but not since Marian came. I feel like we've been given a second chance as much as she has. I want to do some good, see her settled in life, and I must confess that watching her expression of wonder at each new experience has reminded me that I've become jaded by the wealth that constantly surrounds us."

Daniel might never have noticed that his mantle clock could probably feed a family for a year, had Granny not constantly whispered of his privilege and obligations to do good so often as a young man. "So, you want her to stay for your benefit?"

"Of course, I do, but I'd shelter any young woman from harm." Granny whispered, "You do know she's in some sort of trouble, don't you?"

"I do, and that was probably my fault," he admitted. "If she'd never met me, she'd never have left her old life."

"If she'd not followed you, she might have been caught up with those thieves Wilson mentioned."

A near miss, and one she might have endured before. Marian might have been with the old man and boy begging on the roads, too, if not for him.

"It wasn't much of a life to leave behind if my suspicions are correct. Besides, if she'd never met you, you'd already be engaged to Miss Wilson and bound for misery. I have to love Marian more for following her heart—and I mean *you*—for that reason alone."

Daniel smiled, but he'd already known Marian had won

his granny over, and probably from the moment they'd met. "Well, we'll never really know that for sure, will we?"

"It was plain for all to see that you'd made the wrong choice for a wife," Granny murmured. "Will you tell your mother about your change of heart tonight?"

"No. I'm sure she'll figure it out soon enough," he suggested, and then glanced toward the door. "What really kept Marian from dinner?"

"I don't know," Granny confessed darkly, looking utterly displeased. "I lied about that."

Daniel sat up straighter. "Why would you do that? Where is Marian?"

"I don't exactly know," Granny said slowly, glancing his way.

Daniel was on his feet in an instant. "What do you mean, you don't know?"

"Well, I haven't seen her for several hours now and no one can find her. Not since she went upstairs to peek at what remains of your mother's wedding trousseau with Miss Kimble this afternoon. They came back down, but Marian was not with them. Your mother looked rather unconcerned about her absence, and I didn't think much of it until we sat down to dinner without her. With the Wilsons here, I pretended nothing was amiss, but I am truly vexed with her for missing dinner. I was hoping for another story to enliven my evening."

Granny rambled on, but Daniel could hardly listen. Something had happened after he'd been kissed by Marian. She had no cause to avoid him besides embarrassment, unless… "She can't leave!"

"Why would you think she has?"

"Marian was always leaving, Granny," he said with a

growl. "She has no right to make us all love her while waiting for us to look the other way. Now she's probably had ample time to fill her pockets to speed her journey."

"That is an unkind accusation, Daniel," Granny chided severely.

"She was in my chambers this afternoon for a reason," he countered. "Oh, why did I let her kiss distract me?"

"Never mind the money," Granny chortled. "What was that you said about kissing?"

"No time for that now," Daniel cried as he rushed from the room, bounded up the stairs, and went directly to his bedchamber. When he'd found Marian in his room earlier, had he interrupted her first attempt at stealing from him?

The room was empty of her. All the coins in his desk drawers were gone.

He checked every other place where he usually left coins. It was all gone, every penny and pound, which meant she had enough to take her anywhere she pleased.

Since Marian was not in his room, or hers either, he went directly to Mother's bedchamber to ask if she'd seen Marian while he'd been at the dinner table.

At the door, he paused, tugged down his waistcoat and smoothed his hair in readiness to enter a room that had been off limits to him for his whole life. He knocked on the door, but he was panicking. She could be anywhere by now. She could be in danger again, too. He heard a sound inside and put his hand on the doorknob. "Mama, it's Daniel. Are you awake?"

There was no immediate answer, and when he turned the knob, he found the door locked. He was so surprised by that, he put his ear to the door and listened.

He heard a muffled voice. And movement inside.

He drew back and knocked, again and louder. Finally, he heard light footsteps coming toward the door. He stood back and waited. "Who is it?"

"Your son, Mama. Are you all right?"

"What do you want?"

He put his hands on either side of the doorframe, exasperated. "I want to talk to you."

"Can it not wait until tomorrow?"

He ground his teeth and forced tranquility into his soul as he remembered that he shouldn't aggravate her. Mama hated to be disturbed when she'd already retired to bed. "The Wilsons have left."

"Yes, I saw their carriage depart."

He took a deep breath. "You did not return to finish dinner?"

"Obviously not."

Daniel rolled his eyes. "Listen, could we talk face-to-face?"

"Tomorrow."

"No, tonight. I insist upon seeing you. There might be a problem."

It took a long time for the door to be unlocked between them. But finally, Mother stood framed in the doorway, glaring at him, wearing her robe. "Satisfied?"

"Almost," he said. "Why did you not return downstairs?"

"I wanted to give you time to talk with the Wilsons alone. I thought if I were absent from the room, you'd finally discuss marrying Amy. I had also hoped that Mother would have followed me and left you to it. Is it done? Has a date been set?"

"No."

"Then there is nothing at all for us to talk about until you do," Mother said dismissively. "If you don't mind, I'm weary."

Mother closed the door in his face, but he stuck out his foot.

Mother glanced down, her face becoming angry. "Have you no respect for my privacy?"

Daniel ignored that. "Granny believes her companion has gone missing. I'm worried. Have you seen Miss Trill, or know where I can find her?"

"No," Mama answered. "I don't have the faintest idea where she might have gone. I'm sure she's around somewhere. Perhaps she's with the servants or in the kitchens. She's fond of cake, I've noticed."

"Yes, I should have thought of that sooner," Daniel agreed, and jerked his foot back to allow Mother to close the door and go back to bed, while he hurried to the kitchens.

Chapter Fifteen

MARIAN FOUGHT against the bonds tying her to a padded armchair as footsteps in the other room continued pacing to and fro. She'd cry out again, but her initial entreaties for freedom had produced no response.

She had woken in the dark room with an aching head that left her dizzy, and discovered herself bound and gagged. She hadn't reacted immediately. But as her eyes adjusted, she'd recognized she was still at the manor and in a room vaguely familiar to her.

The last thing she remembered, though, was being in Danny's chambers, stuffing her pockets with his money and planning her escape from the manor that night.

She didn't know who was out there pacing in the next room, but they seemed to be taking their time, and for that Marian was grateful.

She shook her head, testing that her dizziness had indeed passed now and noticed no further signs of imbalance. Aside from that, she was not hurt.

But someone must have caught her in the act of stealing and knocked her over the head before dragging her into this small room.

There seemed to be tall cupboards and chests of drawers all around her, as well as a tall looking glass. The chair she was tied to was well-padded. It was very dark, but she was certain she was in an upstairs chamber of the manor. And perhaps a lady's dressing room, though not one she recognized.

But why had she been taken here, of all places? Shouldn't she have been dragged before the lord of the manor to be dealt with somewhere below, like his study?

And what would Danny do when he found out she'd stolen from him, besides send her away? Was he making her wait until the dinner was over before dealing with her? She glanced at the window and thought it must be over soon, if not already.

The footsteps on the other side of the door stopped abruptly when a knock rang through the room.

Marian stilled and listened as her captor spoke to someone at the door, but it was much too far away to make out any words or determine which speaker was her captor.

Marian looked about but found nothing that might help her escape. With her ankles bound to the chair legs, and her hands tied firmly behind her back, she could move only a little. She couldn't move enough to win her freedom, and there was no point trying to overturn her chair when she might hurt her head again.

She cursed under her breath at the audacity of her captor. To lock Marian in a ladies' dressing closet was surely overstepping their authority.

The voices stopped, and eventually the footsteps headed back toward Marian. A key turned in the lock and light flared, blinding her.

And when Marian could make out the figure holding the candle, she discovered it was the countess herself, smiling grimly at her.

"Ah, good. You're finally awake."

"My lady?" she mumbled, utterly shocked, blinking her eyes.

Lady Scarsdale disappeared out the door again, leaving Marian alone for a few minutes at most.

Crockery rattled, and the countess returned to the room carrying a tea tray, which she sat down on a table opposite Marian. The tray contained a teapot, cup and saucer, and a plate of sugar biscuits.

"How did I get here?" Marian mumbled around the gag.

"I put you here, my dear," the countess admitted. "I'm so glad you're not a tall thief or overly heavy. That would have posed a difficulty for me tonight."

So, it had been Lady Scarsdale who'd discovered Marian with her hands in Danny's drawers while everyone was supposed to be at dinner?

Marian would gape if her mouth wasn't already stuffed with a cloth. Lady Scarsdale had seemed so proper and reserved on every other occasion. No real threat to anyone. How could Marian have been so wrong?

Lady Scarsdale folded her hands in her lap. "Now let's start at the beginning, shall we?"

It was quite frightening how normal and calm Lady Scarsdale seemed about holding Marian captive in a dressing closet. She must be far stronger than she looked, too. She might not have even needed help to get Marian from Danny's room all the way to her own, a distance of some twenty yards down the hallway, and then tied her up before she'd regained her senses.

And the knot work on the bindings holding her captive to this chair still defied Marian's nimble fingers and slender wrists, too. It occurred to Marian then that Lady Scarsdale had done this before.

Clearly, the countess meant to handle the business of her thievery herself. And she was in no rush to deliver a punishment.

The older woman poured herself a cup of tea, sweetened it a little, took a sip, and then set the cup down on the table covered by a pretty embroidered cloth. The tea service was one Marian had never seen before downstairs. But the sugar biscuits were favorites of Marian's, and her stomach rumbled with hunger and her mouth watered since she'd missed dinner tonight.

Lady Scarsdale noticed the direction of her gaze. "See something else you'd like to take from us?"

"No," Marian answered immediately around the gag.

"Manners make a lady, Miss Trill."

"No, thank you, my lady," she ground out.

"That's better. A lady must keep her poise in every circumstance." Lady Scarsdale stood and removed Marian's gag, but the moment Marian opened her mouth, Lady Scarsdale stuffed the biscuit in its place. "Never let it be said I was churlish to those in need."

Marian was too busy eating the delicious biscuit to form an answer. The biscuit was so good that when she was done, she thanked the countess, hoping for another.

But make no mistake, Marian was a prisoner of the countess. It was her own fault for underestimating the woman and not checking that she'd remained unobserved.

"Now tell me, and be honest—what you are doing here?"

Marian answered, "Nothing."

The countess dropped all the money Marian had stolen on the table beside the tea pot. "What were you doing in my son's bedchamber?"

There didn't seem much point in lying about it again. "Stealing his money."

Although the truth, that did not seem to satisfy the countess, who straightened in her chair. "Who sent you?"

Marian frowned. "No one sent me."

"And yet a member of the scandalous Trill family suddenly appears in this part of the county, has wormed her way into my very home when you must know I swore swift retaliation should any of your cronies darken our doorstep again. I paid the blackmail in full, as agreed."

Marian reared back from the countess as much as the chair allowed, confused, and shocked at her suggestion. "What blackmail?"

The countess took a bite of the last sugar biscuit and then stood to pace to the window. She peered outside into the dark night and sighed. "How much will you demand this time to stay away from my family?"

"I don't understand."

"I knew what you were here for the moment I saw you, of course," she said as she resumed her seat. "Another bite of the apple, so to speak. But I'm not having it. Not again."

Marian wet her lips before speaking. "I don't know what you're talking about, my lady. I'm just a thief."

"You're also a good liar, too. Charming, beautiful, and cunning, but just as deceitful as all members of your family have been through the years," she claimed. "I will release you at dawn and you will leave this place, empty-handed, but be sure to take the others hiding out there with you. The authorities were warned days ago to be on the lookout for your uncle Crossman and his band of thieves. Perhaps you will escape imprisonment this time. Perhaps you won't. But should you see them, do tell them I'm better prepared than I used to be. If any of them show their faces here, threatening my son or my mother, they will regret it."

"You know my family? We're not murderers." Although, the mood toward their victims had taken a dark turn of late, thanks to Tommy and Beatrice. Given the countess' words, and she had no reason to lie, Marian was a little afraid of what she might have missed the others doing behind her back.

The lady huffed. "I've known your family longer than you can possibly imagine, girl, and there's nothing Crossman won't do for profit. He's a persistent blackmailer, thief and all-around scoundrel, your uncle. It's been four years since I last dealt with him, and I will not pay him another king's ransom to forget he knows my past."

"Your past?"

The countess grimaced. "I did not come from a prosperous family."

"I knew that." Marian's eyes widened as she realized there was so much she did not know yet about the countess and her past. But everyone had one, and it was not always pleasant. The countess did not appear ready to divulge hers, though. "Does Danny know about my uncle's blackmail? He didn't seem to recognize him when they met in Wraxall."

The lady turned pale. "My son knows nothing of our dealings with your dreadful family over the years, thanks to him spending so much time in London, and I had intended to keep it that way forever until you arrived."

Marian gulped. "They don't know that I'm here. My family, that is. I even doubt they heard his name. I never knew he was an earl until Granny told me."

"A likely story."

"It's true." Marian took a deep breath. "The last thing I

ever want is to see Danny hurt, or you and Granny, either. They wanted to ambush Danny's carriage on the road. I argued against that, and they would have done it anyway… Tommy and Beatrice, I mean. So I went to warn Danny to travel armed, so he would arrive home safe and whole, and he did."

The lady pursed her lips, and her eyes narrowed on Marian. "You're a thief."

"I am what I was brought up to be by my uncle," Marian said, lowering her eyes. "I don't remember anything else. My life before my father died is a mystery to me."

"There is nothing else for you to remember besides a life of crime, girl. Your father traded in stolen goods, just like his father did. Goods that Crossman stole from *my husband*."

Marian digested that information. "So, Crossman really is my uncle?"

"Why would you ever question that?"

"I thought he was, but then something was said to suggest otherwise. That's why I left. I didn't trust them not to harm me. They were planning to get rid of me on the road somewhere."

"I see loyalty runs deep in your family still. Phineas Trill, the man my mother talks about so fondly, had two sons. Noel, the heir, and Crossman, the weasel spare. Noel had the looks and charm and, as eldest, took over Phineas' business when he died. But he'd not the head for business and relied too much on his brother for advice. Together, they turned a somewhat respectable family business into a thriving den of iniquity, thus making themself self-appointed kings of the seedy underbelly of Portishead society. There was no one and nothing that pair couldn't profit from if they wanted too badly enough."

"What happened to their money? My uncle roams the roads, claiming he's next to a pauper, and he never returns to Portishead anymore. He's never talked of any business or any trouble with the law."

The countess smiled sweetly. "Probably because there's a price on his head now, my dear, for murder."

Marian reeled in shock. "And my father? What became of him?"

"Dead, by your uncle's hand, over a greater share of the business. Your mother died much earlier," Lady Scarsdale informed her. "Of shame, no doubt, on your mother's part. All the money and gilt furnishing in her parlor couldn't disguise the facts or salvage her reputation after the rumors spread about their methods of getting everything they ever dreamed of."

"Why did Granny not tell me all this when I first arrived? Why didn't she have me arrested?"

"Mother feels strongly about certain matters. She believes everyone deserves a second chance, and we gave you that. You failed when you tried to steal from my son tonight," she said, glaring at Marian pointedly, and then at the money stacked on the table between them. "I've had my eye on you the whole time you've been under this roof, waiting for your true nature to emerge."

Marian bit her lip. "I want to leave."

"You could have gone at any time before this and without the funds you tried to steal from my son," Lady Scarsdale complained, taking a sip of her tea, and setting the cup down again.

"I wanted to get as far away as I could. Before my uncle thinks to look for me here," Marian said. "He should pay for his crimes, but I don't want to see it, or have Danny's wedding spoiled by unpleasantness."

"I assume my son already knows about your bad habits." The countess lifted one brow mockingly. "Afraid you'd hang with your uncle? I'm sure you've stolen from others and done worse?"

"I'm only a thief, madam. I only ever did what I was told, or for my next meal. I never physically hurt anyone," she promised. "If you let me go, I'd never go back to my uncle or near the people who work for him. They're the truly dangerous ones. Tommy and Beatrice were planning to take over Danny's group by force when I left."

"Yes, I know about them. Crossman has always kept a pair of accomplices ready to shoulder the blame," Lady Scarsdale said, sitting back with a smirk. "Orphans, tempted by the promise of riches and raised to do his bidding. And funnily enough, they never seem to end up with any money in their grasping hands. It's only they who wind up in prison, where they're brought to account largely for *his* actions."

Marian gulped. Her thoughts turned to young William, and she feared for his future even more without her. She did not want him to end up in prison, but she hoped the others were caught and sent to trial for their violent crimes.

If she ever got away from Lady Scarsdale's elegant prison, she'd go in search of the boy. Take him with her somewhere safe, where they could live away from temptation and never bother anyone again.

"My lady, I know nothing of blackmail, or any threats made against you and your family over the years. I was a child when I went with Crossman. When I was taken by him and raised a certain way. I had never heard of your family before I arrived here, in fact. I'm not your enemy, madam…

but I could be your greatest ally. I know my uncle's habits and, more importantly, his many aliases and hideouts."

"Why should I trust one word that comes out of your mouth?" the countess snapped.

Marian could tell a good sob story that would make other women weep, but the countess appeared not to be like other women. She was strong-minded, cynical, and not easily swayed by a glib tongue. "Because I made a mistake when I followed your son home. I thought…well…something foolish. Now that I know him better, and you, I would never let anyone harm him or the people he loves."

"Oh well, if that is the case, you won't mind spending the night right there, and very quietly," the lady said, and then smiled as if she knew Marian wouldn't last the whole night without complaining or attempting an escape.

Marian didn't like the idea of being kept a prisoner, even in a cell as comfortable as this. Captivity did not suit her nature one little bit. Yet, compliance might be the only thing that could convince the countess to consider her trustworthy by morning and win her freedom. She'd rather not be sent to trial, or to hang along with Crossman and the others.

If the countess was going to have her arrested, wouldn't she want everyone to know?

But Marian was fairly confident Lady Scarsdale hadn't told anyone about her capture.

Marian wriggled in the armchair, then glanced down at the inviting, thick rug on the floor beneath her bound feet, then at the window, which didn't admit a single draft, and inhaled the lightly perfumed air. She let out a soft sigh. Her future, her life, was entirely in the countess' hands now. "I've slept in worse places."

"Have you?"

"I won't sully your ears with the details of my early life. I know you don't care," she said without any malice. "But could you close the door on your way out? I'm told I sometimes talk in my sleep, and I don't wish to disturb you more than I already have."

The lady, however, sat there sipping what remained of her tea, studying her like an insect captured under glass. Marian wriggled a little bit more, but then lowered her head and tried to fall asleep while the countess was still in the room.

"When?"

Marian raised her head slightly. "When what?"

"When did you and Crossman meet my son?"

"In the last village, the night before he returned home."

"Explain. In detail."

"Uncle had followed his carriage from the previous town, and then had a chance to test his generosity when faced with someone in need of his charity. Your son was too generous and painted a target on his own back, I'm afraid."

"I see."

"But I didn't like the plans they were making to take his carriage the next day, so I went to warn him to arm his men."

"You betrayed your own uncle for my son? A man you'd never met before that day, or so you claim."

"Yes. I don't really understand why I did it even now. It just… I felt I had to protect him for some reason."

The countess shook her head violently. "That is a tale you've heard my mother speak of."

"It's no tale. That's how I met Danny. Just ask him," Marian suggested. "He could have been wounded or even killed. I couldn't bear the thought, so I did what I had to do."

"No—that can't be how it happened," the countess scowled. "Mama told you the story of how I met my husband without giving you the full details, and you've twisted it for your own scheme to deceive us all. It won't work."

Marian blinked. "You protected the late Lord Scarsdale from thieves, too? From Crossman?"

"You know I did."

"I didn't, I swear. So, we both did foolish things for the men we—" Marian choked on what word almost came next…but then decided, what was the point of keeping that secret when her feelings about Danny had never mattered and never could? "The men we fell in love with at first sight. No wonder Granny was so amused when I told her how I met your son."

She shrugged away the pain that followed her confession. The countess' eyes had narrowed on her, and Marian bravely continued.

"Your experience with my family should tell you there's no way to win against Crossman forever, but you might with my help. He's wily and skilled at avoiding capture. My leaving won't guarantee your safety, but I can help you to stop him coming back to bleed you dry."

"I thought you said you wanted to protect my son," Lady Scarsdale taunted, as if she didn't believe any of her claims. "If you say you love him, how could you still want to leave him?"

"I don't, not really." Marian lifted her chin. "But I'm not good enough for your son. Nor can I stay to watch him marry Miss Wilson. She deceives you. She cares for nothing but the title she'll gain in marriage. The power this marriage grants her will make Hammersley Lodge her own. All your attention and devotion to grooming her to take your place will make that happen in ways you don't yet fully appreciate."

"You're wrong about her," Lady Scarsdale insisted. "Amy's perfect for my son. She's almost a daughter to me already."

"But you're not a mother to *her*, are you?" Marian held the countess' gaze and saw a flicker of discomfort appear in her eyes. But she smoothed it away almost instantly. "You know I'm right. Deep down," Marian whispered sadly. "She'll do as she pleases, no matter what you want. Then she'll pack you off to the dower house or send you off to Portishead with your mother before the first year is out."

"That is enough."

"I'm only telling you what I see. And what I've seen with my own eyes…a slight sneer when you talk. She'll drive a wedge between you all. It's already happened with your mother, hasn't it?" Marian shrugged. "Amy is the real reason you don't get along anymore. I'll go at first light, and I promise you will never see me again."

"You'll go where you're told to go and not a moment sooner, young lady," the woman answered, standing abruptly, snatching up the candle and heading away without a backward glance.

She stepped out and shut the door behind her with a loud bang, leaving Marian in total darkness with the money she'd stolen piled up beside her. She heard the turning of the lock and then nothing but the creak of bed ropes after that.

Left alone in the dark dressing closet, Marian let out a heavy sigh and lowered her head again. She didn't want the family torn apart by deception and greed, but there was nothing she could do to stop it from happening…unless the countess heeded her warnings and accepted her help.

Chapter Sixteen

MARIAN WAS GONE. Daniel could hardly believe the woman really had left so suddenly or quietly. Yet she could be found nowhere in the manor last night or anywhere out on his estate grounds this morning, either. No one had seen her in nearly an entire day, in fact.

Granny had sent a message along to the Kimble residence, just in case Marian had gone there without remembering she should tell anyone.

But the news back was not what he'd hoped. Miss Kimble had not seen Marian since yesterday afternoon, when they had been in his mother's chambers together.

Daniel seemed to be the last person to talk to Marian, and when she'd fled him, there appeared to have been no further sightings.

He stared out over the garden, brooding about what to do; worried, but trying not to show it. Her uncle had been in their village, and he wondered if she'd met up with him.

Daniel was also conflicted. He'd not wanted Marian to be here in the first place, but now he'd gotten used to the idea, he didn't want her ever to leave without him. He'd only just understood the depths of his interest in Marian, and what it might signify for his future if she stayed in his orbit.

Because it wasn't every day a grown woman followed him home and ended up taking employment as a paid companion to his granny. He'd not voiced much opposition to her staying on in that role, either. Granny liked her, liked her stories and company. Mother hadn't raised an objection either and she usually would. He'd thought nothing would drive her away—not even the knowledge he'd come home to marry someone else.

But she didn't know he'd changed his mind about that.

When alone, they got along very well as friends, and still shared a passion for kissing each other. He'd grown rather fond of doing that, too. Kissing Marian. He'd expected that, having decided not to marry Amy Wilson, he would be able to devote his energies to a pursuit of Marian.

But she was no longer around to be pursued, wooed, *or* kissed. There would be no more conversation and no longing looks for him to enjoy.

And it was not just the kisses he missed. It was the certainty inside him that Marian would always be somewhere around when he had time for her.

The behavior of women often confused him, but with Marian, he'd always been certain that his attraction to her was fully returned. There had been the potential for romance between them all along, and a budding friendship that might have outlasted almost anything thrown their way—even his marriage.

Theirs should have been a brief acquaintance, but it had already become so important to him. Certainly, more than his unsatisfying and brief affairs with other women had ever amounted to.

Granny had cautioned patience when it came to love, but mother had constantly promoted a match with Amy Wilson instead. She believed only Amy could become the next Countess of Scarsdale. But Amy was not so perfect after all. She was not a woman he wanted to talk to at all hours of the day and night. Not the woman he wanted to share his life with.

Marian might have stayed long enough to realize what was under his nose.

He'd had Papa and Mama's romance as an example in the back of his mind for his entire life. Granny had explained theirs had been a love match, and at first sight too, although Papa's greater age had prevented him from declaring himself soon enough for her taste.

Daniel did not know if that ache he felt in the pit of his stomach when he thought of Marian was the same sort of thing, but it might just be close. Now they were apart, he was sure he could not live without knowing where she'd gone and why she hadn't at least said goodbye to him.

But if she felt the same yearning for his company, she really ought to have stayed.

His heart was fully aware of Marian's absence, and it argued he'd have to do something about finding her again. He toyed with the ring in his pocket, wishing Granny had given it back to him much sooner than she had. The trinket that had brought Marian into his life probably couldn't accomplish that a second time. Not unless she wanted to steal the bauble.

He smiled as he thought of their first meeting, but jumped when a small hand crept into his.

Daniel turned, hoping it was Marian sneaking up on him. But it was only Granny, and he put the ring away in his pocket. "Any sign of her yet?"

"No." He held Granny's worried gaze and then put an arm around her frail shoulders to give her a gentle squeeze. "She's been looked for everywhere I can think of at least twice now."

Granny turned her face into his chest, and he heard a muffled sob of frustration. "I cannot believe she's gone without a word of goodbye to us. Something must have happened to her. Where could she be?"

Daniel felt the same level of concern, but he didn't want to worry Granny any more than she already was by speaking of his worst fears. She might have been taken from the estate by her uncle and forced to return to a life of petty crime.

"People disappoint us," he said, exhaling. "Marian had no ties to us."

"She had ties to *you*," Granny complained.

Daniel sighed again. Since he'd announced he would not pursue a marriage with Amy Wilson, Granny had carried on as if he'd immediately go down on bended knee to Marian instead.

But he was a long way from deciding if he had any lasting future with a known thief and runaway paid companion. He could not join his family name to hers, either, without knowing more about what sort of people she came from.

Oh, he had experienced enough with her uncle Crossman to have concerns aplenty about that side of her family. But did she have any other relations who might prove even worse?

"I've never been completely certain she cared for any of us."

"You don't believe that for one moment," Granny protested. "She's a kindred spirit. She belongs here, not out there picking pockets for a living and putting herself in danger for no good reason. Why, if I saw her again, I would have you put her over your knee and give her the spanking she deserves for the worry she's put me through!"

Daniel squeezed his granny again. It was a sign of her distress she'd threaten Marian with a spanking—and that he be the one to dole it out. He'd never harm any woman or child, and Granny knew it very well. He was not a cruel man. "I agree with your wish that she wasn't picking pockets or spending time with her family. And I don't want to believe she played you false either, but what am I to think? She's disappeared, and she took money from me last night."

That last discovery had saddened him more than he wanted to admit, and he'd been careful to let only Granny know about it. But he'd really only told her to reassure Granny that Marian had enough money to take care of herself and didn't need to steal.

If Marian had told him she wanted money to continue her flight from her uncle and associates, he would have given her plenty, and of his own free will.

Daniel gave the garden one last inspection and turned for the manor house, taking Granny with him.

They walked slowly back. "If Marian doesn't want to be your paid companion, we can't force her to remain."

"She liked her new life here with us more than any money she stole," Granny insisted, patting at her eyes with a scrap of linen she called a handkerchief. "She could have taken my jewels, but they're untouched. It must be your fault she never said goodbye."

"Mine?"

"You should have asked her to stay," Granny said, sniffing back tears. "Does she even know you changed your mind about marrying that awful girl your mother favors? I can't imagine the distress she must have endured, watching you fawning over another woman instead of her."

"I hardly ever fawn," Daniel promised. He'd done

nothing so obvious or in any way improper in front of or behind Marian's back while trying to get to know Amy Wilson again. Conversation and a walk in the gardens were as much as that pursuit had ever amounted to.

He'd done so much more with Marian in secret, it was laughable to feel any guilt or ashamed. He and Marian had kissed and embraced, held hands, and exchanged more than a dozen heated looks in this last week. "I'm not the reason Marian has taken herself away."

But he might just have been a reason she'd stayed as long as she had. If he had told her of his doubts about Amy sooner, would she have remained to talk to him? Kiss him?

"You better be the reason she comes back, young man," Granny warned, pushing him away impatiently. "Get on your horse and go after her."

"I can't do that," Daniel complained. "I don't have the first idea where to look for her."

"You can start in the village. She would have to go there to find a carriage. Find out where one is headed and go after it." She pushed at him twice more, sending him stumbling backward. "Your horse is saddled. Go."

Daniel turned to see that his horse, led by his valet Sunday, was almost upon him.

"Granny, you go too far," he warned.

"*You* had better go as far as it takes to bring that sweet girl back home to us. After all the fun we had together and the plans I was making for her future, her first season would have been a wild success. I will never speak to either of you again if you shatter my dreams."

Since his horse was already called for, and Granny was now almost shouting at him in her panic and distress, he had little choice but to humor the old lady and seek out Marian.

He took the reins from Sunday and mounted the impatient beast, ignoring Sunday's propensity to ask questions.

But he was mounted now and ought to at least find out for his own peace of mind and Granny's that she had truly gone. He kicked his horse to a gallop almost immediately, and Sunday quickly followed him down the long drive.

When the estate gateway loomed, Daniel slowed his mount to a walk and Sunday fell into step beside him. "Where are we headed, my lord?"

"Don't you know?"

"You're really chasing after the paid companion?"

"Perhaps I am." Indeed, he was. Marian's happiness or unhappiness was uppermost in his mind right now, a stark contrast to the fact he hadn't cared at all if Amy was disappointed that he had not proposed to her yet and never would.

"Well, that's grand, if you don't mind me saying so."

Daniel glanced at his valet in surprise. "What makes you happy about my interest in Miss Trill?"

"Well, it's clear to see your family is taken with her," Sunday enthused. "The servants all like her, too. My mother, especially, and she told me your mother rarely takes an interest in young ladies the way she has with Miss Trill."

"I'm not sure how Mother feels about Miss Trill."

"Well, she must approve, because she was with your mother last night. Better her than me," Sunday said, and then winced. "No offense, but I wouldn't want to be alone with your mother. She's terrifying."

"Wait. What?" Daniel pulled his horse to an immediate stop. "When was Marian with mother?"

"Last night," Sunday frowned. "Is Lady Scarsdale not speaking to you again? What did you do this time?"

"Yes, Mother is speaking to me. But she did not mention seeing Miss Trill when I spoke to her." Daniel wiped a hand over his mouth, utterly confused.

"Well, she did. They were arm in arm. Very cozy indeed."

"Mother told me she'd not seen Marian since the afternoon," Daniel said slowly. "Why would she omit seeing her last night?"

"Must have forgotten about it. She *is* getting older, your mother, if you don't mind me saying so," Sunday suggested.

"I wouldn't say that around anyone else if I were you."

"Course not. Sorry, my lord. I know better than to risk your mother's wrath. At first glance, you'd think she was a sweet lady who wouldn't hurt anyone."

"Of course, she is. Why would you think otherwise?"

"Well, there isn't a lad around who'd dare sneak onto the estate to steal even an apple from the orchard these last dozen years or more. Not after that nasty business she dealt with."

Daniel's lips parted as he struggled to recall exactly what the nasty business had been. Something to do with an intruder? "Oh yes, I remember now. An intruder in the house. I'd almost forgotten about that."

"No one else who was here ever will. That thief was up to no good, but he was no match for your mother in a temper. The servants had little to do after she was done with smashing a vase over the fellow's head. She had him tied up nice and tight and scared the wits out of him into the bargain. Heard he got himself transported too. Anyone with sense learned to avoid the manor and grounds after that affair."

Had Daniel ever had that complete story told to him?

Apparently not by mother, because there was so much more to the encounter than he'd ever dreamed existed, including her bravery.

But that had been years ago. Surely, she wouldn't attempt to restrain a thief who…

He gasped out loud.

Marian had stolen from him yesterday…and she was still missing this morning. Was there another conclusion to reach?

Mother might have Marian locked up somewhere in the manor, and had kept the news from him to take care of the matter herself.

She'd done it before.

It would explain why she'd been so unwilling to speak to him last night or help with the search for Marian this morning! She might have known exactly where Marian was the whole time.

Dread washed over him. What exactly did she intend to do with Marian? Call the magistrate?

He couldn't have that. Marian could wind up transported to a penal colony or even hung!

"We need to go back home," he whispered, and wheeled his horse around and kicked it to a gallop, heart in his throat. If Mother had found Marian with her hands in his drawers, he didn't want to imagine what she might do.

If Marian was in any way harmed, there would be hell to pay. Even if it had been at mother's hands.

Chapter Seventeen

Marian listened to the comings and goings of the house early the next morning and, upon hearing utter silence, removed her hands from the bonds that had held them all night.

Well, half the night.

Once she'd gained her freedom from the ropes, Marian had stayed where she was. She'd had a lot to think about. About the countess' troubles with her family, her reasons for trying to leave the way she had, and about discovering she was in love with Danny, particularly.

Danny would not be pleased about that or to learn she'd fallen back into old habits. She was sorry that she had because she did not deserve his love or trust because of the latter.

The countess would surely tell Danny all about her thieving, if he didn't already know, and he would never respect her again.

Though what was keeping Danny away this morning, and the countess from having her sent off to the magistrate, she couldn't possibly imagine. The countess would surely have gloated about catching her red-handed, preparing to escort her out the door with his blessing. Clearly, Danny's mother would never trust her again to not be like the rest of her family. She never had to begin with. It gave her pain to be tarred with the same brush as blackmailers and murderers, though.

Her rushed decision to leave had been a mistake. Taking money certainly had been, too. She'd forgotten the first rule of thieving—always know where every soul was before even beginning. A week here and she'd forgotten all the basics of her early training.

She'd assumed the countess would be occupied at the dinner and never imagined anything could bring her back upstairs so early. It was her own fault she'd been caught. The countess had been watching her every movement.

Marian brought her hands forward and inspected her wrists, pleased they were not terribly chafed. The bonds hadn't been tight enough to cause any lasting harm to her skin. In fact, the countess had been much too gentle with someone of her unsavory habits.

She'd been tied not with rope, but with a soft linen sash belonging to a pretty robe of the countess', which in the end had allowed her wiggle room. Marian wound the material around her fingers, neatening the creases so it would not be too much work for the laundress to press flat again.

With that chore done, she set it back neatly on the small table and moved to look out the window. The sun was high in the sky now, and it was going to be a beautiful day for everyone but her. She imagined Danny somewhere out there, glad to be almost rid of her presence. Had he washed his hands of her already, perhaps, resumed courting Miss Wilson in earnest?

He could be an engaged man at this very moment, and the thought of it made Marian unbearably sad. She bit her lip. There was no reason for him to continue delaying a decision he'd obviously made long before they'd ever met.

Her tender feelings for him hardly mattered in the end.

What was next for her, though, was the unknown. The countess' behavior suggested she was used to taking matters into her own hands, no matter how unpleasant. Would the countess turn her over to the authorities for trial immediately, or worse, drag out her captivity and deal with her in the most final terms here—at gunpoint—with a ditch behind her in some distant field?

Marian would put nothing past the countess now. She was no prim and proper lady, unused to dealing with unpleasant people. She protected her family, and Marian grudging admired her for being so strong.

Marian was prepared for the first and the second outcome, but she'd fight hard to avoid her own death, of course. Escape was still possible, and possibly her only option left. She searched about the chamber for potential weapons to defend herself with if the worst came to pass, but saw only a needle and thread lying forgotten near the windowsill. It wasn't much, but it might just make enough of a difference to make someone release their grip without inflicting severe injury on them.

Marian carefully wove the needle into the sleeve of her gown, in a spot easy to reach, and then paced the chamber for a brief time to warm her muscles in readiness for flight.

She heard horses' hooves on the gravel drive and rushed to the window, expecting to see the magistrate and his men. But it was only Danny on horseback with one other horseman. He slid to a halt in front of the house and looked directly up to her window, or rather, at the countess' windows, and then rushed inside, while the other man took the reins of his horse and hurried to lead it away.

Marian's heart sank. Danny must have good news to

share with his mother. It could be one of two things—his engagement, or the magistrate was hot on his heels.

Marian slumped against the window, all hope lost for an easy escape or for anything more pleasant to befall her beyond that.

She wished she didn't have to face Danny again.

She'd never dare tell him what was in her heart now. She would give anything, beg the countess for her silence, to avoid him learning about her love for him. Anything to spare them all the embarrassment.

All there was left to do was wait for the magistrate. She hadn't seen the countess since daybreak, and a servant had not come to make up the bedchamber beyond, either, in these past quiet hours as far as she could tell.

She jumped as she heard a heavy thud from the adjoining room, followed by the crash of a door. Footsteps rushed through the other room, but not of the same light quality she expected from the countess herself or a maid.

It was someone else.

Male.

Danny?

Marian rushed to the door and put her ear to the wood.

"Marian," he hissed. "Are you in here somewhere?"

Marian hesitated. Danny hadn't known about her night of captivity. Perhaps there was a chance she could escape.

She slapped her palm against the dressing closet door. "I'm here," she cried, surprised Danny had actually come looking for her before she was dragged away. "I'm here."

The door rattled nearly off its hinges, but it did not open, much to her disappointment. "It's locked," Danny called to her. "I'll throttle Mama for this!"

Marian breathed a sigh of relief. He hadn't ridden ahead

of the magistrate after all, but come directly to rescue her instead.

She couldn't keep the smile off her face. But then she remembered his mother. This situation would put an end to any appearance of affection between mother and son, most likely, and though she couldn't fault his anger, it was all Marian's fault. If she'd not come, if she'd not wanted money to leave again, the countess would never have resorted to such drastic measures, and Daniel would never learn his mother was a woman of many secret talents.

"It's only stuck," Marian called out, lying through her teeth about her situation. "There's a trick to opening the door that only the countess knows."

"A trick only my mother knows," Danny repeated. "A likely story. She's gone too far this time."

"No! No. It's true. Ask Granny if you don't believe me. Her own door gets stuck all the time," Marian promised, wincing at the lies spilling from her tongue. But she did not want to cause any trouble in the family.

There was a long silence after that, and then Daniel asked, "Marian, are you tied up?"

"Of course not," she promised.

"Can you open the window and show me your hands?"

"I suppose so. Why?"

"Just do as I say and poke your arms out," Daniel said with an exasperated sigh.

"I'm not climbing out on the ledge to win my freedom from this room," she warned him. The room and window were much too high from the ground to mount that sort of escape. There was nothing but flagstones beneath the window.

"I'd never ask you to put yourself in danger for me, but I

need to see you, Marian. Just open the window and show me you're really all right."

"Oh, very well," she agreed and rushed to the window. When she threw it up and poked her head out, she risked a single glance down. Yes, a fall from this window's height would surely kill her, or ensure a slow and very painful death. An escape in that direction would be foolish in the extreme.

Another window rattled open to her right.

"Thank God," Daniel said as soon as he saw her. "I thought you'd gone without saying goodbye! Thought I'd have to chase you into the next county to find you again."

"I'd never leave without saying goodbye to you," she promised.

Daniel was at a window in his mother's bedchamber, and he grinned at hearing her promise. Marian grinned back, then showed him her hands, and that she really was free and well.

"You stay right there, and I'll be back with an axe if need be, to get you out," he promised.

Marian smiled at the thought of him butchering a door to get to her. It was rather a romantic gesture, but utterly unnecessary. She was almost certain that the countess would relent now that Danny knew. "Danny, wait?"

He returned to the window. "I'm sorry I borrowed money from your room last night without asking permission," she admitted.

"Borrowed? I think you mean stole. But why did you wait until now to take it? I expected it days ago."

She was taken aback by his question and took a moment to think of the right way to answer. Of course, she'd hoped not to have to leave him. But the fact of the matter was, she'd almost forgotten she didn't really belong here.

She'd made friends, ladies who expected better from her, and she'd betrayed them all. And there was Danny now, smiling at her as if she was already forgiven, and *he* was going to marry someone else.

"I liked it here too much," she admitted at last. "I liked your family. Enjoyed having, well…not having to steal for my supper every day."

"Can you still like my family when my mother has locked you up?"

"It was an accident," she promised him. "No harm done."

"Except to my nerves, and Granny's. If it was an accident that you were trapped in Mother's dressing closet, Marian, wouldn't she have heard your cries for help and done something about it? She has excellent hearing."

But before Marian could answer him, Danny disappeared.

Yes, that was a huge flaw in her insistence of mistaken entrapment, but she would not change her story now. The countess had spent last night sleeping in her own room and could have released her long before this if she'd wanted to. However, Marian would not drive a wedge between the lady and her son.

Marian ducked back inside the dressing closet and closed the window again, locking it for good measure. She turned to face the door to wait for Danny—but the countess was standing directly behind her now, the door closed at her back. A key clenched in her hand.

She had the oddest look on her face, too.

Marian curtsied, marveling that the countess had managed to surprise her yet again. She hadn't heard the woman let herself into the chamber, and neither had Danny. "Good morning, my lady."

"You freed yourself?"

"Yes."

"And lied about me to my son?"

"Of course, my lady," Marian agreed. "There's no need to bother your son with trivialities, provided you grant me my freedom, that is."

"The bonds. How long did it take you?"

"The bonds were not as tight as they could have been. I can teach you to do a better job with that later if you'd like."

The countess' eyes narrowed and then she nodded. "I'd like that."

"Good," Marian said, smiling. "Perhaps we ought to leave this chamber before your son returns. He's gone to look for an axe, and I would hate to see the manor damaged on my account."

"So would I," Lady Scarsdale agreed as she walked to the door and opened it.

She gestured Marian from the room ahead of her. Marian slipped out into the countess' bedchamber and waited for the woman to join her. "May I have some paper and ink to write those aliases and addresses my uncle uses most often so you can finally catch him?"

"I hadn't thought you were serious about that," the countess admitted, appearing taken aback by her keeping her word.

"I will never lie to you again, my lady. If I'm quick, I can get it written out and slip away before Danny comes back. He'll never hear a bad word against you from me, I swear."

"Well, if that's the case, you'd better get to writing," the countess said briskly, opening a beautiful writing desk for Marian and placing a quill and a single sheet of parchment on its surface.

Marian scratched out all she could remember about her uncle and handed it to the countess, wincing slightly that in her eagerness to detail everything she knew, she had made rather a mess of her handwriting. "I hope that helps you."

"Excellent. But I don't believe your leaving is required now."

"I should go," Marian promised. "I can't stay if Daniel is engaged."

"He's not engaged as far as I am aware," the countess admitted, brow rising. "Nor likely to be if you leave, I now suspect."

Marian shook her head, confused. "I thought he'd gone to see Miss Wilson this morning. He rode home in such a rush that I suspected he had good news to share with you."

"My son rode out in search of you at my mother's urging, dear, and came back directly to my chamber."

"Oh," Marian said. "Why would he imagine I was here?"

"Probably those loose lips of his valet. Never tell that boy a secret you want kept from my son."

"Sunday is very loyal to your family."

"As are you, it seems," the countess observed, nodding her head slightly, and folding the paper she'd been handed. "I had not expected you to be loyal to anything but your *own* family. I think you should go in search of my mother now. She's had a fretful night worrying about how you fared with me. Tell her she was right."

"Of course…but about what?" Marian asked as then dipped the countess a properly deep curtsy.

"About everything. Oh, and Marian, you will join me for tea at four o'clock in the conservatory each day from now on. Is that understood? We can discuss those knots you were talking about, and other matters."

"Yes, milady," she said, agreeing to the tea and all that would entail. It would also be an hour each day listening to Miss Wilson prattle on, while Marian pondered what Daniel saw in the woman he meant to marry.

She headed out into the hall and headed directly to Mrs. Nolan's chambers, so she could avoid Daniel when he came back.

The old lady's face was wreathed in smiles as soon as she saw Marian poke her head around the door. She extended both her hands, and Marian rushed to the woman to be pulled into a fierce embrace.

"I see you passed my daughter's little test."

Marian closed her eyes and then shook her head. These women would certainly keep her on her toes. "She said to tell you that you were correct."

"Hates to admit she was wrong, and still hasn't, since she had *you* tell me rather than admit it herself," Granny said and then chuckled. "My daughter is a delight, isn't she?"

"You knew she had me the entire night?" Marian laughed. "Is there nothing that escapes your notice?"

"Not much. Not much that happens *here*, really. But that valet Sunday was almost no help in the end. I sent him off on horseback with Danny so he'd have another chance to remember to mention he'd seen you and my daughter together last night."

"Why didn't you just tell Danny where I was, and that I was perfectly safe with your daughter? She had every right to be angry about what I did."

"Were you really safe?" Granny asked, raising one brow. "My daughter has dealt with thieves before and detests them on principal. I assure you, you were in considerable danger from her initial temper. I had to promise a great many things for her to go along with my little play. The first promise she extracted from me for leniency was to be nicer to her little protégé." The older lady pulled an unhappy face about that.

"Miss Wilson," Marian said. "The woman destined to take Lady Scarsdale's place here."

"Have you ever noticed that fate has a funny way of choosing its own direction?" Granny asked, and then smiled. "Now, you must be famished after your ordeal. Come and eat."

When she gestured to the table beside her, Marian noticed more sugar biscuits and a glass of milk had been laid out. "You were expecting me?"

"Of course," Granny promised. "Eat up, dear girl. The day is about to become even more exciting than even I could have foreseen. After you eat, I think you ought to take a dip in the grotto pool."

Marian paused with the glass of milk partway to her lips. "Why the grotto?"

"You never know what the day will bring," Granny answered. "I want you looking your best, and as ravishing as possible. Wash your hair."

"Yes, madam," Marian was too hungry to ask any more questions, so she finished the biscuits, drained her glass, and let herself be ordered out of the old lady's room after promising to take a nice relaxing soak in the hot spring.

Chapter Eighteen

DANIEL DROPPED the head of the axe to the hardwood floor, causing the little bottles on Mother's dressing table to rattle in their places. "Mother, where is she?"

Mother turned slightly. "Where is who?"

"You know I can only mean Marian Trill. She was locked up in that dressing closet of yours not ten minutes ago. What have you done with her?"

Daniel hefted the axe into the air, with half a mind to use it on something else in the room to lessen his frustration and anger. He'd expected Marian to be here so he could rescue her from her prison. It would have been romantic.

Mother glanced at the axe, but was utterly unruffled by his display of aggression. "I can't be expected to know every movement the Trill girl makes about the manor. She's not my daughter."

"But she was locked in your room all of last night," Daniel pointed out.

"Yes, so I heard, but she's clearly left it now," Mother answered, setting a string of pearls about her neck, and smiling at her reflection.

Her attention remained on herself in the mirror, as if her appearance was the most fascinating and important matter of the day. It was almost as if she was trying to make out that Marian's night of captivity hadn't even happened. But Daniel couldn't quell the certainty that a disagreement of some sort had occurred between Mother and Marian. A disagreement that Marian curiously denied, as well.

Mother looked around, acting surprised to find him still in her room. "Oh, did you speak with the carpenter yet about the sticking doors?"

"No, I've yet to have time to seek him out," he admitted, annoyed by the attempt to change the subject. Mother always did that.

He prowled the room and peeked into the dressing closet, where he'd last seen Marian. Nothing was out of place except a rolled-up length of cloth left on a small table. Daniel found that curious. He picked it up and unrolled the length, and discovered it was actually *four* lengths of cloth. Each one with creases.

He studied the two chairs in the room and the fabric ties with growing suspicion.

Marian *had* been tied up at some point but lied to him about it. He'd bet his life on that.

Why not tell him? He would have done something about his mother. He would have banished Mother from the manor or something far worse to protect Marian.

He returned to Mother's bedchamber and threw the four lengths onto the table in front of her. "Explain this if you can."

Mother shrugged. "Are you incapable of sticking to a singular subject today? It is the attention to detail that matters most when running an estate of this size. I've no idea what these are, but I'll have my maid put them away later."

"Mother!"

"Son, if you hadn't wasted your time in London, you would know that the change of season always plays havoc with this old house. The carpenter could have told you that doors stick all the time."

"This isn't about sticking doors. It's about Marian."

Mother sat up straighter. "Why all the concern for my mother's new companion? She's hardly worthy of your notice."

Daniel sighed. What was the point of keeping secrets from her? He was fairly certain Mother already suspected his interest was not that of a distant employer. "She's more than that to me."

Mother's brows rose high. "Is she really?"

"Yes." He bit his tongue then over what he could have said to explain why Marian mattered to him so much. Mother didn't need to know the particulars of his amorous pursuits, and she probably didn't want to know either. All she'd wanted was for him to marry and to get an heir, ensuring the estate passed to the next generation while she was still here to see it happen.

But he wasn't sure yet if that was what Marian could be to him, so he held his tongue for now. "Where is she, please?"

"For heaven's sake, she's probably with my mother at this hour, or she might have gone out to the grotto to bathe. I've heard she's like a duckling in that respect," Mother warned.

"A duck?" he echoed, but brightened at this news. His favorite place was the grotto, and to have Marian like it too was an unexpected boon.

"What is it about her that holds your interest, son? You act like a jealous lover and now demand to know where Marian is, as if she belongs to you?"

Daniel thought for a moment. "Marian has always made me feel good about myself."

"Or it could just be lust," Mother suggested, and then burst out laughing when he gaped at her. "Oh, you remind me so much of your father when he was courting me, it's almost painful to watch again. I knew what he wanted from me, but it took a while for him to pluck up the courage. I loved your father from the moment we met. That need for Marian that you're trying to deny will only grow stronger." Mother leaned toward him. "You're in love, my dear boy."

Daniel gulped because his mother was rarely wrong. He might have committed violence on Mother, or her room, if she had tried to keep him and Marian apart.

"Mother, if you will excuse me, there's somewhere I need to be."

She turned back to her mirror. "Of course, Danny. I'll always be here to guide you," she murmured. "No matter what happens."

And for a change, her promise comforted Daniel a great deal.

He hurried out of the bedchamber and headed for Granny's room—only to come to an immediate halt and spin back to stare at his mother's door.

Mother had called him *Danny*.

She never did that, but Granny did, and so did Marian.

It had been Scarsdale this, and my lord that, and nothing less for years and years since he'd inherited. But today, Mama had spoken to him with affection, and even laughed in his presence.

A smile broke over his face, beyond his power to control. What on earth had occurred last night between Marian and Mama to bring about such a change of heart?

He had to find out, and he quickened his steps.

Granny was more than happy to confess that Marian had

gone for a dip in the grotto. Her knowing smile made him blush, and he hurried after Marian with a spring in his step.

Daniel heard splashing well before he saw the slender form frolicking in the water alone. He breathed a sigh of relief. Everything was right again.

He desperately wanted to talk to Marian about what had gone on last night, and everything else. Although she seemed no worse for wear, she had lied about her entrapment, and he wanted to know why she would.

He walked to the edge of the pool as Marian ducked her head under the sparkling water. Having her out of sight was only a temporary obstacle. She had to come up eventually for air, and then they would speak. They were always at their most honest when they were entirely alone.

He stood beside the pool and then turned for the bench. He removed his coat and waistcoat and placed them beside Marian's clothes, and then sat to remove his boots.

Marian surfaced only to float, obviously naked from top to bottom, in the exact center of the steaming pool, seemingly unaware of his presence.

Her pert nipples suggested she was in the much cooler part of the pool since they peaked just above the waterline invitingly.

He yearned for a taste of them, and another kiss from the vexing woman, too. How could he have nearly let this woman slip through his fingers? How could he not have recognized the love of his life when Marian had first appeared, wearing his promise ring, and when she had so much trouble giving it back to him?

He cleared his throat, but Marian didn't hear him.

He skirted around the water's edge, trying to catch her notice.

Her eyes remained stubbornly closed, and he set his hands on his hips, irritated with her for unwittingly playing hard to get. Was he going to jump into the water just to speak with her?

Instead, he leaned down and flicked water over her face.

She spluttered, thrashed about as she wiped it away before looking around at him. "That was mean."

"I don't like to be ignored."

Her gaze traveled from the top of his head to his toes. "Well, what are you standing there for still dressed? Come and join me."

"Did you follow me home so you could always tempt me, Marian?"

"Perhaps I did, but now I just want to get you wet," she said, and then flicked water at him.

Daniel dodged back, avoiding the worst of it.

"Did Granny send you?"

"Yes."

She laughed softly. "Then you'd better come in and play."

Marian flicked handfuls of chilly water at him until his breeches were in danger of becoming drenched, he hurried to undress and jumped into the deepest part of the pool.

He came up sputtering and flicked his wet hair away from his eyes. "All right, you have me where you want me."

"Not quite where I want you. Where I've always wanted you."

"We're I've wanted you too," he promised.

"Well, come get me, my lord," she taunted.

He waded across to her, and Marian smoothly rolled into his arms. Her added weight ducked him farther under the surface, and the silken glide of her bare limbs against his almost made him moan. "I didn't know you could swim," Daniel said, moving closer to the edge of the hottest part.

"I'd hardly call this swimming. But it's so lovely to float here, and I've never been able to resist taking a dip at every opportunity."

Marian turned in his arms and abruptly stood up, pushing her damp hair over her shoulders and her full breasts into his face.

Water cascaded off her skin and revealed her tiny waist and beautiful pale breasts. Her body glistened in the reflected light from the dozens of glass panels set in the roof openings over their heads.

He could barely drag his eyes away from her ravenous beauty. He'd never been one not to look at an alluring body when it was so proudly put on display in front of him.

"It's hotter in here today than I thought it would be," he noted, mopping his brow. He'd welcome a plunge in the icy part if there weren't a thousand reasons to stay with Marian.

She smiled and ducked back under the water. "Granny warned me it gets hot enough to burn."

"I don't mind the heat," he told her, winking.

"I like a little friction to warm my blood, too," she said, skimming her hands up to her breasts and cupping them so he could see.

Daniel's cock stiffened under the water.

She ducked back down, giggling, covering herself up to just under her chin, and studied him with dazzling eyes. "You do look a little hot and bothered, my lord," she teased. "Is there anything I can do for you?"

"Yes." He pulled her into his arms again. "I've been worried about you."

She wrinkled her nose, as her arms wound about his neck. "I'd never come to harm in this place."

"I always thought so, but all I've thought of lately was how to get my hands on you. You're in real danger around me."

"You could never hurt me, Danny," she promised, releasing him to swim to the edge of the pool. She lay her arms upon the edge of the pool and then kicked her legs out behind her. She laughed softly. "Never in a thousand years."

"What of mother then? What went on between you two last night, anyway?" He slid his hand under her, fingertips on her belly, to support her up while she kicked her legs harder. "I'm sure she held you captive, but now it seems to me she's suddenly mellowed overnight."

"That's between us women."

"Is that right? And I'm supposed to just forget all about you being locked inside her dressing closet. Tied up."

Marian looked at him over her shoulder, her eyes considering. "Could you? It would make things easier with your mother."

So, she *had* been tied up and didn't want any fuss made about it. He frowned, confused but willing to accept her decision. "I suppose I could, if I had assurances that it won't happen again."

"I can promise you nothing like that will happen again," she murmured, smiling. "Your mother and I want the same things. I like it here, and so does she. I wouldn't want to change a single thing, or for anyone to be banished."

Daniel nodded, finally understanding. He'd been angry about Marian's night of captivity, but she was a peacemaker. She wouldn't make a fuss; she would never pit him against his mother or grandmother the way Amy had already tried to do.

He grinned. No wonder he loved her, and that Mother was in such a good mood today. "I'm glad to hear it," he whispered.

Marian's eyes grew soft. "I like the way you're looking at me now, my lord."

"I'm looking at someone I like very much," he said, biting his lip.

"So am I," she whispered. "What are you waiting for?"

"Permission."

"Gladly given, my lord. Always and anywhere."

"Stay there," Daniel whispered and moved toward her feet, caught both her ankles, and parted her legs under the water. Her breath hitched, and she held his gaze as she looked at him over her shoulder, as he waded into the space he'd created between her thighs.

Marian held tight to the ledge in front of her as Daniel pressed his sex against hers. "Mama knows there is something between us."

"Is there?"

"You know there is, or there will be from today," Daniel whispered.

Marian moaned as their bodies connected, and his cock brushed her sex.

He fairly trembled with anticipation of what would happen next. The minute he'd seen Marian, touched her, a pleasant weight of certainty had settled over him. She was his, and he belonged to her. Marian made him feel both at ease and excited. She would change his life certainly, but only to make it better.

Marian suddenly stiffened. "Is Miss Wilson expected today?"

"I hope not." He slid his cock back and forth between

her thighs, creating friction against her sex for a moment. "Marian, I will not ask Amy to marry me after all."

"No?"

"No."

Marian turned around, her expression one of utter astonishment. "You're really not going to ask Amy? Ever?"

"Never," he admitted, pulling Marian so their lips were inches apart. What a miscalculation he'd almost made with his love life. He could not marry someone who cared so little for harmony in his family or ignore someone who made his heart sing with lust and hope. He'd come home to make a marriage, and only Marian could make that possible. "How could I want her when there's you?"

"You could have both of us," Marian whispered, and then winced. "I could be content to be your mistress."

"Never." Daniel was so shocked by the suggestion, he dropped her. She sank like a stone and came up spluttering.

Daniel hauled Marian against him and closed the distance to seal his lips to hers. His kiss was not subtle, nor anything but possessive. He urged Marian's arms and legs to wrap around his body and made sweet love to her mouth.

When they eventually parted, both of them were panting hard, he pressed his head to hers. "I would never dishonor you like that," he whispered, meaning every word. She could only be his wife. "I want you and only you in my bed."

"I want that too," Marian whispered back, and her grin returned, bright and joyful.

Daniel captured Marian's face between his palms and kissed her again. He'd never shared his grotto with a lady he loved before and found it freeing to be alone with Marian here like this.

But he knew such an interlude could only last so long.

Someone would come looking for them both, eventually. They would have to go back to the manor, and he would proudly tell his family of his new plan to marry Marian.

They could hardly be surprised.

For now, Marian was his alone, and she seemed to revel in the grotto's delights, the cozy atmosphere, the candlelight, the water sliding over her naked curves, and having his nakedness between her legs, too. Daniel had always thought the grotto would be romantic with the right partner, and Marian was the one.

He'd make love to her here and now, before propriety tore them apart again. He would propose later and give her his ring.

She'd already stolen his heart.

With Marian, he wouldn't even have to put his scandalous habits behind him. Marian wasn't prim and proper. She would be right by his side as he showed her the wonders of his world.

"You look very serious all of a sudden, my lord," Marian murmured.

"I'm a serious man," he told her, pushing back her hair.

"No, you're not. That's just what you want everyone else to believe since you came home. Especially her." She shook her head. "But I know you now. You're a wicked man, under all that finery. You don't have to be anything other than who you are around me. Be yourself. The man who saved me," she admitted. "The man who's first thought has always been to wonder if he could lure me into his bed."

"Who needs a bed? Debauching you here and now appeals to me."

"Would that be so wrong? I know I'm not at all like other women. I'm not an innocent like her and—"

Daniel put a finger over her lips to stop the flow of words. He was sure she was going to say something ridiculous. "Proper women have never appealed to me," he promised her.

He kissed Marian again, and his heart rejoiced at the rightness of doing wrong with her.

How foolish was he to imagine he could change his preference just by coming home?

He held Marian more tightly in his arms and lost himself in the pleasure of her kiss. This was what he wanted. Passion with Marian and more days of bliss to follow.

He stood and waded out of the pool, carrying Marian in his arms.

He found a length of towel and laid it near the edge of the hottest part of the pool. And then he lowered them both down to the ground and continued to make love to her mouth.

He ended up on his back, Marian rising above him, gloriously naked, her body beaded with sweat and water.

Before he was even ready, Marian was bearing down on his erection and making love to him.

"At last," she whispered, tossing him an impish smile.

He loved her impatience. "Eager to have me, were you?" he asked, strumming the tips of her nipples with his thumbs.

"I never thought I would be with you like this," she answered, her face flushing as she moved up and down with more haste. "I thought you wanted her."

"I never did. Not like this," he swore.

Marian had the most luscious body of any woman he'd ever made love to, and he was grateful to be under her at last.

He let her have her way and lay back, one hand cushioning his head as she languidly stroked his cock with her innermost walls. With his other hand, he toyed with her nipples, her curves, and then slipped his fingers between her folds.

Marian quivered and gasped as they made love in the steaming air of the grotto. He watched her closely as her first climax neared, watched her lip's part and her breath speed from her lungs as he teased her body to the very heights of desire.

When her release hit her, Marian dragged his own climax out of him, and he roared with the thrill of a perfect joining.

When Marian relaxed at last, she finally met his gaze. There was no regret, but a dazed smile of contentment that pierced his soul with immense satisfaction. What would it be like to have this woman look at him that same way every day, every time they made love, every time he returned to find her waiting just for him?

Daniel rolled them into the steaming hot water because he knew already that a happily ever after was possible for them, no matter that their lives had begun so differently. She was his fate. His one true love. His happiness.

Chapter Nineteen

The countess pursed her lips. "Miss Wilson, would you care for more tea?"

"Yes, thank you, my lady," Amy Wilson murmured, thrusting out her cup to have it filled again. Her second that afternoon.

Amy gave Marian a superior smirk when the countess declared the tea pot empty, which meant that Marian could not be offered another cup.

"Cake, Miss Wilson?"

"I couldn't eat another bite, my lady," Amy assured her, hand going to her slender middle as if it was in danger of bulging from the first tiny slice she'd consumed.

"Miss Kimble? Miss Trill? I'm sure I can tempt both of you to indulge."

Marian nodded, and she and Gabby accepted another slice of cake from the plate. Only one slice remained, and the countess took that one for herself.

Marian devoted herself to her plate, but couldn't help noticing that Amy Wilson was twitching in impatience at being the odd one out now.

Marian knew that feeling well.

Since her return from the grotto, she was feeling uncomfortable. Danny had been an attentive lover three, determined to bring her pleasure with every stroke of his fingertips and cock. But it had been hours now since they were together. As soon as Marian had returned to the manor, Granny had dragged her away and his mother had been waiting to talk over a matter of estate business with her son.

Marian had assumed Danny would come to find her long before now, but he was off with Mr. Kimble talking somewhere.

She and Danny had made love with little to no discussion of their future together beyond the next kiss or climax, which had suited her very well at the time.

But that was then, and this was now.

Being stuck in the same room with the woman Danny promised he would never marry was definitely making her uncomfortable. Largely because Amy Wilson was clearly unaware that his interest and intentions toward her had changed. And the longer she spent with Amy, the easier it was to see the differences between them were so great.

Now back in the manor for hours, Marian was growing a little disappointed in Danny. He ought to have done something to make it clear to Amy that his interest had waned. Instead, she sat there looking around the drawing room with a decidedly content expression on her face, as if it would soon be all hers.

It did not matter if Danny kept their affair a secret. She would have been content to become his mistress if he'd wanted that. She was not ashamed of her attraction to him, ashamed of being his lover, though she would rather not continue their affair right under his mother's nose.

Danny had not mentioned any desire to continue making love to her, though.

Since Marian's arrival in the drawing room, Lady Scarsdale also carried on as if nothing was different between them.

But it certainly was.

They knew things about each other that they'd both rather the others never learned. Marian kept to her role as companion, seen but not heard as the countess commanded the room and the conversation. Lady Scarsdale was gracious to her two guests, but she largely ignored Marian's existence, as was her usual habit.

"What do you say, Miss Trill?"

Marian looked up guiltily because she hadn't the faintest idea what everyone had been talking about. "Forgive me, my lady, what was that?"

"The countess asked you a question," Gabby whispered, her expression concerned. "Are you feeling unwell?"

"I am perfectly well, but I thank you for your concern," she muttered.

"Her face is very pink and blotchy," Amy noted, as if that was unbecoming of a lady.

"I hadn't noticed any difference, but perhaps you should move nearer to a window, Miss Trill, with my mother. You'll catch a breeze there," Lady Scarsdale suggested, though it sounded more like an order.

Marian nodded and rose to obey, "Yes, my lady."

"We could take a turn first, if you like," Gabby suggested quickly.

"A breeze is all I need."

"Nonsense," Gabby offered, and rushed to lead Marian on a circuit of the room. "I feared we'd never escape," Gabby whispered.

Marian had to laugh at that. "Escape from what?"

"Can't you feel it?" she whispered. "Something momentous is about to happen."

She looked around the room and at the occupants. "I sense nothing different."

"Didn't you notice how Lady Scarsdale and Miss Wilson keep disagreeing today? They are usually so in tune."

"That is true."

"Something has changed." Gabby gave her a look of glee. "Amy was acting superior, and the countess wouldn't let her for a change. That never happens, let me tell you. You know what that could mean, don't you?"

Marian wet her lips and studied the countess, who was nodding to something Amy was telling her. She noticed nothing but the countess smiling at Amy as if she was her daughter already.

Danny claimed he didn't want Amy Wilson, and she believed him. But the lure of the young lady's dowry was a powerful incentive, as was the pressure of family expectations to make a respectable match. He'd said he only wanted Marian. A woman with no family, position in society *or* dowry. But it occurred to her that Amy Wilson might not let Danny go so easily. He was quite a catch, being titled and wealthy.

Thanks to Gabby's shared confidences, she was more aware of what society women looked for in a husband, and it wasn't what Marian believed important in any match.

Marian settled on the window seat and so did Gabby.

They chatted for a while until Granny sent Miss Kimble off to the pianoforte to play for her.

Granny urged Marian to come closer. "You look pale. What's on your mind?"

"Will you still leave when your grandson marries?"

"Goodness, yes. I decided that long before he came home,

too," the old lady promised in a whisper. "There's always been strife between my daughter and me. We have distinctive styles and opinions about, well, almost everything there is to disagree about. Add in a new wife, and I would rather not spend all of my days disagreeing over the smallest unimportant things. I think it is best if I make myself scarce until everything is settled down again. I'll renew my friendships with old acquaintances and perhaps make some new friends."

"I'll come with you."

"No, my dear. You can't now."

Marian bit her lip. "Why can't I come with you?"

"We are very much alike, you and me. Neither one of us will ever be proper, nor truly fit in here."

Marian wanted to weep, cut to the quick by Granny's assessment.

"Besides, once Danny's married, everything will work out for the best, I expect."

"What do you mean?"

"My daughter is completely won over, and my grandson is obviously smitten. It's only a matter of time before he pops the question."

Marian lowered her gaze to her lap. Had Danny lied to her? "He said he wouldn't marry."

"Oh, he must someday soon, but if I were him, I'd jump now rather than be pushed to the altar."

"He would never do that. He loves his freedom too much."

"And he loves *you*, though I'm not sure he's confessed what's in his heart, judging by the shocked expression on your face."

"He would never! Lady Scarsdale would hate him to…"

"Marry someone like you? No, you would not have been her first choice."

She looked up to see the lady herself watching her with an odd expression. Marian's face grew uncomfortably warm.

"You know, I sometimes think it a great pity my daughter ever loved the late Lord Scarsdale as much as she did."

She glanced at Granny, surprised by her words. "What is wrong with loving someone?"

"Love hurts, and my daughter has never been comfortable with potent emotions. Danny is much the same. She found it difficult to go on without her beloved husband by her side," Granny admitted. "That's why I stayed as long as I have. For her, and for my grandson."

"Oh," Marian said, but she didn't know what else to say. Lady Scarsdale came across as a distant woman, critical of her son's misbehavior and disapproving of any sort of fun. But she'd never realized the woman might still grieve for her late husband, too. Knowing that went a long way to understanding her better.

"Now, you help me up and I'll take myself off. I'm much too tired to listen to more banging on the pianoforte this afternoon. But I want you to keep an open mind about what I said and see that girl off the property for me."

"Yes, Granny," she promised. "But I doubt I can."

The old lady patted her cheek and smiled. "My dear. You think too little of your importance and too much of hers. What my grandson needs most is not a proper lady, but an original."

The old woman shuffled off, and Marian watched her head out the door. When she turned back to face the room, Gabby rushed to join her again.

"Now you're white in the face," Gabby hissed. "Are you

sure there's nothing wrong with you? What did Mrs. Nolan say to you?"

Nothing that could be repeated.

The sound of the gentlemen arriving at last turned Gabby's attention toward the door, and she saw Amy sit up straighter, too, push out her tiny bosom a little higher, and plaster a welcoming smile on her face as Danny and Mr. Kimble strode into the room.

But Miss Wilson's smile wasn't genuine. Forced and calculated and designed to make herself stand out. To make a particular man notice her.

Mr. Kimble went to join Amy and the countess, but Danny's gaze sweep over Amy as if she wasn't there and then he turned toward Marian.

Instant relief swept over her as he headed her way, beaming a smile. "There you are."

Gabby sat forward a little, startled. "Were you looking for me, my lord?"

"No. I was looking for Marian, actually."

"Oh, well, here she is. Catching a cool breeze coming through the window. She was looking a little pink, and the countess was concerned she was too hot."

"You are good to be so concerned," he said, as he turned his smile fully on Gabby. "Would you excuse us for a moment? I should like to have a private word with Marian if you don't mind."

"Of course," Gabby agreed and took herself off without asking if Marian minded. Halfway across the room, she turned back, and her expression was one of some confusion.

She'd obviously realized Danny had used her given name. An odd thing for an earl to say to the paid companion.

But not to his lover.

Daniel settled into the window seat at her side. "Are you all right?"

"Of course," she promised. Yet, she couldn't keep her irritation from her tone, and he noticed.

"You're vexed about something," he drawled.

"I'm not," she promised, hating that he could read her mood so easily.

Daniel laughed softly. "Yes, you are. You wear the same look as my mother does when she's disappointed in me. What did I do?"

"Nothing. You did nothing."

"Ah, so it's the thing I *didn't* do that has your nose up in the air," he continued. "You know, when I started for home, I had decided I was tired of being alone. When I say alone, I mean, I was lonely even in a crowded room. I could look at a woman and know that being with her would never satisfy me beyond a few hours. My friends have all married for love, but I did not ever think that was my destiny. So, I came home to make the only match I thought made sense."

"I can understand why that held some appeal," she admitted. "Having someone to come home to must be nice."

"That is what I hoped for," he said. "I think—"

"My lord," Amy Wilson said, and they both looked up. "Would you care to hear me play?"

Danny waved his hand. "I don't mind if you use the instrument."

"Perhaps you'd be so kind as to turn the pages for me?"

"Not now. Perhaps Kimble will do the honors," he suggested, and his decision sounded so final that Amy's smile vanished in an instant.

Miss Wilson huffed and spun on her heel, almost stomping her way to the pianoforte. Marian was glad such a woman would not become Daniel's bride. Amy Wilson was not worthy of the honor of taking Lady Scarsdale's place. Danny needed an easier woman who would bend to fit into his life here without causing much of a ripple amongst the family.

"Did you have a pleasant afternoon?" he asked.

"I have. Granny wants to teach me to paint watercolors," she admitted, which seemed to make Danny laugh for some reason.

"You don't have to do that, or anything else you don't want to do, you know."

"A companion does as she's told, if she wants to be paid at the end of each term," she quipped. "I'm sure learning to paint will be no great hardship."

Daniel studied her. "You're funny, do you know that?"

She shrugged. "I do what I can to bring levity to the world."

"You do it very well," he assured her. "I think that's why I like you so much. You're amazingly easy on me."

"You're no great hardship, either, my lord."

"Don't start 'my lording' me now. Save that for when we're back in London."

"London?"

"Mm, you don't think I could let Granny unleash you on society without me being there to protect you? There are more dangers in the world than brigands on the road. You haven't met a duchess in a bad mood yet."

"I thought you were staying in the countryside?"

"That was when I thought my life had to be a certain way. I've revised my opinion on that, thanks to you, and especially about who could be the right sort of woman for me to marry."

"I see." Marian froze and didn't dare glance at Danny. She hoped he was simply thinking out loud and not planning to wed some other woman already. In fact, she wished he'd never discuss his marriage with her ever again.

Thinking of him with another woman made her pea green with envy. She wanted him, and to let no other lady put their hands on him.

She liked Danny just as he was. A bachelor with no ambition to wed a proper lady anymore.

"I should check to see if Granny needs me," she whispered, and then burst to her feet. "She said she was tired."

"Did she ask Miss Kimble to play the pianoforte?"

"Yes."

"Then she's not tired. She will be dancing with the butler somewhere no one can see them. She's an original, my grandmother. Likes to do as she pleases. When I was growing up, she always delivered her opinion about something terribly important and then left me alone to ponder her words. She's always right."

Marian could feel another flush sweep over her skin. Did Danny love her?

He might, but surely he would not offer marriage that would make her a countess. Surely Granny was mistaken about that.

Gabby rushed over. "Did Lord Scarsdale tell you the news? Miss Trill, will you come to dinner tomorrow night? Lord Scarsdale has already agreed to come, and I must invite another lady to make up the numbers. It will be my first dinner as hostess."

Dine as if she was a proper lady, travel with Danny alone in a grand carriage? It was hard not to immediately look forward to such an event. "I'd best speak to Mrs. Nolan about it."

"Oh, she's already agreed you must come," Danny promised.

Gabby clasped her hands together before her chest. "Please? I need to practice my skills as a hostess for someone who will forgive any faux passes."

Marian glanced toward the countess, who inclined her head graciously as if knowing what was running through her mind. She gulped. "I'd be very pleased to join you all."

"Gabby, are you ready to go?" John Kimble called.

"Yes, John," Gabby answered with a giggle. "I've got the answer I hoped to hear."

"Ah, excellent," John said. "Until tomorrow night, Miss Trill."

The music stopped abruptly as Marian curtsied to the pair.

"We'll see you out," Danny said, and caught Marian's elbow in his grip. He propelled her after the Kimbles and kept her on the top steps until the carriage drew away. "Take a walk with me?"

"I don't think—"

"Thinking has never been my strong suit, but let's do it anyway," he teased, and then hooked his arm through hers. "I haven't taken a stroll in the garden with you yet."

"What about Amy?"

"Mother will look after her. Besides, there's something we need to discuss," he whispered. "When I said I wanted you earlier…I really meant to say that I want to marry you."

Chapter Twenty

Daniel caught Marian as she swooned into his arms and then hoisted her into the air. He stood bemused for a moment by her response to his offer of marriage, but then took advantage of her apparent helplessness. He carried her off into the garden.

When he found the secluded alcove he wanted, he sat down on a garden bench with Marian on his lap. She roused and suddenly fought against him to sit up straighter. "What are you doing?"

"I caught you and lifted you up, swept you away so I could profess my love and devotion," Daniel said as he grinned. "I thought it rather gallant of me."

"You cannot mean that," she warned, looking around with an expression of panic on her face now.

"But I do. Every single word." He tapped the tip of her nose. "I love you, Marian Trill. Thief of my heart."

"How could you?"

"It's your own fault. That and this ring," he said, producing it from his pocket to show her. He waved it before her eyes and her attention fixed on it.

"I don't understand," she whispered, even as her fingers reached for the ring.

He let her take it and sighed when she slid it back on her finger. Where it had always belonged, he realized now. "Shall I tell you the other story about this ring? My granny made my mother put the promise ring on, to make it seem she was already promised to another man. All so my father would become jealous and finally propose to her."

"Your grandmother was devious."

"Yes, but also wise too. They, my mother and father, had been acquaintances for almost a year, but my father thought he was too old for her. Too old to love.

"Well, the ring worked its magic. Made my father see he couldn't live without Mama in his life. They became engaged and married and seven months later, I was born. My mother is embarrassed by that ring now, and the story that goes with it, especially when I was born so soon after they married. I wouldn't mention that if I were you."

"I would not dare," she whispered, her gaze on the ring as she fiddled with it.

"Seeing Mama wearing that ring was the push my father needed to admit his feelings for her. It's become mine, too. The image of you wearing the ring, and how you couldn't seem to give it back, lingered in my mind since we came home. You look upon this ring as if it was irreplaceable and instantly treasured. It took me a while to understand the magic in the air was true love,"

He caught her hand in his. "This ring embodies everything I love and hope for. It's a sign, a pointer, to my best chance of happiness in this world, and that is you, my darling Marian."

"I can't marry you."

"Why not? I have it on good authority that I'm quite the catch."

"My family are thieves," she reminded him with a scowl.

"Yes, well. We all have our black sheep in the family," he admitted. "Even mine has several thoroughly awful scoundrels in our ranks, including me, I must confess. But that was before I met the love of my life, in a seedy inn, and we spent a night together in bed and spoke of our hopes and dreams all night long.

"Say yes, Marian. Marry me, not for the money in my pockets or the title, but because we fell for each other the moment our eyes met."

Marian stared at him for a long time without speaking.

"I don't think my mother or granny will forgive either of us if we say no to love. They are both rather determined women and accustomed to having their way."

And still she hesitated.

Daniel lifted Marian up and deposited her on the bench seat, then got down on both knees before her. He took hold of her hands, deciding he may as well do the whole proposal rigamarole to prove he was serious, since she clearly had trouble believing he was. "Please, my Marian. Let me shout out my love for all to hear."

"I don't deny you an answer to be difficult, but to give you time to truly consider what you ask. I will become a countess. I must take lessons in deportment before I ever meet your friends and…oh, dear God, I have a lifetime of your mother's scolds to endure when I inevitably make mistakes."

"Mama's scolds don't hurt that much, and I'm sure she'll be far gentler with you than she ever was with me. She always wanted a daughter to mold in her image."

"She has Amy for that," Marian said, folding her arms across her chest stubbornly.

"Amy never could meet Mama's expectations. Surely you see that."

"They are so very high," Marian said, wincing. "I've

already failed her once, and I don't know if she will ever completely trust me."

"Trust always takes time to build. But it is also about loyalty to the family," Mother said, startling him because she appeared right behind him, and he hadn't heard her coming.

"Amy would have betrayed what I did to you in an instant," Mother admitted.

Daniel glanced over his shoulder at Mama. "I'm still waiting to hear what you actually did, Mother?"

"You'll never hear it from me," Marian warned, catching hold of his face, and turning his attention back to her.

Daniel sighed. "Ladies, keep your secrets if you must. It's none of my concern what you get up to behind my back, but I would ask that you always support each other in the years to come."

"Of course, we will. That is what family is for," Mother quipped. "Do excuse me, I must return to my guest."

"Yes, Amy," Marian said slowly.

"She will be made to understand," the countess promised as she turned away.

Marian bit her lip, clearly worried about how that conversation would go.

"Miss Wilson will always be mother's favorite, but you will be my wife. A countess. She can do nothing about that now," he promised. "My mind is set upon you."

"Don't keep Marian out here too long, we've a wedding to organize," the countess called out.

"Yes, Mama," he answered.

"I'll be along as soon as I can, Mama," Marian added.

Mother turned back and smiled at them both.

It still astonished him that Mother would not be upset about his ultimate choice of bride. Not that Marian had agreed to marry him yet. For her, it must still be quite the shock.

He sat back down next to Marian, crossed one leg over the other and lay his arm lightly around Marian's shoulders. "I can't wait for you to meet my friends and their wives in London next season. I'm sure you'll get along famously."

"Next season?"

"Well, I thought you'd still want us to go along to support Gabby in her quest to find a husband worthy of her. Mama will need your help with her, too," he warned. "As much as I like my friend's young ward, I find her a tad exuberant for my taste. She'll need all the help she can get to make a good impression."

"I'll need all the help I can get for that, too," Marian quipped rather gloomily.

He pulled her closer. "You'll have me, and Mama, and probably Granny there beside you, too. I hope our family is all that you ever need."

She turned to face him suddenly. "My delay really has nothing to do with you, Danny, or your family. I promise it's not that. I just don't know the first thing about high society, and you've marquesses for good friends and dozens of acquaintances with titles. It's just…"

"You're right to be scared, and my proposal came out of the blue from your perspective, so of course you don't know what to say. But it's the right decision for us both. Marry me now or marry me later, I don't mind waiting, as long as you'll always be nearby. I love you. The rest can be worked out as we go along."

"Shouldn't it be me begging you to put a ring on my finger?"

"We already did that," he said, catching up her hand and

kissing the bauble, where it fit perfectly forgotten but cherished on her delicate ring finger. "The rest is destiny."

"I never believed in destiny before I met you," she admitted. "I never imagined I'd want or could have a life like this."

Daniel pulled her onto his lap again. "I never did either."

"What about my family?"

"Crossman and the others?"

"Yes. There's likely more to the connection than your mother and grandmother told you about."

"But they will tell you, which is almost the same as telling me," he said, not surprised. "I suppose if we put our heads together, we can figure out a way to deal with them."

"Together?"

"Of course. I can't have you constantly living in fear and looking over your shoulder whenever we leave the estate. We'll send for Bow Street Runners tomorrow and set them on their heels."

"I'd like that, but Danny, I beg you, there's one among them who deserves mercy. He's just a boy."

"Oh, you mean the one who crashed into me and emptied my pockets before I knew what he was about," Daniel recalled, trying to remember if he'd ever seen the boy's face clearly. He'd a vague remembrance of overlong hair and shabby clothes.

"I want to find him and take him away from Crossman as soon as I can," she warned him.

Daniel could see she was determined. She wore exactly the same expression as his mother often had when he argued with her. "I can't let you go alone. You would be putting yourself in danger. Perhaps Bow Street can catch your uncle, and we'll catch the boy separately. If we try for him first, the others will notice and flee," he warned.

"Very likely," Marian admitted.

"See, there you go. We've already got the start of a plan. I'll be the next victim he steals from, and when the others catch up to me, they'll walk into a trap or suchlike."

"That is a very smart idea," Marian agreed. "I have some others."

"I thought you might," Daniel said, kissing her brow. "You know, loving you has changed me in ways I never imagined. But it will never be a hardship to become your husband."

Marian burrowed into his arms, and he held her close.

"Oh, marry me, Marian," he whispered. "Make me the happiest of all men. If it's any incentive at all, I've a safe full of jewels that you can try to steal, even though they will all be yours to wear . There are many pretty baubles for you to wear on your fingers and neck and to our bed," he said, and then glanced down at her, grinning, to see if she was at all tempted.

"Oh, well, that's decided it for me," Marian said with a laugh and then met his gaze. She stared at him for quite a while, and then she uttered a sigh. "I'd be a fool not to want to be your wife, Danny. I've loved you from the moment we met."

Daniel set his head against hers and knew his heart was finally in the right place, and it was happy in Marian's safekeeping. "Well, that makes two of us."

Epilogue

Daniel flicked a coin up into the air as he strolled along the narrow, dirty alleyway behind a row of wooden town houses as if he'd not a care in the world. He'd grown a beard and had his hat pulled low over his eyes to further disguise his identity and the back of his neck continued to tingle as he walked along alone, moving toward his ultimate destination, leading his quarry toward capture.

It was hard not to turn around to see how close they were, but he had faith in the plan. Marian's former friends and family had led them on a merry chase across the countryside, evading any attempts to lure them into committing another petty crime.

Until now, that was.

Daniel had painted a large target on his back when young Billy had picked up and kept a bright, shiny coin he'd dropped earlier. The boy had run off ahead of him now, and Daniel had already given the word to let him pass unmolested. He could afford to be lenient for a worthy cause, because the Bow Street Runners were lurking nearby to catch the bigger criminals.

Daniel would not have put himself in such a dangerously outnumbered position without knowing he had experienced men watching his back.

The thieves had picked up his scent as soon as he'd left the tavern where they'd stayed under an assumed name, weaving slightly on his way. Marian had chosen the most likely town and conditions for them to spring their ambush, and although she'd wanted to remain by his side for this part, Daniel had insisted she was kept out of it.

Besides, she had her own job to do elsewhere that was more important to her.

The woman Beatrice had already been detained at the inn, caught going through his luggage. She'd broken into his rented chamber there to see what she could steal and found herself in the company of three Bow Street Runners who had been disguised as his valet and grooms when they'd first arrived.

Crossman and the man called Tommy, who now seemed to be giving all the orders, had followed him from the inn and into this alley, where Daniel would pretend to empty his bladder.

Daniel tucked the coin away and heard the scuff of a boot behind him. Instinct had him turning to face the threat.

Knife held threateningly, the old man Crossman accosted Daniel without words. But his expression turned to shock as Daniel was recognized and his lunge was clumsy and desperate. Daniel easily caught him instead.

Daniel struggled, though, to hold him still. The old man was stronger than he looked. "How dare you threaten a peer, sir!" he growled in the old man's ear.

At his words, the alley swarmed with Bow Street's finest, and Crossman was quickly taken off Daniel's hands. Far behind them all, a heated scuffle was currently underway.

It took four Bow Street men several long and concerning minutes to subdue Tommy, but they eventually dragged him away, slumped in their grip.

A Bow Street man rushed up to him, grinning. "Well done, my lord. We got them all. Are you all right?"

"Not a nick, not a scratch," Daniel promised, adjusting the set of his coat, and trying to act as if he did this sort of thing every day. "That will teach the scoundrel to tangle with the Earl of Scarsdale."

Crossman's head snapped around to stare at him. "Scarsdale?"

Daniel nodded. "My mother sends her regards," he answered with a smug smile. The fellow turned pale, which made Daniel all the more curious about the things that mother still refused to tell him about her past with Crossman. However, he did not want to dredge up matters that might sully his mother's reputation.

He also did not offer the man any message from his niece, Marian, or tell him she had become his wife. The less Crossman knew about how he'd been found so easily, the better, in his opinion. He wouldn't like the old fellow to come after his wife for what he might see as a betrayal.

Daniel glanced down the alleyway to where the young boy had disappeared. There was no sign of him, thankfully, and Daniel could only hope that he'd escaped down the path they'd planned for him to take.

Marian promised young William would hide at the first sign of trouble. She'd taught him that and made him promise that he'd always try to find her when it was safe to come out again. She believed his caution would serve them well when he was separated from the rest.

Marian also believed Daniel's presence at her side might spook the boy at first. He didn't know that they were to be married soon, and that Daniel was no threat to anyone Marian loved.

With the thieves caught and being dragged away, Daniel was now at liberty to pursue a reunion with the woman who had stolen his heart.

The alleyway widened, and Daniel moved at a slow pace toward a somewhat open space directly. In the center sat Marian on an apple box, a fresh coat for the boy laid across her lap and a tempting pie for his empty tummy sitting to one side.

Daniel sighted the boy between himself and Marian, hidden under a stack of empty crates, watching Marian closely. Daniel strolled past the boy, as planned, and hoped he wouldn't turn tail and run in the other direction before Marian got a chance to speak with him.

He paused beside Marian, stooped to kiss her cheek and, as planned, moved on a little farther to wait against a far wall. This was not exactly a safe area for a wealthy earl and his countess to take a picnic lunch. But the boy would be uncomfortable in any place more refined, Marian believed.

"Are you hungry, Billy? I've food for you," Marian said gently to the shadows of the alleyway where the boy hid.

The boy remained in his hiding place, but Daniel was certain he'd heard her words.

She gestured to him. "This is my husband, Danny. He's helped me look for you. The Runners have what they came for and are gone away again. Crossman, Tommy, and Beatrice are with them now. It's been so many months since we've been together that I hope you still remember me, even in my new finery?"

The boy emerged from the shadows, eyes wide, and his gaze darting around the alley, looking for any others. He was filthy from top to toe.

Daniel's heart bled for the boy. He had not fared well

without Marian to look after him, and Daniel was glad he'd promised to take the boy on no matter what condition or situation they found him in.

For now, it was just him and Marian in the alleyway with a skittish child, afraid of being captured. The boy's gaze settled on him for some time and then returned to where Marian sat patiently waiting.

The child, obviously half starved, edged toward her at last.

"Do you like my fancy dress? I'm to live like a lady now. In a grand house, and I don't have to steal to fill my stomach anymore. Neither will you if you trust us. There's a warm bed waiting for you, Billy, if you want to come and live with us. I hope you will, but the food beside me is yours with no strings attached, as is this larger coat I bought."

The boy froze when Marian stood up from the wooden crate. He was halfway to her now, and Daniel watched intently as she continued to speak to the boy about her new life as a lady.

The boy was truly a frightened animal, expecting cruelty and capture at every turn. For months, he'd listened to Marian talk and fret over the boy's absence from her life.

Daniel would do nothing to spook the boy today. They might never get another chance to turn him from a life of crime. But they could not stay here forever.

"It will be dark soon," he warned Marian.

She nodded. "Are you always thinking of your stomach, my lord?"

"Always."

"We'll have roast duck and potatoes for dinner tonight. Are those still your favorites, lad?"

The boy nodded, and Daniel smiled to himself. The way

to a man's heart was often through his stomach. Marian was clever to have used that.

The boy glanced at him again—and then he suddenly ran at Marian. Her arms enveloped the boy, and she cried out her joy. Daniel rubbed at his eyes, pressing back an unexpected emotional response to the scene, too.

He straightened and, after giving them a few moments, drew near the pair. "I'm glad you found each other again," he whispered, so he didn't alarm the boy.

The boy was startled though, and he spun to stare at him, arms still wrapped around Marian's waist.

Daniel approached and held out his hand. "I'm Daniel. Danny, if you prefer."

After long consideration, the boy extended his hand. He did not give a name, but he gave a very firm handshake and slipped the coin back into Daniel's palm. Marian had said he'd been taught never to steal from anyone in their family. It seemed he had earned some trust today.

"It's a pleasure to meet you, William. Marian has been so worried about you." Daniel grinned, tucking the coin back where it came from, and then looked over at the uneaten pie they'd brought with them. "We should have bought two meat pies; you know, looking at that pie now, I'm utterly famished."

The boy narrowed his eyes and deliberately stuck the fingers of his free hand into the pie they'd bought for him. It was obviously done so Daniel wouldn't want a taste, and he laughed softly, delighted by the boy's spirit.

"That's what I used to do, too, when I didn't want to share with my friends," he promised, even as Marian chided the boy for the display of bad manners. Daniel shrugged.

"Maybe I'll buy another pie, or even two, on the way to the inn."

The boy quickly stuffed a bite of pie into his mouth.

Marian scowled. "You'll do no such thing, my lord, or you'll spoil both your dinners."

"I doubt that," he promised, noting that while they were talking, the boy had eased his grip on Marian and had almost finished his pie. "Shall I buy another just for you, lad?"

The boy looked at him, and the smallest of smiles appeared on his lips.

"Well, now you're done eating, we'd best be on our way to see if there's any left at the shop. Oh, but that reminds me, in case we become separated, this is for you." He returned the coin the boy had stolen, along with a piece of parchment, neatly folded. "The coin is your quarterly allowance, and just in case we ever become separated, this paper will help you find your way back to us. It is directions, so you can always find Marian again."

The boy nodded, stuffing the coin and paper into a pocket with one hand, as he held onto Marian with the other.

"All right then. Come along, you pair. We'd best be going before anyone unpleasant comes along to spoil our day."

Marian leaned toward him. She offered a smile and then kissed his cheek. "Thank you."

"No, thank you, Marian, my love." He grinned at her and then at the boy. "What good fortune I had that day we all met. I swear, I am blessed to have had my heart stolen by two softhearted former thieves."

After a few steps, a small hand crept into Danny's, and his heart lightened further as the boy smiled up at him at last.

They would get along just fine. Become a family who could face any obstacle thrown in their path.

It would be an unconventional family they'd have, full of black sheep and thieves, but it would be strong because they knew how to love and compromise.

The End

More Regency Romance...

DISTINGUISHED ROGUES SERIES

Chills ~ Broken ~ Charity ~ An Accidental Affair

Keepsake ~ An Improper Proposal ~ Reason to Wed

The Trouble with Love ~ Married by Moonlight

Lord of Sin ~ The Duke's Heart ~ Romancing the Earl

One Enchanted Christmas ~ Desire by Design

His Perfect Bride ~ Pleasures of the Night ~ Silver Bells

Seduced in Secret ~ Yours Until Dawn

No Ordinary Lady ~ Miss Kimble Bites Back

SCANDALOUS BRIDES SERIES

Wicked with Him

Desperately Seeking Seduction

Love and Other Disasters

WILD RANDALLS SERIES

Engaging the Enemy ~ Forsaking the Prize
Guarding the Spoils ~ Hunting the Hero

*

SAINTS AND SINNERS SERIES

The Duke and I ~ A Gentleman's Vow
An Earl of Her Own ~ The Lady Tamed

*

REBEL HEARTS SERIES

The Wedding Affair ~ An Affair of Honor
The Christmas Affair ~ An Affair so Right

*

MISS MAYHEM SERIES

Miss Watson's First Scandal

Miss George's Second Chance

Miss Radley's Third Dare

Miss Merton's Last Hope

About Heather Boyd

USA Today Bestselling Author Heather Boyd believes every character she creates deserves their own happily-ever-after—no matter how much trouble she puts them through. With that goal in mind, she writes steamy romances that skirt the boundaries of propriety to keep readers enthralled until the wee hours of the morning. Heather has published over fifty regency romance novels and shorter works full of daring seductions and distinguished rogues. She lives north of Sydney, Australia, with her trio of rogues and a four-legged overlord.

Find out more about Heather at:
Heather-Boyd.com

facebook.com/HeatherBoydRomanceAuthor

instagram.com/heatherboydbooks

bookbub.com/authors/heather-boyd

goodreads.com/Heather_Boyd